# Past Due for Murder

Also available by Victoria Gilbert

Blue Ridge Library Mysteries

*Shelved Under Murder*

*A Murder for the Books*

# Past Due for Murder

## A BLUE RIDGE LIBRARY MYSTERY

## Victoria Gilbert

**CROOKED LANE**

NEW YORK

Published in the United States by Crooked Lane Books, an imprint of The Quick Brown Fox & Company LLC.

Crooked Lane Books and its logo are trademarks of The Quick Brown Fox & Company LLC.

Library of Congress Catalog-in-Publication data available upon request.

ISBN (hardcover): 978-1-68331-874-3
ISBN (ePub): 978-1-68331-875-0
ISBN (ePDF): 978-1-68331-876-7

Cover illustration by Griesbach/Martucci
Book design by Jennifer Canzone

Printed in the United States.

www.crookedlanebooks.com

Crooked Lane Books
34 West 27th St., 10th Floor
New York, NY 10001

First Edition: February 2019

10 9 8 7 6 5 4 3 2 1

Dedicated to all who rescue, support, love, and protect the animals who share our beautiful planet with us.

# Chapter One

I t's amazing how much easier it is for people to learn something when you turn lessons into stories.

I surveyed the fifteen Girl Scouts seated around the bonfire we'd lit at the organic farm owned by the Fields family. The girls huddled on the blankets they'd spread across the cold ground, their wide-eyed gazes focused on the woman who circled the fire as she recounted folktales and legends from the Blue Ridge Mountains.

I elbowed Sunny. "They're never this quiet when we host their troop at the library. I'm usually hoarse at the end of the session from trying to shout over all the shrieking and giggling."

"I told you Mona was a great storyteller." Sunny sniffed the end of her long blonde braid before she flipped it over her shoulder. "My hair smells like burnt toast. But I guess it's worth it to prove to the town council that young people *do* participate in library events. And even on a Friday evening."

I gazed back at the fire, studying the middle-aged woman dressed in a flowing peasant skirt and a quilted embroidered jacket. Ramona Raymond, a folklorist and lecturer from nearby Clarion University, held her flashlight under her chin, allowing its beam to transform her angular face into a macabre mask.

1

"And then the girls dashed off in their lace-trimmed, beribboned white linen dresses, chasing the mountain lights, and were never seen again." Mona waved her flashlight toward the nearby woods. "This happened on the first of May, after the town's traditional May Day celebration. Sadly, the warmth of the day soon gave way to a cold, cold evening. Most people claim the runaway girls were lost in the mountains and eventually died from exposure, but some say"—Mona stepped closer to the fire, smoke as ephemeral as the dresses she'd just described spiraling up into the star-sprinkled night sky—"that they were lured into the underground court of the fae, forced to dance at fairy balls forevermore."

A collective gasp escaped the girls' open mouths. Only Cicely Blackstone, the mayor's daughter, appeared unmoved.

*That isn't surprising*, I thought. *Cicely would probably yawn and proclaim her boredom if a herd of unicorns pranced out of the woods right now.*

Sunny leaned into me. "My grandparents claim it was a UFO, not fairies."

"Of course they do," I said with a grin. "But you know . . ." I raised my hand to my lips and mimicked a smoking gesture with my fingers.

"Yeah, there is that." Sunny's blue eyes shone with good humor. Her grandparents—Carol and Paul, whom everyone called P.J.— had once been part of a commune briefly housed on the Fields family farm. Now they were respected members of the community, and their business supplied fresh vegetables to local restaurants and food co-ops. But I'd spent many nights in their cozy farmhouse kitchen when I was younger. The sparkle in Carol and P.J.'s eyes when they recounted tales of their time as members of the '60s counterculture had told me that they'd never entirely given up their rebellion against the more staid elements of society.

Cicely tapped a pointed stick against the packed earth bordering the bonfire. "But how can there be fairies here? I thought they all lived in Ireland and Scotland and places like that. How'd they get to America?"

"Oh, they've always been here." Mona tossed her wild mane of curly, silver-streaked, dark hair away from her face as she knelt beside the girl. "My theory is that the fae live in another dimension, so they can appear anywhere. They travel through interdimensional portals." She rose to her feet, brushing some dust from her skirt. "Anyway, if you don't want to believe that, can't you imagine that fairies might have immigrated here, just like your ancestors did?"

"Guess so," the girl said, squirming under Mona's intense gaze.

"Now there's a new wrinkle." I glanced over at Sunny. "Interdimensional portals?" While assisting Mona with the research she'd been conducting at the library, I'd recently read more than I'd ever wanted to know about the mountain lights but had not run across this theory.

Sunny shrugged. "She mentioned it when I took her classes at the university. I did wonder how much of that talk was an act, though. I figured it might be part of her bag of tricks as a storyteller, like the bohemian chic clothes."

My gaze swept over Sunny's fringed suede jacket, tie-dyed T-shirt, and artfully patched jeans before resting on the leather boots that encased her legs up to her knees. "Thinking about taking up that profession, then?"

Sunny wrinkled her nose at me. "Only if you're signing up as a grunge band groupie."

I yanked on the ties of my well-worn hooded sweatshirt. "Hey, just because I like to wear flannel shirts over concert tees . . ." I glanced down at my faded jeans and battered leather sneakers. "Okay, point taken."

"Should we go ahead and set out the food?" a voice called from off to my right.

I turned toward the speaker. It was Bethany Virts, the owner of the local diner, The Heapin' Plate. She was flanked by Scout leaders and a few other volunteers. Two battery-operated lanterns cast intersecting ovals of light, illuminating the food spread across the table.

Bethany waved a package of marshmallows. "I didn't want to open these bags too soon. I know how quickly they dry out."

"Go ahead. I think Mona is wrapping things up," Sunny called out. "She always finishes her presentation with the fairy lights story," she added, addressing me.

"This tales-by-the-fire event was a good idea," I told my friend. "Thanks for organizing it. We might as well get something more than just a dry lecture out of Mona's research."

"Especially since the town council is paying for it."

"That does put the cherry on top. Although it's a shame we aren't getting any additional pay for the extra work it took to set this up. Especially you. Hustling tables from the Lutheran church and picking up all the stuff for the s'mores is above and beyond the call of duty."

"You expected extra pay from the Taylorsford town council?" Sunny quirked her pale eyebrows. "How long have you lived here again?"

"Over two years, and yeah—I should have known better."

Since the public library where I worked as director also maintained the town archives, Sunny and I had recently spent numerous hours assisting Mona, and the students she'd dragged along as part of some extra-credit assignment, with research into area folklore. Her grant from our notoriously stingy town council had shocked me until I learned that Cicely's father, Mayor Bob Blackstone, was planning a revival of Taylorsford's long-neglected May Day traditions.

He probably thought that since the fall Heritage Festival was such a success, a spring event might also drum up tourism.

As Sunny and I strolled toward the snack table, two young people stepped in front of us.

"Hello, Ms. Webber and Ms. Fields," said Hope Hodgson, one of the three students who'd accompanied Mona Raymond on her library research trips.

"Hi there." Sunny flashed a smile but didn't stop walking. "And excuse me, but I'm needed over at the s'mores station."

"Wait," Christopher Garver said as Sunny strode away. "We just wanted to know if you'd seen Lacey."

Noticing the concern etched on the faces of both students, I paused. "No, I haven't run into her this evening."

"We haven't seen her either." Chris's deep-brown eyes were shadowed by his dark lashes. "Not since Thursday morning. She had studio yesterday, so she couldn't catch a ride with us, but swore she'd be here tonight."

"And she isn't answering her phone. It must be broken or something, because I can't even leave a message." Hope tugged on one of her head-hugging braids, popping loose a few of the vibrant green beads entwined in her dark hair. The beads sailed into the darkness, momentarily illuminated by the lanterns on the table behind her.

"She probably forgot the assignment or someone asked her out on a last-minute date or something," I said.

Hope shook her head. "That isn't like Lacey. She's kind of flaky about some things, but she usually stays in touch."

"Too much, sometimes," Chris said. "She's always blowing up my cell with her texts."

"And as for dates—I don't think there's anyone in her life right now. She was seeing some mysterious guy for a while, but that must've fizzled. At least she stopped hinting about it, which is all she'd do before." Hope frowned. "Now all she does is complain about relationships not being worth the pain. So I can't see her suddenly changing her mind, especially if it meant jeopardizing a good grade in this course."

"Did you ask Mona if she'd gotten any message?"

Chris rubbed the smooth dome of his shaved head. "We did, but she claims she hasn't heard from Lacey today either. She didn't seem too interested in pursuing the issue, but Hope and I are worried. We don't think it makes sense. Lacey's already on academic probation, and she's sure to fail this class if she doesn't complete the extra-credit work."

"It's really weird that she'd blow off an easy assignment like this," Hope said. "Especially since Professor Raymond only allowed her to participate in the project because she felt her workload was unfair."

"Yeah, the prof thinks Lacey's dance training is too demanding and that's why she's failing," Chris said.

"She's a dancer?" I called up an image of the third student in Mona's group. Lacey Jacobs was a willowy blonde who had to be constantly reminded to remove her earbuds when anyone spoke to her. *Listening to music while rehearsing steps in her head.* I should have recognized that habit. It was something my boyfriend Richard, a dancer and choreographer, also did quite often.

"I thought you'd know that, 'cause she's in Richard Muir's studio and . . ." Hope's eyelashes fluttered over her dark eyes.

"Is she?" I thrust my hand into my pocket and clutched my cell phone. Although I was sure I'd spoken Lacey's name once or twice when I had complained to Richard about Mona's research demands, he'd never mentioned that she was one of his contemporary dance students.

*Yet another instance of his odd behavior lately.* As Chris and Hope continued to express their concerns over Lacey's absence, I pulled out my cell phone and tapped the darkened screen.

Still no return call or text. I pocketed my phone. I hadn't heard from Richard all day, which had raised my anxiety level higher than the pitch of the Girl Scouts' usual squeals.

After receiving a phone call from his mother asking him to come home to help arrange a surprise birthday party for his favorite aunt, Richard had told me he planned to drive to his old hometown after his Thursday classes. We'd chatted on the phone the previous evening, so I knew he'd reached his parents' home safely, but I'd heard nothing since that call. I hadn't been too worried at first, since he'd warned me that he'd be forced to run errands and undertake other chores related to the party. But when he hadn't even sent a text, my mind had conjured visions of accidents and other dire events. Realistically, I knew my fears were foolish. He was with his family, not alone, and if something bad had happened, I would've been informed. No, he had to be okay. He'd just gone silent. Which, like not mentioning his connection to Lacey Jacobs, wasn't like him.

"There you are, standing around, useless as usual. Why aren't you helping with the s'mores?" Trisha Alexander, Mona's graduate assistant, appeared at my elbow, her gaze fixed on Chris and Hope.

"Aw, come on, Trish. We aren't here as babysitters." Chris lowered his eyes and hunched his shoulders. Even though he towered over the graduate student, the expression on his face made him look like a cowed puppy.

Trish was so tiny that even I topped her by several inches, despite my slightly less than average height. With her feathered cap of nut-brown hair and sharp-featured face, Trish looked like a pixie, but I'd caught her bullying the other three students often enough to know her Peaseblossom fairy appearance was an illusion.

My lips twitched. *A fairy, but not the Tinkerbell type.* She'd be one of Mona's supernatural creatures—the kind that lured away unsuspecting humans and trapped them underground.

Trish curled her hands into fists and placed them on her hips. "You're here to assist Mona and the organizers of this event. And right now it doesn't seem you're doing either."

Hope pointed toward the bonfire. "Looks like Mona's just answering a few questions, so maybe we can ask her what she wants us to do." Hope stared down her nose at Trish. "And where Lacey is."

The other young woman gripped her own upper arms with both hands as if stricken with a sudden chill. "Lacey lives on campus. That's probably where she is right now."

"But she promised she'd meet us here tonight, and none of us has seen or heard from her since yesterday morning." Chris shoved his hands into the pockets of his fleece jacket. "Maybe you don't care. I know you don't like Lacey and probably hope she flunks out."

"That's not true." Trish rocked back on her heels.

I narrowed my eyes and examined the graduate assistant. I'd never seen her display any anxious tics, but the mention of the absent dancer had certainly unnerved her. "You really haven't heard anything from Lacey?"

"No, but then I'm not her nanny," Trish said shortly.

"Neither am I, so if you'll excuse me, I need to help Sunny and Bethany." I stepped around Chris and Hope and headed for the borrowed banquet tables.

The students trailed me.

"Almost ready to go." Sunny waved a half-eaten chocolate bar at me.

"I hope you're saving some of that for the s'mores," I said.

Sunny made a face at me as Bethany looked up from breaking

graham crackers into squares. "Oh hi, you guys. Where's your friend?" she asked the students.

"That's what we want to know." Chris cast Trish a dark glance.

"She didn't call you?" Bethany wiped the crumbs from her fingers with a paper napkin. "That's odd. She promised me she would."

"What do you mean, Ms. Virts? Did you see Lacey today?" Hope asked.

"Yes, around two o'clock. She was waiting outside after I closed up the diner. She told me she'd hitchhiked from the university and needed a ride up to the Twin Falls trailhead." Bethany scrunched her thin face as she stared at the three students standing beside me. "She really never called?"

"No." Chris rubbed his forehead. "Did she explain why she wanted you to take her up into the mountains?"

"She said she'd lost something up there when you all went hiking last weekend. Some piece of jewelry that had sentimental value." Bethany lifted and dropped her bird-wing shoulders. "I thought it was strange and didn't like leaving her there alone, but she swore she'd call one of you later for a ride back into town."

"But she hasn't, and she isn't answering our calls or texts. And I don't remember her saying anything about losing any jewelry last weekend." Hope shared a look with Chris.

I studied the pair, curious why they seemed so shaken by Bethany's information. Sure, they were probably worried about Lacey wandering alone in the mountains at night, but there was something more . . .

*Something resembling frustration, or fear, rather than simple concern.*

Hope elbowed Chris. "Come on, let's take your car and drive up to that trail right now."

"Hold on—you won't be able to see anything, and besides, you haven't completed tonight's work yet." Trish tightened her lips over any additional admonitions under the withering stares from the other students. "All right then, go. I'll ride back into town with Mona."

Chris and Hope took off at a sprint. As I followed their progress to a cluster of parked cars, I noticed a cell phone screen flicker like a firefly near the perimeter fence.

There was someone standing there, hidden in the shadows. I stepped away from the table, coughing as a puff of wind blew smoke from the fire into my face. Rubbing my eyes with my fists, I squinted at the stranger. I didn't particularly care for the idea of someone lurking at the edge of the field, especially after all the other adults had headed over to the bonfire to supervise the marshmallow toasting.

This was a tall, lean figure. A man, if my eyes didn't deceive me. As he held up his phone to his ear, it illuminated his face for a moment.

I took a few stumbling steps forward. No, he couldn't be here. No way was Charles Bartos, pianist, composer, and music professor, lurking at the edge of a small-town library event geared toward teens.

*Except maybe to talk to you, Amy.*

I moved away from the table, my gaze fixed on Charles. We'd never spoken after the night two years ago when I'd discovered him fooling around with violinist Marlis Dupre at a reception given in honor of their new classical music group, the Alma Viva Trio. After humiliating myself by tossing a glass of champagne at him—and hitting the dean of music instead—I'd rushed back to his loft apartment while he'd lingered at the party. Devastated by his betrayal of our yearlong relationship, I'd snatched up the few items I'd kept at his place and fled without leaving a note.

*He never tried to reach out after that, so why would he now?* I reminded myself as I walked toward the man leaning against the fence. *Although perhaps, after his recent loss, he's reconsidered some of his past actions.*

*But how would he know to find me here?* I frowned as I picked up my pace. *He couldn't have known I'd be at this event unless he stalked the library's website.*

Which was possible, but definitely put a different spin on his actions. It betrayed a determination to track me down that I'd never have imagined. Perhaps he was serious about making amends, even after all this time.

"Where are you going?" Sunny called out. "Seriously, Amy, I thought you were going to help supervise . . ."

I ignored her and picked up my pace. I hadn't spoken to Charles in over two years and had been shocked when I'd heard that Charles and Marlis had purchased land in the mountains outside Taylorsford. According to local gossip, they'd renovated the pseudo-Swiss chalet on the property into a retreat where they spent long, private, weekends away from their jobs at Clarion University. Since I'd had no desire to unexpectedly run into either of them, this had been unwelcome news. But I'd never seen them together since that fateful night when I'd discovered their affair, and now I never would. This past February—only four months after they'd finished renovating their vacation home—Marlis had been struck by a car while jogging on a side road near the university. She'd tragically died at the scene.

Richard, who taught dance at Clarion, hadn't provided much information on this situation, despite my efforts to persuade him to share any details with me. I wasn't surprised, as I knew Richard went out of his way to avoid Charles due to a bad experience he'd had when they'd worked on a single collaborative project two summers ago. All Richard had heard through the campus grapevine was that

Charles had been granted a leave of absence to deal with his grief and had taken off to travel throughout Europe. But it seemed that he'd returned.

My stride shortened as the space between us decreased. Despite my new life, and love, my stomach clenched over the thought of speaking to Charles again. He'd been my first mad love—the kind that made one do foolish things. Oh, I'd had a few casual boyfriends before Charles, but none of them had left much of a mark. He had slammed into my heart, and smashed it, like a sledgehammer.

Now he was the one suffering. Strangely, that thought didn't bring me satisfaction. All I felt was pity.

I reached Charles and managed to squeak out a hello before someone rushed up behind me.

"You!" Mona swept past me and stopped short in front of Charles, shining her flashlight in his face. "What do you think you're doing, showing up here? Planning to steal more of my work?"

"I'm not trying to take anything from you, Mona." Charles shadowed his eyes with his hand. "I'm simply enjoying a little break from sitting alone in an empty house. Now—please remove that light from my face."

I instinctively took two steps back as Mona flew at Charles like an avenging angel, striking his shoulder with her flashlight. "You lying piece of garbage! Get out of here before I kill you!"

# Chapter Two

I retreated while Charles threw up his arms in a defensive gesture, forcing Mona to step away.

"What's he doing here?" Trish said under her breath as she appeared beside me.

I glanced down at her. "You know Charles Bartos?"

She stared at her leather sneakers as she shuffled her feet. "Of course. He's one of the most famous professors at Clarion. And there's been a lot of talk about him lately, what with him tragically losing his girlfriend." Trish looked up and stared toward the tableau at the fence. "Besides, he and Mona have history."

Fortunately, it appeared that Trish was not aware of my own relationship with Charles. "What do you mean?"

"You never heard that story? Mona usually tells it to everyone she meets."

Although they'd lowered their voices to the point where I couldn't make out their words. I could tell by Mona's furious gesticulations that she was still arguing with Charles. "No, she hasn't mentioned anything about it to me."

There was no way I'd admit to Trish that I knew exactly why Mona wouldn't have shared this story with me. Having worked at

Clarion for many years, the folklorist undoubtedly knew of my previous connection to Charles.

Trish was apparently too focused on her mentor to detect the tension in my voice. "Mona says he stole some of her work and used it as the basis for a composition that made him a pile of money. He never credited her, even though he clearly used the folk songs she'd discovered. Mona claims the lyrics were copied practically verbatim from her research."

"Not the *Moon and Thistle Cycle*?" I snapped my mouth shut before I said anything more. Although Charles had completed this song cycle before we met, we were dating when it first received accolades, so I knew how pivotal it had been to his career. He'd already achieved renown as a concert pianist, but the piece solidified his reputation as a composer, especially after a prominent soprano recorded it and the album won a Grammy.

Trish side-eyed me. "That's the one."

"I used to work at Clarion, so of course I heard about it. You really couldn't escape all the hoopla about that on campus." I turned away from her suspicious gaze. "It looks like Maestro Bartos has had enough. Which I can understand, especially with what he's been through recently."

Charles walked into the shadows created by the cluster of cars as Mona strode over to me and Trish. "That man thinks he's God's gift, when he's really a spawn of the devil." She glanced at my face and tightened her lips.

"Why did he show up here tonight? Did he say?" Trish asked.

The tremor in her voice made me cast the graduate student an inquisitive glance. She was definitely upset about something. Perhaps it was simply the fear that her mentor would get into trouble for assaulting another professor.

"Not really, or at least he offered no reasonable excuse. He claims he's simply trying to find ways to deal with his grief, but I find that hard to believe. How can your heart be broken if you don't have one?" Mona turned to glare at me. "Did you know he'd be here?"

"Of course not. We haven't even spoken in two years. I had no idea he was even in the area, much less that he'd crash your presentation."

Trish's boots scattered some dirt clods. I could feel her eyes on me but refused to meet her gaze.

"But you do know him well, right?" she asked.

"Know him?" Mona snorted. "They lived together a few years back."

"Well, not full-time," I said, as I caught a glimpse of Trish's dark expression. "I came back to Taylorsford on the weekends."

"Still, you were his significant other."

"Not so significant, as it turns out. Since he cheated on me with the woman he's now mourning." I allowed my tone to sharpen on my last words. It was true that Charles had betrayed me, but now, while he was struggling with grief, I found Mona's harsh attitude distasteful.

"That was you?" Trish's voice rose like a peacock screech. "The dean of music thing? I heard that story when I first transferred to Clarion, but I didn't connect it with you."

"I'm not surprised. I left my university job and moved here to take over the management of the public library immediately after that debacle."

Mona's frigid expression thawed. "It's true—he treated you abysmally. But that's Charles Bartos for you. He takes whatever he wants and uses it with no thought for anyone else."

I sucked in a deep breath. "That's in the past. As I said, we haven't spoken for over two years. I'm just as shocked as you that he showed up here tonight. I don't know, maybe after everything that's happened, he wanted to apologize . . ."

Mona snorted. "Apologize? Hell will freeze over before that happens." She looked me up and down. "You know you're better off without that snake, I hope? Especially since you've found a much nicer man."

"True," I said, because it was. Even if that nicer man had been behaving strangely lately.

Mona turned to her assistant. "After that encounter, I'm done. Let's go, Trish." Mona bobbed her head at me. "Sorry, I didn't mean to fly off the handle like that. Thank you again for setting this up. I did enjoy telling the old tales to the Scouts."

"I'll share your thanks with Sunny," I called out as Mona and Trish turned away and headed for Mona's car.

After they drove off, Charles stepped out of the shadows and walked over to me. Tall and slender, he wore his blond locks a little too long for current tastes. But I knew he would never cut his hair. He was quite aware how seductively it veiled his face when he leaned over the piano keys.

*And how it flowed back like a glorious mane when he lifted his head in exultation during some dramatic passage*, I thought, recalling the time I'd caught him practicing just such a gesture in a mirror.

"Hello, Amy," he said in a cultured voice that bore the slight trace of an English accent. Although he'd been born and raised in the Midwest, he'd picked up that affectation when he'd spent several years studying at a prominent London conservatory.

*It does play well with his fans.* I had to admit that it was also one of the things that had first seduced me, once upon a time.

"Hello again, Charles." I brushed a lock of my straight brown hair out of my eyes. "What are you doing here? I thought you were in Europe."

"I was, but I had to cut my travels short. I have a few concerts that I couldn't reschedule. I had to return to honor those commitments." Charles lifted one of his fine-boned hands. "So I decided to spend a few days here between trips. A small respite before flying off to Chicago."

"Solo piano concerts?" I asked, examining him with concern. Always lean, Charles was thinner than I'd ever seen him. In the dim light, the shadows under his sharp cheekbones dramatically hollowed out his face.

"Yes, as the Alma Viva Trio is no more." Charles took a shuddery breath. "At least for now."

I laid my fingers on his tensed arm. "I was very sorry to hear about Marlis. Truly."

"Thank you." Covering my fingers with his other hand, he stared into my eyes. "I can see that you're sincere. Of course, that doesn't surprise me. You always were much nicer than I deserved."

It was a vague sort of apology, but I latched on to it nevertheless. "Not really. And anyway, I know Marlis was an integral part of your musical career as well as your life. It must be terribly difficult for you. I don't know how I'd cope if I lost my boyfriend."

"Ah yes," Charles said, lifting his hand off mine. "You're dating that dancer, Richard Muir, aren't you?"

"Yes, and I can't imagine . . ." I shook my head. "I thought I'd lost him once, last fall, and that was truly dreadful. So I believe I can understand a little of what you're going through."

"Perhaps." His lips twitched, but the resulting smile resembled a grimace. "Anyway, I'm heading out of town this evening on a red-eye flight and decided that I wanted to see you before I left."

"Really? Why?"

Charles shrugged. "I've spent a lot of time in reflection lately. One of the things I've realized is that I need to make some sort of amends after the unfortunate way things ended between us." He massaged his temple with his fingers. "Having seen how quickly someone can be swept out of my life, I felt an urge to speak to you again."

"You sound like you're leaving Taylorsford for good," I said, not sure if I was happy with this idea or not.

"No. Or maybe. I'm not entirely sure at this point. But I'll be returning to the mountain house after these concerts, at least for a little while. I need to spend some time there before I decide whether to sell the place or not." He reached out and clasped my right hand. "I should be back by Tuesday or Wednesday. Perhaps we can get together sometime after that, just to talk? I would like that very much."

He was gazing at me with a familiar, soulful look in his blue eyes. I knew he'd just lost his lover and was hurting desperately and was lonely, but . . .

*Surely he doesn't think we could ever be anything to each other again?*

I cleared my throat and slid my hand from his grasp. "Maybe, although I'm awfully busy these days. How about contacting me when you get back and we'll see?"

"All right. And thank you again for your condolences, Amy. They mean a lot to me."

"You're welcome. But I would offer the same to anyone in your situation."

"I know," he said, flashing his most dazzling smile. "Which is why I want us to be friends again."

"We'll see," I repeated, my thoughts spinning like pinwheels. "Anyway, I need to go. This is a work event and I'd better hightail it over there to help with the cleanup, since I'm sure I've missed assisting with the s'mores."

"I understand. But I promise to contact you again very soon."

Charles inclined his head slightly and said goodbye before striding off toward the parked cars.

I stared after him, thinking how curious it was to hear him say he wanted *to be friends again*, when, despite our intimate relationship, we'd never been friends in the first place.

\* \* \*

By the time I arrived back at the turn-of-the century Queen Anne revival home I shared with my aunt, I'd dissected my conversation with Charles down to the bone and still had no idea why he was so interested in seeing me again. Mulling over this odd turn of events, I simply said good-night to Aunt Lydia, who was watching some mystery series on BBC America, before I headed upstairs to my bedroom.

I resisted checking my cell again until after I'd brushed my teeth and changed into my "Wake Up Smarter, Sleep With a Librarian" nightshirt. Flopping across my bed, I held my breath as I tapped the phone screen.

Finally, a message. "Call me" was all it said, but at least it was something.

I clicked on the shortcut that dialed Richard's phone.

"So where the heck have you been?" I asked as soon as he picked up.

"And hello to you too, Amy."

Was it just my imagination, or did Richard's typical teasing tone sound a little forced? "I thought perhaps you'd decided to take a road trip to Siberia."

"Sorry. My mom's had me running all over the county . . ." As Richard's voice trailed off, I heard something odd in the background. It almost sounded like a public announcement—the type of thing you'd hear in an airport or train station.

"And you couldn't text me until now? All today without a word . . ." I closed my lips over my next words, disliking the hectoring tone that had crept into my voice.

I didn't want to become one of *those* girlfriends—the kind that panicked if they weren't in touch with their significant other every other minute. But I *had* been worried, especially after seeing Charles and remembering how he'd lost Marlis in an instant.

"I really am sorry. Time just got away from me and then my parents insisted on changing the venue for the party, so we had to transport all the decorations and supplies to a new location. Honestly, today's just been crazy, what with running from one store to the next."

Maybe that's what I'd heard—someone making an announcement in a big-box store. Yes, that had to be it. There was no reason for Richard to be in an airport or train station. No reason I could imagine, anyway.

"It's okay," I said, after a deep breath. "I was just worried. I thought maybe you were lying lifeless beside the highway or something."

"No, I'm fine." The moment of silence following this assertation stretched a little longer than usual, making me wonder if Richard had also needed to calm his breathing. "It was just one thing after the other, that's all."

I considered mentioning seeing Charles at the bonfire and Lacey's disappearance but thought better of it. Those were probably conversations we should have face-to-face. "The party's tomorrow, right?"

"Yeah, but I think I may stay on a few days. Diedre offered to cover my studio, so I don't have to teach again until Wednesday, and there are still a few things here I need to look into . . . I mean, take care of, so I probably won't be home until Tuesday evening." Richard raised his voice at the end of the sentence. Although not quite fast enough to cover the sound of hydraulic brakes in the distance.

"Wait, where the heck are you? It sounds like a bus station."

Richard cleared his throat before replying. "Just traffic outside. Anyway, with the party craziness, I may not be able to call again, but I promise I'll stay in touch by text."

"Sure, okay." I stared at my cell phone screen, wondering what in the world could prevent him from calling me between now and Tuesday evening—a full three days from now.

"And there's Mom again," Richard said, although I'd heard no beep or buzz on the line to indicate an incoming call. "Must go, sweetheart. See you Tuesday." There was a slight pause. "Love you."

"I love you too," I said just before he hung up.

But not before I heard another announcement.

I stared at the darkened screen of my cell for a minute before gently placing the phone on my nightstand, right beside a pile of books I hadn't yet found the time to read.

Richard had lied to me. I knew that as surely as I knew he was not in any store. Not tonight. He was standing in either a bus or train station.

What I didn't know was why.

# Chapter Three

Since the library was closed on Sunday, we were typically over-whelmed with returns on Monday. I blew a strand of my dark hair out of my eyes as I plucked individual books from the stacks on the circulation desk and arranged them in call number order on a pro-cessing cart.

"Is this everything out of the book drop?"

"So far." Sunny was wearing the aqua plastic–framed glasses she'd recently been prescribed for close work. Although she'd fussed, I'd reassured her that they just made her look more adorable. Which they did. "But I'll check again after lunch. You know how some people like to dump stuff out there even when we're open."

I flashed her a grin. "I guess some of our patrons don't appreciate our smiling faces." My words were accompanied by the sound of rain pelting the library's deeply recessed tall windows. "Just don't forget your umbrella. It doesn't look like this storm is letting up anytime soon."

Sunny glanced at the windows and sighed. Our book drop was not connected to the library building, which meant dragging the inner bin back and forth through the workroom door. It had been easier to manage book drops when they were cut into the outside wall of library buildings and returns could be collected from an inside bin throughout the day. But bitter experience had forced most public libraries to install stand-alone drops outside. That way, if someone decided to deposit something flammable, the resulting fire wouldn't spread to the library itself.

I shook my head as I contemplated such behavior. How tossing firecrackers or lighted rags, or even garbage, into a book drop gave anyone pleasure transcended my ability to identify with my fellow humans.

"So, what did you and Brad do this weekend?" I examined one of the returned items—a book on American history—with disapproval. Someone had inserted sticky note flags throughout the volume. I sighed and began peeling the adhesive bits of paper from the pages.

"Um . . ." Sunny stared at her cart, a plastic DVD case dangling from her beringed fingers. "Nothing actually."

"Oh right, what was I thinking? I bet he was busy with various investigations, including looking into Lacey Jacobs' disappearance. I imagine it's become more of a priority since she hasn't been heard from in over forty-eight hours."

Sunny slid the DVD into its proper location on the cart before glancing over at me. "True, but to be honest, we didn't have anything planned."

"Something you want to tell me?" I asked, noticing the wariness shadowing Sunny's typically open expression.

"It's no big deal." Sunny straightened and tossed her shimmering blonde hair behind her shoulders. "We're just cooling off for a bit, that's all."

"Your idea or his?"

"Both, actually." Sunny shrugged. "You know I'm not too keen on getting married."

"As in, you really don't ever want to. Yeah, I know."

"Well, so does Brad. And that's created a problem."

"That's not really surprising, especially since he is a bit older than us. When we celebrated his birthday last month, he even mentioned being forty-one and still unmarried a couple of times, so maybe his age is making him anxious. Honestly, they say women are the ones who worry about such things, but I find men are often worse. Richard is only thirty-six and he still jokes about being an eternal bachelor." I grinned. "I just come back with the fact that I'm thirty-four and thus an old maid, so we match. Which makes him laugh, of course."

Sunny shrugged. "I suppose you're right. I should've realized the age difference would come into play, although I'm only six years younger than Brad. I suppose I was lulled into a false sense of security. It was okay for a while. Even though I told Brad up front that I wasn't interested in marriage, I guess he thought . . ."

"He could change your mind? They always do, don't they?"

Sunny shot me a grin. "You know it, girl. No matter how many times they're thwarted in such attempts."

"As long as you're okay with it, I guess a little hiatus won't hurt." I considered my own reaction to Richard's lack of communication over the past few days. "You *are* okay with it, I hope?"

"Sure. Mainly because I knew this was coming. It always does." Sunny turned to stare at the pile of DVDs on the counter. "Sometimes I wish I'd been young back in the sixties. Free love and all that."

"I doubt it was actually any easier." I pulled a recycling can from under the desk and swept the pile of Post-it flags into it. "Romance always seems to complicate things."

"For sure. Since you brought up the investigation, I guess you've heard the latest news about Lacey?"

I shoved the recycling bin back under the desk. "I read they found her car parked near her dorm, with an empty gas tank."

"Which explains the hitchhiking, I guess."

"Typical broke student." I shook my head as I recalled my own days of stretching one month's money to cover two.

"Yeah, apparently after she hit a deer earlier in the year, she had to spend a mint to fix the damage to her car, so I guess she's been strapped for cash."

I massaged the back of my neck to loosen my tight muscles. "Why hitchhike though? Couldn't she have called Chris or Hope, or even Trish, for a ride?"

Sunny shook her head. "I saw Chris and Hope on Saturday, and they told me they drove in from Clarion on Thursday afternoon while Lacey was still in class. Chris has a boyfriend who lives in town and they were all going out to dinner that evening. As for Trish, she doesn't have a car right now."

"Oh? I thought she did. An old clunker. I remember her parking it out back earlier in the semester."

"Not anymore. I know because I had to drive her back to Clarion one day when she missed her ride with Chris and Hope. Trish told me her car died when she drove it home a couple of months back. Since it would've cost more than it was worth to repair it, she took a bus back to Clarion and decided to use public transportation or rides from friends instead. As for her helping Lacey"—Sunny glanced over at me, her golden eyebrows arched—"you do realize Trish hates Lacey for some reason, right?"

"Yeah, although I'm not sure why." I rubbed my neck again. "Seems like there's definitely some ill will there."

"Apparently. Anyway, I hope Lacey's okay and we hear something from her soon." Sunny held up a brightly colored DVD case with the title *Fairy Tale: A True Story.* "Oh, look. This is the third return I've seen that touches on that topic. I guess Mona's storytelling sparked some curiosity in a few of our patrons."

"But the fairies Mona talks about aren't quite so sparkling." I frowned. "The ones connected to the mountain lights stories actually sound pretty horrid. Dragging people underground and trapping them forever . . ." I shivered as a memory surfaced. I'd once spent time stuck in a dark, tight space filled with filthy muck and dank stones, uncertain if I'd live or die. "Not something that appeals to me."

Sunny slid the DVD into its proper slot on the reshelving cart. "I get that, especially after what you went through in that well."

I looked out over the main room of the library. Shadows filled the corners where the light from its antique hanging pendants didn't reach. "I try not to think about it, although I still have nightmares."

"Understandable." As Sunny placed the last DVD on the cart, she glanced at her watch. "Oops, almost story hour. My turn, so I'd better dash back to the children's room."

"No problem, I'll finish up here," I told her as she sprinted off.

After clearing up the returns, I scanned the reading room. Seeing that no one needed my assistance, I strolled back over to the circulation desk computer.

It was time to answer a question that had been gnawing at me since Sunny had brought it up—why Trisha Alexander might bear a grudge against the missing Lacey Jacobs. I pulled up one of our full-text newspaper databases to begin my search.

It didn't take long to score a hit. Surprisingly, it was a group photo of teenagers dressed in camouflage fatigues and holding rifles. I peered closer and spied Trish kneeling in the front row. The caption identified the group as a regional skeet shooting team.

My lips tightened. Trisha Alexander as a sharpshooter was the last thing I'd ever have imagined, but then, I'd never really spoken with her, or any of the other students working on Mona's project, about anything outside of their research. I did know that Trish had been raised in a rural area, but that was it.

The second item retrieved by my search was more enticing. It was an article from a city paper that referenced a cheating scandal at a large state university close to DC.

I leaned in and stared at the screen. The story mentioned that several students had been dismissed from the university after purchasing the answers to a final exam. But it was the photograph accompanying a linked article that caught my eye. The girl in the picture had long hair dyed a matte black, but it was obviously Trish. Accused of cheating but cleared, she'd brought a countersuit, claiming that the professor who'd exposed the scandal had falsely targeted her for unspecified reasons of his own.

The professor's name was Arnold Jacobs.

I whistled, drawing the attention of the patron Sunny and I had dubbed "The Nightingale" because of her well-meaning, but inaccurate, attempts to help reshelve library books.

"Sorry," I said. "I just ran across some surprising news."

The Nightingale made for the desk. "They found that girl with marks on her arms from alien probes, right?"

"No, nothing like that," I said, forcing a smile. "Just some unrelated research." The lie tripped easily off my tongue. The last thing I wanted was to encourage the Nightingale to spread more of her outlandish ideas.

Disappointment drew down the Nightingale's thin lips as she turned aside.

I refocused on the computer screen and typed in a new search.

Pulling up the university website, I zeroed in on the biographies of its faculty and staff.

And there he was—a full professor in the anthropology department. Looking over his biography and photo, I soon realized that my suspicion had been correct. Arnold Jacobs was Lacey's father.

I knew from some of Mona's comments that Trish had received her undergraduate degree from Clarion, but only after transferring from a larger university. The notoriety of the scandal had obviously forced Trish to leave a much more prestigious institution for a smaller college. I frowned. No wonder Trish disliked Lacey. It wasn't surprising that she'd despise the daughter of the professor she thought had sabotaged her.

I glanced up at the wall clock, calculating whether I could reach Brad Tucker before lunch. This revelation about Trish's connection to Lacey might mean nothing. But it was certainly as likely a motive for violence, or even murder, as others I'd stumbled over in the past.

# Chapter Four

I called Brad while Sunny was at lunch, He was clearly interested in the information and promised to conduct a follow-up interview with Trish as soon as possible.

"It's definitely pertinent," he said. "Especially with this new wrinkle . . ."

"What's that?"

He cleared his throat. "I probably shouldn't say this, but you'll hear it on the news soon enough—some hikers found Lacey Jacobs' cell phone up in the mountains, off the Twin Falls trail."

"No wonder no one's heard from her. Even without foul play, she's had no way to call for help."

"Right. We're now looking into it as a lost hiker scenario and have mobilized additional search teams to cover the area. The phone was found near old Delbert Frye's property, so we're checking with him, as well as with that guy who bought property up there several months ago. He's not at home right now, though. Off performing somewhere. You know, that musician whose girlfriend was recently killed."

"Charles Bartos?"

"That's the one."

"I didn't realize his property was close to Mr. Frye's."

"Adjacent, actually. I even informed Bartos and his girlfriend about old Delbert when they moved in. Warned them to steer clear, as he's basically a hermit who doesn't welcome strangers."

"Yeah, I've heard from my aunt and others that he likes to chase off any trespassers with a gun." I took a deep breath. "You don't think Mr. Frye would take a shot at someone like Lacey if she wandered onto his property by accident, do you?"

"Hard to say. We're looking into that angle, of course. But I don't want anyone speculating about such things until we know more." Brad's tone held a clear note of warning.

"I promise not to say anything. Not until the info's released to the news media, anyway."

"Good. Now I'd better get back to work. So much going on right now." There was a significant pause before Brad spoke again. "Say hello to Sunny for me, would you?"

"Sure thing," I said, before wishing him a good day.

When Sunny came back from lunch, she barely reached the desk before blurting out the news about Lacey's recovered cell phone.

"I saw that online," I said, debating whether to mention my call to Brad. I decided against it, despite my promise to give her a hello from him. I wasn't ready to share my suspicions about Trish and didn't want to have to lie to Sunny about the original purpose of my call. "I wonder what Mona will have to say about that? Since she seems so convinced that Lacey just took off for a date or something." The bang of the front doors drew my attention. "Speak of the devil, there's Mona now. Headed this way like a woman on a mission."

Sunny straightened and adjusted the neckline of her loose peasant top. "I helped her last time, so if you don't mind . . ."

"Sure, if you'll keep watch over the desk."

"No problem. I'll even double-check all these returns before the volunteers arrive to shelve." Sunny cast me a bright smile. "Anything to avoid hearing more local folklore. It's interesting at first, but I think I've reached my limit, especially with the interdimensional whatevers."

I wagged a finger at her. "I thought you liked all that new age stuff."

"This isn't the same. No illuminating aspects to it. Pretty dark and dour, at least the way Mona tells it."

"Exactly the one I need!" Mona reached the desk just as Sunny hurried toward the workroom.

"Hi Mona, bye Mona," she called out. "Need to grab some more carts, sorry."

"It's Amy I want anyway." Mona shook the rain from her curly hair.

I leaned forward and encircled a stack of returned books with my arms to protect them from a shower of water droplets. "Hello, Mona. Have you heard the latest news on Lacey?"

"Yes." Mona's dark eyes flashed with what looked like irritation. "It appears that foolish child did come into Taylorsford on Friday but then took off hiking on a whim and ended up lost. I hope they find her soon, of course, but honestly, the way she's carried on . . ." Mona tightened her lips over whatever she'd been about to say and shook her head, flinging more water across the desk. "I'm not here to discuss that problem, but I do need to talk to you. It's critical."

I flicked a few drops of rain off the top of a glossy paperback and pushed the stack toward a drier section of the desk. "How can I help?"

Mona's gaze darted left and right. "Not here. Can we go somewhere more private? The archives building, perhaps?"

"That's out back and it's raining."

Mona leaned in, pressing her palms against the top of the desk so hard that veins popped up on the backs of her hands. "It's extremely important."

"All right. Just let me get something to keep from getting soaked." I strode into the workroom. Sunny rolled her eyes at me as I grabbed my rain slicker and umbrella before pocketing the key to the archives.

"You're enabling her," she said.

"We live to serve." I made a face. "Or so I'm told. Anyway, can you watch over things?"

"Sure." Sunny followed me back to the circulation desk.

As I stepped away from the desk and slipped on my coat, I noticed that Mona was already waiting for me at the back of the library. Impatiently, if the tapping of her water-stained suede boots was any indication.

I crossed to the back door and opened it, grimacing at the steady downpour. "Let me lead the way. I'll unlock the archives so you can dash inside, since it seems"—I looked Mona over—"you left your rain gear at home."

Mona patted her damp hair. "A little water doesn't bother me. I've traipsed through worse than this when I've collected stories from mountain folk."

I nodded and made a run for it, zigzagging to avoid splashing through the puddles that dotted the gravel lot behind the library. When I reached the small stone building that housed the archives, I fumbled with unlocking the door. Shoving the umbrella handle under my armpit so I could use both hands, I swore under my breath as the umbrella slid back, exposing my head to the pounding rain.

*So much for staying dry.* I stomped into the archives behind Mona and hovered near the door. As I closed my umbrella and slipped off my coat, my gaze landed on the pale oval that marked one section of the floor.

The sight of that lightened wood still rattled me. The previous summer someone had died on that spot, and although the wooden planks had been thoroughly scrubbed, the bleach mixture used to clean the blood had lightened the area until it shone in vivid contrast with the age-darkened boards surrounding it.

"Okay, here's the thing." Mona circled behind the large wooden table that sat in the middle of the room. "I need to know two things."

She was trailing water everywhere. I sighed, knowing I'd have to come out later with a mop. "What things?" I asked as I hung my coat and umbrella on a hook on the back of the closed door.

"First, whether you've ever heard of any scandals concerning the two girls who disappeared back in 1879. The ones I mentioned in my fairy lights story."

"No, what scandal could there have been?"

"Oh, I ran across something in my research that seems to suggest . . ." Mona waved one hand through the air in a dismissive gesture. "Well, never mind. If you haven't heard anything from your interactions with library patrons or from your aunt and her friends, I guess it isn't a widely circulated rumor these days."

I studied her while I brushed water droplets from my hair. She appeared almost manic, as if she was barely able to prevent herself from bouncing up and down like an overactive child. "Why would some old scandal matter, anyway? Assuming there was one."

"Perhaps it shouldn't, so many years later. But it's been my experience that families can be very protective of their history. I just thought that I might be able to use the information I found as leverage, you know?"

I wiggled my toes inside my shoes to free them from the uncomfortable cling of my damp socks. "No, I don't know. Leverage to do what?"

"Get some of the more reticent folks to talk." Mona twisted one of her tight curls around her finger. "I haven't been having much luck with a few of them, even though I suspect they could provide information that would greatly benefit my research. That old man who lives up in the cabin in the mountains refuses to have anything to do with me, even though his family"—Mona lowered her head, staring at her hands—"has been around forever, so I'm sure he could share some great stories."

"If you mean Delbert Frye, I doubt you'll have much success there. From what I hear, he doesn't talk to many people, and certainly not strangers."

"Oh, I don't know. He might be interested in talking to me. Once I share a bit of information with him, that is." Mona slowly curled her fingers into fists.

I narrowed my eyes. Mona was looking entirely too smug. It made me wonder what information she could possibly have dug up on old Delbert Frye or his family. Probably nothing pleasant. "It's your funeral. Go ahead and try to talk to him without an introduction, but be prepared for him to chase you away with a shotgun." I shrugged. "Anyway, that's one thing and you said you had two questions for me. What's the other one?"

Mona lifted her chin and met my stare with a defiant little smile. "I want to know whether Charles Bartos ever confessed his crime to you."

"Crime?" I strolled over to face her across the table.

"He stole my research and benefited from it without ever compensating me. Or even acknowledging my contribution to his composition. I'd call that a crime."

"If you're talking about the *Moon and Thistle Cycle*, I don't know anything about that aspect of the piece. He composed it before we started dating."

"But weren't you involved with him when it won all those prizes, including that Grammy, and when he was awarded grants for future compositions?" Mona uncurled her fists and placed her hands on the table.

"Yes," I said, recalling that Charles had not invited me to be his guest at the Grammy Awards celebration. He'd claimed that he needed to take some musician who'd mentored him in the past.

*Yeah, and you thought that was just fine at the time. A noble gesture. But you might as well admit, at least to yourself, that he probably invited someone who'd cut a more glamorous figure on the red carpet. You were so blinded to the truth that you just smiled and said you understood.*

I rolled my shoulders, shaking off such useless regret. "Anyway, if you're wondering if he ever confessed to plagiarizing your research, no he did not. At least not to me."

Mona sighed deeply and gazed down at the hands she had pressed against the tabletop. "I had hoped . . . Well, never mind, then." When she looked up at me, I was shocked by the fury blazing in her eyes. "I hoped you'd be able to give me a confession, even if it was second-hand, so I wouldn't have to go after him with the really dirty laundry. But now there's nothing else I can do and, trust me—I'll force him to admit his guilt, no matter what it takes."

I stared at her, confused by the vicious edge to her tone. There seemed to be something more than mere professional jealousy fueling her anger, but I couldn't imagine what that might be. Since campus gossip had never even hinted at such a thing, I was certain she'd never had any romantic involvement with Charles.

*But face it, Amy, that might be true only because Charles would never date someone older. Maybe Mona made a few romantic over-tures and he brushed her off with that offhand cruelty he so often displayed . . .*

"You can try, but to be honest, Mona, I doubt you'll ever get him to confess to anything. He never likes to admit that he's wrong."

Mona lifted her hands from the table and flexed her fingers. "Did he ever apologize to you? For cheating on you with that violinist?"

"No. And now that Marlis is dead, I certainly wouldn't demand it." I studied her furious expression with concern. "Look, Mona, even if you despise him, I think you should cut Charles a little slack right now. The man has suffered a great loss."

"He plays the grieving lover well, anyway." Mona's lips curved into a sardonic smile. "But I doubt he'll be alone for long."

"It's no concern of mine," I interjected, not interested in hearing any more gossip about my former boyfriend. "Given that you intend to pursue this vendetta, exactly how do you propose to prove that Charles stole your research? I'm not saying he didn't, but after all this time, I wonder how you plan to make your case."

Mona rubbed her hands together. "Oh, just like with old Mr. Frye, I have collected some information that I think may compel Charles to confess. If he knows what's good for him, that is. I was hoping to have your corroboration on the theft of my work, but that's not abso-lutely necessary."

I noticed the color that had risen in her cheeks. "Well, he did tell me that he'd be back at the mountain house tomorrow or Wednes-day, but I don't know if confronting him is the wisest choice. The man is in mourning. He's likely to call the sheriff on you if you show up unannounced." I lifted my hand to silence Mona's retort. "Not that he'd harm you, but you might miss your chance to get him to talk if you attack him while he's still so raw from Marlis's death. Maybe it would be best if you arranged a meeting a few months from now at the university, with some other members of your department available for support."

"No, it's now or never." Mona walked around the table and headed for the door. Pausing with her hand on the doorknob, she gazed back at me. "I can read the disapproval in your face, Amy, but you wouldn't think me so heartless if you knew the truth."

She was definitely alight with some secret passion. I walked over to her and laid a hand on her arm. "I just don't want to see you stir up something that might backfire. Charles isn't above bringing a defamation of character suit against you."

Mona threw back her head and laughed. "Character? Just wait until I can expose Charles Bartos's true character to the world. He'll have to slink away with his tail between his legs like the mangy cur he is."

I eyed her as I slipped on my rain slicker. "Here," I said, holding out my umbrella. I can pull up my hood if you want to use this."

"No thanks." Mona stepped outside. "I welcome the rain. It's washing all my troubles away. Just like my talks with Delbert Frye and Charles will, soon enough."

She dashed across the parking lot, leaving me to follow her.

Back inside the library, I headed straight for the workroom so that I could hang up my wet coat and pop open my umbrella to dry.

"Sorry to bother you again," Sunny said, poking her head around the workroom door as I slipped my feet out of my soaked loafers. "But you have another patron asking for you."

I muttered something not suitable for public consumption. "And here I am in my socks."

"But they're such cute socks."

I lifted one foot and pointed my toes inside my socks. "They are, aren't they?" I admire the tutu-clad pink elephants dancing across a field a navy blue.

"Just to give you a heads-up, it's Kurt Kendrick. Looking very dashing, I must say." Sunny lifted one hand, pinky up. "Dressed like a proper gentleman in one of those British spy trench coats."

"Meanwhile, I look like a drowned rat." I shoved my damp hair behind my ears. "All right, I suppose if I've dealt with Mona this morning, I can handle Kurt too."

"That's the spirit." Sunny pushed her glasses up her nose and gave me a bright smile.

Slipping around the circulation desk, I spied Kurt Kendrick standing in the middle of the reading room. Since he was as white-haired as my aunt, and well over six feet tall, he was hard to miss.

As I drew closer, I saw that Kurt was engaged in a lively conversation with none other than Mona Raymond. "Hello, Kurt, I heard you were looking for me?"

"Amy, so nice to see you. It's been too long." Kurt, whose childhood nickname had been "The Viking," was over seventy but still exuded a virility that many younger men would have envied.

"I'm sure we've both been tied up with work." I gazed up at him, feeling, as always, dwarfed by both his size and his vitality.

"Ah yes. Work. Just what I was discussing with Professor Raymond." Kurt gestured toward Mona. "I hear she's conducting research into the mountain lights, so I've invited her to meet someone who might be able to provide some deeper insights into local folklore."

My damp socks let out a squelch as I pressed my feet into the carpet. "Who's that?"

"Mary Gardener. She's ninety-two but still as sharp as a tack." Kurt tapped his forehead with one finger. "She probably remembers more than I've forgotten, to tell you the truth."

"I've heard of her. An old lady who lives by herself up on the mountain. She's an expert on local folklore and has researched the history of the town by talking to the older residents over the years, if what Zelda Shoemaker tells me is true."

"Yes. She once worked as a maid at a local orphanage"—Kurt shot me a significant look—"but fortunately she left about the time I did, before either one of us fell ill from that contaminated well water."

"You really believe this lady can give me deeper insights into the fairy lights, Mr. Kendrick?" Mona, her hair still shedding water like a fountain, tilted her head and looked up at Kurt. If I hadn't known better, I'd have sworn she was flirting with the wealthy art dealer.

*Or maybe I don't know anything.* I narrowed my eyes as Mona stroked the side of her face with one damp hand. It was a gesture that could be interpreted as simply wiping away beads of rain, but it also drew attention to her admittedly sensual lips.

I glanced at Kurt, wondering how he'd react. On a superficial level, I understood Mona's interest. Regardless of his age, Kurt was a handsome devil and could be devastatingly charming when he wished.

Mona fluttered her dark lashes. "I would love to meet your friend, Mr. Kendrick."

I opened my mouth and closed it again. It wasn't any of my business, even if I suspected Mona was barking up the wrong tree.

Kurt smiled, his craggy features and white teeth making him look like the storybook wolf I often imagined him to be. "Wonderful. I'll take you to meet her tomorrow afternoon. I had a visit already planned, so I'll simply have to let her know to expect two additional guests. That is, if you'd like to accompany us, Amy." Kurt turned his bright blue gaze on me.

"Sure thing. Honestly, I'd love to make a connection with Mrs. Gardener. She can probably share stories perfect for the archives. Stuff about the history of the town, I mean."

"It's settled then. I'll pick up both of you tomorrow afternoon. Can you get off a little early, Amy? I was thinking around three o'clock."

"No problem. I'm sure Sunny will cover for me, especially if it means we might be able to collect some good oral history recordings."

"Great. Just meet me in front of the library." Kurt turned his attention back to Mona. "By the way, you might want to watch your terminology, Professor Raymond. Mary calls those glowing orbs that people claim to see the *mountain* lights, with no mention of fairies. She says it's best not to name the 'Folk' so directly."

"Please call me Mona, and of course I'll be careful." Mona widened her dark eyes. "She's a believer, then?"

"Oh yes. Most definitely. She's informed me on numerous occasions that she's seen the lights and even heard some sort of unearthly music that's pulled at her, luring her away. But she tells me"—Kurt flashed a toothy grin—"that she doesn't enjoy dancing enough to do it for eternity."

Mona tossed her mass of dark hair behind her shoulders. "It's very kind of you to arrange a visit, Mr. Kendrick. I'm looking forward to meeting her."

"It's Kurt. And I must confess I'm mostly doing this for Mary's sake. I think it would be nice for her to have your company. She needs to see something other than my weathered old face now and then."

"Now Kurt, I'm sure she loves your visits." Mona pressed her fingers lightly against the arm of his elegantly tailored coat. "Besides, I don't think you're quite as ancient as all that."

Covering her hand with his, Kurt graced Mona with a dazzling smile. "Nice of you to say so, but I'm sure your lovely face will be much more welcome."

I eyed him with suspicion.

Kurt, looking at me over Mona's shoulder, winked.

# Chapter Five

The late April weather was warm enough that I was forced to shed my sweater and tie it around my waist while I waited outside the library on Tuesday afternoon. Kurt was late, which was perhaps for the best, as Mona Raymond also hadn't shown up yet.

I'd found this odd enough to call her a few times, but all my attempts had only reached her recorded message. It was strange. The folklorist was such a punctual person that I'd expected to find her pacing the library lawn when I'd stepped out the front doors.

Kurt pulled up in front of the library in his glamorous black Jaguar. Always the gentleman, he climbed out and waited for me to reach the car before opening the passenger side door. "Mona isn't coming?"

"I guess not. We could wait a little while longer, but she's one of those people who's always on time, so this probably means she had to bail," I said, climbing into the car. "She isn't answering her phone either, which makes me think something important has come up. Maybe she's dealing with a sensitive situation, something where she can't take time to contact us. You know—like a critical meeting with a student or something. I know how emergencies like that can pop up without warning."

"Then I'm afraid we must go without her. I'm already twenty

minutes late, and I don't like to keep Mary waiting. She frets over such things." Kurt closed my door and circled around to slide into the driver's seat. "I'll arrange a visit for Mona another time."

"Okay. I'll just send her a text so she knows not to bother showing up."

Kurt drove out of town, turning on a narrow side road that led up into the mountains. "From delving into local history, I understand that this was an old logging route," he said, expertly navigating the road's twists and turns. "Makes me wonder how they maneuvered those big trucks around these corners."

His comment reminded me of some research I'd done on the history of the lumber industry for one of our patrons. "It was probably wagons, not trucks. Major logging operations had pretty much shut down by the twenties, at least in this immediate area. My family's wood lots were farther south."

"Ah yes, the Baker fortune was built on lumber, wasn't it?"

"Not that there's any of it left, but yes." I stared out my window, admiring the bright splashes of color provided by the blooming rhododendrons nestled in the hollows. Shadowed by pines and hardwoods, their magenta and pink blossoms gleamed brightly against the dark green undergrowth. "You knew Mary Gardener at the orphanage?"

"I did. The truth is, she was the only person on staff who treated me with any sort of kindness. I suppose you could say we bonded over our mutual sense of being outcasts." Kurt cast me a sidelong glance from under his bushy white eyebrows. "Like me, she wasn't born in Taylorsford. She moved here with her husband after World War Two. He was a native of the area, but she was born and raised in North Carolina. Still a mountain girl, but that didn't count. She was an outsider, just like me."

"I didn't know she'd been married. I've always heard she lived alone."

"Sadly, her husband died young. He was only in his late thirties. That would've been back in the early sixties, when Lydia was still young and long before you were born. I'm not surprised you've heard nothing about him." Kurt turned the car onto a gravel road. "They never had children and Mary had no interest in remarrying, so she was left alone."

"Except for you?"

Kurt flashed me a grin. "I stayed in touch, even after I left Taylorsford. I like to honor my friendships, rare as they are."

I studied his rugged profile. "You never married? I mean, I know you might not have been so inclined . . ."

"No, I never found anyone I wanted to impose myself on quite so thoroughly." He cast me another amused glance. "In case you're trying to put two and two together in that inquisitive brain of yours—yes, I enjoy the company of women as well as men. Romantically, I mean. I hope that doesn't give you pause."

"Not at all." I sank back in my seat, realizing I needed to rearrange a few of my conclusions about him—something it seemed I had to do on a regular basis. "By the way, that road we were on, right before the last turn, does that lead to Delbert Frye's property?"

"And the old Patterson place, now owned by your former boyfriend."

I shot him a sharp look. "More of your little birds keeping tabs on me?"

"Could be. But don't take it personally, I keep tabs on everyone in my life."

"I didn't know I was *in* your life," I said, before staring back out the side window.

"Of course you are. I'm quite fond of you, as well as Richard." Kurt casually dropped one hand off the steering wheel and tapped my knee. "You should be flattered. I don't say that about many people."

I turned my head and examined him with a critical eye. "I can imagine."

He grinned. "Ah, here we are."

We pulled up in front of a small box of a house. One story, with white siding and a low concrete porch covered with a simple roof, it looked nothing like what I'd imagined.

"Not what you expected?" Kurt slid his keys into his jacket pocket and opened his car door. "I'll bet you pictured a rustic log cabin or something along those lines."

"I guess I did," I said as I climbed out of the Jaguar.

Kurt met me at my car door. "This house was built in the late forties, right after the war. It's had a few upgrades since then, like the siding and a new roof."

I turned to stare up into his face. "I'm guessing you've helped her with that, and some other things, over the years?"

He shrugged. "Army pensions and social security don't stretch very far these days."

"Careful." I wagged a finger at him. "I might actually believe you have a heart."

Kurt laughed and laid his hand over his chest. "Alas, like the Tin Man, I assure you I am quite hollow."

"But the Tin Man proved," I said, as we made our way to Mary Gardener's front door, "that he didn't actually require a heart to have a heart."

"Yes, he did, didn't he?" Kurt's blue eyes sparkled as he glanced down at me. "All right, let's see what Mary has to say today. I never know what stories she's likely to tell, which does at least keep things interesting."

The doorknob turned easily in Kurt's hand. This didn't surprise me. My aunt had always left her doors unlocked until I'd recently badgered her into changing her ways.

I followed Kurt into the house. The front door opened directly onto a small living room. Paneled in polished wood, its dark walls were enlivened by windows framed with white lace curtains and numerous pictures of flowers. Examining one of the paintings, I narrowed my eyes. This was not some amateur piece picked up at a flea market.

"Did you give her these paintings as well?" I asked.

Kurt paused in an archway leading to what looked like the kitchen and glanced at me over his shoulder. "Several of them, yes. They aren't masterpieces—just things I bought off professional artists because I thought Mary might like them."

"They're lovely," I said, my sweeping gaze taking in more of the paintings.

As I trailed him into the other room, I heard him tell someone, "Don't get up."

The kitchen surprised me once again. It was unabashedly modern and boasted robin's-egg-blue solid surface countertops that contrasted beautifully with gleaming stainless appliances and pale-yellow walls.

Studying his broad back as he bent over the woman sitting in a wooden rocker beside a built-in electric fireplace, I mulled over the very likely possibility that Kurt had paid for all of the upgrades to Mary Gardener's modest home.

"Mary, may I introduce Amy Webber?" Kurt straightened and stepped aside, motioning toward me. "She's the current library director in Taylorsford."

The seated woman was so tiny that her feet did not touch the floor. Although her face was as lined and grooved as a walnut shell, her hazel eyes sparkled as brightly as water in a shallow brook. "Hello, my dear," she said in a reedy voice. "I'm very pleased to make your acquaintance." She held out one arthritis-twisted hand.

I crossed to her and clasped her knobby fingers firmly. "Very nice to meet you as well, Mrs. Gardener."

"Please, call me Mary." The old woman squeezed my hand in a surprisingly strong grip while tossing back the wool blanket covering her legs with her other hand. "Karl, can you please get this thing off me? I'm about to roast."

For a moment, I thought that Mary had forgotten who was in the room, then realized my error. Naturally, Mary Gardener would've known Kurt by his original name of Karl Klass when she met him at the orphanage back in the late 1950s.

*Her memory is better than yours, it seems.*

"But weren't there supposed to be two guests?" Mary asked, proving my point. She motioned toward one of the counters, which held a crystal plate filled with sugar cookies and four glasses of lemonade.

Kurt lifted the blanket and draped it over the back of the rocking chair. "I'm sorry, Mary. Professor Raymond couldn't make it today. But I promise to bring her another time."

"That's fine. Just means I get to see you again sooner." Mary offered Kurt a smile that lit up her wizened face. "Now Karl—show some manners. Pull up a chair from the kitchen table so Amy can sit herself down. After that you can serve the cookies and lemonade."

"Yes, ma'am." Kurt's face and tone were both humble. But he gave me a wink as he slid a chair over to where I stood.

"Amy, Karl has asked me to share some local stories. I hope you'll allow me to tell the tale of the mountain lights. That's the one I thought the professor would want to hear."

"That will be perfect," I replied, taking a seat. "I have to ask, though—do you mind if I record you? It would be for the town archives. We like to collect local stories from the people who know them best."

Mary waved her hand. "Laws no, I don't mind. As long as I never have to listen to it. Don't much care for the sound of my own voice these days. It's all thin and whiny, like a weasel caught in a trap."

I smiled as I extracted my small voice recorder from my purse. "I promise I won't make you listen if you don't want to."

Mary settled back in her chair, crossing her hands one over the other in her lap.

"Go ahead, Mary," Kurt said, before grabbing a TV tray and setting it up between his chair and mine. "I'll play waiter while you talk."

"All right then." Mary fixed her bright gaze on me. "Well, I'm sure you've heard this story before, Amy, but listen close—most of what you've been told is nothing but a shadow of the tale, spun by those who don't know the truth."

"But you do?" I asked, after thanking Kurt for the drink and the two cookies he'd set on a napkin on the tray beside me.

"Yes, I do. Now, you've heard how it was May Day . . ."

Mary spun her tale, mesmerizing me to the point that I didn't even take one sip of my lemonade. Her story followed the general outline of what I'd heard before but included many more details.

"Wait," I said at one point. "You're saying one of the girls was related to Delbert Frye?"

"Yes indeed. His great-great-aunt Ada Frye. She was his great-grandfather's sister and was only eighteen when she disappeared. The

Frye family has always sworn she just ran away with her friend, Violet Greyson, but . . ." Mary tented her fingers and narrowed her eyes. "I think they were lured away by the Folk."

"To dance forever in the hall of the Mountain King?" Kurt took a sip of lemonade, but the rim of the glass couldn't hide his smile.

"Pshaw, Karl. There you go, making fun again. I bet you wouldn't be so high and mighty if you were to catch a strain of that unearthly music rising up from under the hills."

I scooted forward in my chair. "You've heard it?"

"Laws yes, child." Mary tipped her head. "Times are I can hear it still."

"On the other hand," Kurt said, stretching his long legs out in front of him, "there is another, more reasonable explanation. The Frye girl didn't want to marry the man her family had chosen for her, which I can understand. From what I hear, he was a bit of a brute."

"That's true enough and may have been why she ran off. But why did she never return? Can you answer that one for me, young man?"

I almost giggled at the thought of Kurt being called a young man, as well as at the bemused look on his face, but took a long swallow of my lemonade instead.

Kurt shrugged. "She and her friend probably settled in another town, changed their names, and lived happily ever after. Why should she have come back here? All those bad memories . . ."

Mary cast him a sharp look. "Didn't keep you away."

I widened my eyes as I turned off the recorder and slipped it back into my purse. Mary might've been over ninety, but she was no one's fool. She'd punctured Kurt's ironclad air of invulnerability with one short phrase.

Of course, Kurt, being Kurt, instantly composed his face and came back with a quip. "Only for you."

She waved him off. "Always such a charmer. Heaven knows why you're still single."

Kurt shot me a swift glance before replying. "No one could match up to your finer qualities, Mary. My first love." He bent forward in a gallant bow.

Mary snorted. "Don't you believe him, Amy. He's always been a rascal. Probably broke as many hearts as he captured. Although"—a beatific smile lit up her wrinkled face—"I must confess he's always been a dear to me."

I glanced over at Kurt, who was, of all things, blushing slightly. "As he should be."

"Now he wouldn't tell anyone this, but he's helped me out quite a bit over the years. Kept me in this house—sending in nurses and handymen and cleaning ladies and such. And all because I was a little bit nice to him back when he was young."

"More than a bit," Kurt said gruffly. "You were the only one who treated me like a human being; like someone with actual feelings. Well, you and then later Paul Dassin."

"Paul was a good man, though I know many around here didn't care for him. They always called him an outsider, just like me." Mary fixed her gaze on my face. "I understand you're dating his great-nephew."

*Does nothing get by this woman?* I side-eyed Kurt. "Yes. Richard Muir. He inherited Paul's house."

"The old Cooper place." Mary brushed a loose strand of her gray hair away from her face. "I was happy to hear that poor Eleanora Cooper had finally been cleared of suspicion in her husband's death. You had a hand in that, I'm told."

"Yes, last summer." I squirmed in my chair. Mary Gardener seemed to know an awful lot. I didn't mind her knowing; it was the fact that Kurt Kendrick had obviously seen fit to share so much information about me, as well as Richard, that unnerved me.

*As if we really do mean something to him*, I thought, casting him a questioning glance.

"She was an outsider too," Mary murmured. Looking at Kurt, she raised her voice. "Oh, by the way, I wonder if you could do me a favor before you leave today."

"Certainly," Kurt replied. "Whatever you need."

"Carry that jug out to the compost heap." Mary pointed toward the sink. "The one filled with peelings and coffee grounds. I usually take it out myself, but my rheumatism is acting up today."

"That's no problem." Kurt rose to his feet. "But you do have a garbage disposal, you know."

Mary muttered something about "newfangled gadgets" and plucked at the faded material of her floral print cotton housedress.

Kurt shook his head. "What am I going to do with you? All right, I'll take care of that right away. Amy, you stay and talk. I'm sure Mary appreciates the company."

"You've known him a long time," I said, after he had grabbed the jug and exited through the kitchen door.

Mary smiled. "Yes, indeed. Almost sixty years, I guess it is now." She tipped her head. With her bright eyes and her thin hair pulled into a knob of a bun on top of her head, she reminded me of some inquisitive bird. "You're Lydia Litton's niece, aren't you? Strange, you don't look a thing like her."

"I am her niece, although it's Lydia Talbot. She married Andrew Talbot, you know. And you're right, I don't take after her. I resemble my mom, Lydia's younger sister, Deborah."

"Of course, what was I thinking? Lydia married that artist, and Debbie moved away . . ." Mary closed her eyes for a moment. "I only saw your mother when she was a little slip of a thing. But now that you mention it, I do recall she had dark eyes and hair, like her grandmother." Mary's eyes fluttered open. "That's why you look familiar. You're the spitting image of Rose Baker Litton."

I made a face, as I always did when I was compared to my great-grandmother.

Mary eyed me with interest. "Don't much care for that? Can't say I blame you. Rose was not near as sweet as her name."

"No, apparently not," I said, thinking about my great-grandmother's involvement in the death of Eleanora Cooper. "Did you know her well?"

"Laws no. What would a fine lady such as her have to do with the likes of me? No, I only knew her by sight, and reputation. She liked her money, that I do know. Didn't approve of Paul Dassin turning over land to the town, and for an orphanage no less. Guess she was probably happy when they tore it down after all those people died."

"At first, maybe," I said, considering how the deaths of the children and others at the orphanage had revealed a secret that had contributed to Great-Grandmother Rose's mental decline. "Speaking of money, you said something a little while ago about a treasure connected to the mountain lights? I've never heard anything about that before."

"Oh yes, supposedly there was gold collected by the Folk." Mary stared over my shoulder, her eyes clouding as if she were peering into another realm. "At least I've heard tales about people around here searching for some such thing. Seems to get all muddled up in the story about those lost girls, like maybe that's what they were actually doing up here in the mountains." She huffed and blinked the shadows from her eyes. "As if such gold could be carried away. Would turn to dust if you tried, you know."

"But that never stops anyone from searching, I bet. People always want to believe in hidden treasure." I stood and pointed at Mary's empty glass. "Would you care for more lemonade?"

"No thank you, my dear. But please, help yourself."

I crossed to the counter to refill my tumbler from the pressed-glass pitcher, taking the opportunity to sneak another cookie. Between bites, I garnered a promise from Mary to relate more stories for the archives whenever I chose to visit.

Kurt shoved open the side door so hard it banged back against the wall. "Sorry," he said as he set down the empty jug and grabbed my arm, forcing me to abandon my glass.

"Everything all right?" Mary asked.

"Yes, just used that rake in the shed to tidy up the compost pile while I was at it," he replied, pulling me to the other side of the kitchen.

"What is it?" I mumbled through a mouthful of cookie.

"I saw something out there, on the edge of the woods." Kurt kept his voice low. "Can you call Brad Tucker and tell him to get out here right away?"

"Sure," I whispered, "but what did you see?"

"A footprint, and not from Mary's galoshes." Kurt narrowed his eyes. "This imprint included toes."

"So possibly a woman's bare foot?"

"Or a child's. It is rather small, but I suppose a petite woman's foot could have made that mark."

"It could've been Lacey Jacobs." I gnawed the inside of my cheek. "If she lost her shoes . . ."

"Which is why I believe the authorities need to be alerted. They should scour this area." Kurt ran one hand through his thick white hair. "If the girl's wandering around barefoot, she could be in real danger."

I let fly a swear word that made Mary straighten in her chair.

"Now, Amy," she said. "I'd prefer not to hear that sort of thing in my house."

I apologized profusely as I crossed the room to clasp her hand. "I'm also sorry to say that I must leave rather abruptly. It's been such a pleasure to meet you," I added, my fingers reaching for the cell phone in my pocket. "I'll come back soon."

"You are welcome anytime, young lady. Just see that you leave that language at home." Mary shook one bony finger at me.

I swallowed and nodded. "Sure thing. Bye now." I fled the kitchen and headed out the front door, pausing on the porch to punch in the number for the sheriff's office.

Kurt was right—we had to alert the authorities about his find as soon as possible. Because if what we suspected was true, we might have stumbled over the best clue to Lacey's current whereabouts.

And she might be in worse shape than any of us had imagined.

# Chapter Six

B y that evening, I was in no mood to be sociable. Not only had I been pulled into yet another criminal investigation, I'd also received only two texts from Richard since our phone call Friday night.

My aunt was not sympathetic. "In my day, we often went a week without any communication with our friends, especially if they were out of town. There was no such thing as texts or emails, and long-distance phone calls were expensive. It didn't mean that people were no longer interested in us. Even now, Hugh and I don't talk every day." Aunt Lydia pointed a cake knife at me. "Now, cheer up—we have guests."

I leaned back against one of the butcher-block kitchen counters. It was fine for her to talk about her relationship with art expert Hugh Chen, whom she'd been dating for several months, but they were both older. Surely they had different expectations. *Although, to be fair*, I told myself, *that's probably just showing your age bias*. I shook my head and stared morosely at the cake she was slicing. Three tiers of delicate yellow cake layered and topped with fluffy white icing and flakes of fresh coconut, it normally would have made my mouth water. But that evening I was fighting off nausea, partially due to exhaustion. Since Kurt had elected to stay with Mary after Brad questioned her, I'd had to wait for one of the deputies to drive me back. Starving by the time I'd gotten home, I'd scarfed down—far too quickly—a plate of leftovers from the dinner Aunt Lydia had prepared for her close friends Walt Adams and Zelda Shoemaker. Not the best choice for my already nervous stomach.

"It just seems odd. Richard is usually so attentive." I clutched my coffee mug to my chest.

"You mean he spoils you." Aunt Lydia looked over at me, her blue eyes narrowed in disapproval. "Really, Amy. The man is helping out his family. He can't drop everything to soothe your fragile ego."

"Should've known you'd take his side," I muttered, staring down at the stains inside my empty mug. The streaks made the shape of a heart. It wasn't tea leaves, but I hoped it was a good sign. "Anyway, you're right. Whatever is going on, I shouldn't take it out on you, or our guests."

"Quite right." Aunt Lydia dropped a few dessert forks on my tray. "Perhaps this will cheer you up—I just heard from your mom. She said that she and Nick want to come for a short visit next weekend. I thought it sounded like a lovely idea and agreed."

"My parents are coming here?"

"Yes. It will be the first time Debbie's been back to this house in quite some time. I suppose we'll need to give everything a good cleaning, but we do have a week to take care of that."

"It will also be the first time they have the opportunity to meet Richard." My fingers tightened around the edge of the tray. "Whenever I've visited since we met, he's either been traveling for his choreography projects or couldn't get away from campus."

"I know." My aunt walked over to the counter to pick up a silverplated coffee carafe. "Strangely, you've always chosen weekends when he was busy. Not that I suspect you of doing that deliberately, of course," she added as she crossed back to the kitchen table and set the carafe on a second tray.

"I'm guessing you planned this, knowing he said he'd be home next weekend."

"Could be." Aunt Lydia's smile confirmed my suspicion. "Anyway, it's time they met. Now—how about you carry the cake into the sitting room? I'll bring the coffee." Aunt Lydia placed ceramic cream and sugar dispensers, spoons, and a few mugs next to the coffee pot.

I swallowed back a sharp retort. She was right—I had deliberately delayed my parents meeting Richard. Not because I thought they wouldn't like him. Quite the opposite. I was more concerned that they would immediately rush out and rent a hall for a wedding reception.

But they did need to meet him sooner or later, so I might as well make the best of it. I cleared my throat and pointed toward the coffee tray. "Maybe I'd better carry that one. It looks heavy."

Aunt Lydia raised her chin and stared down her aristocratic nose at me. "Are you suggesting that I've grown feeble in my declining years?"

I snorted. "Declining? Seems to me you're more active than ever these days."

"Exactly. So don't treat me like an old lady. I'm only sixty-five. Not ready for the nursing home yet."

"I just meant your bum leg might make it more difficult . . ."

Aunt Lydia's white eyebrows rose in two delicate arches. "My leg is just fine, thank you very much. Now, grab that tray with the cake and follow me, missy. And please, for the love of heaven, try to smile." She strode out of the kitchen and down the hall, forcing me to quicken my pace to follow her.

As she stepped back to allow me to enter the sitting room, she leaned in and whispered, "Richard is madly in love with you, Amy. Anyone with eyes can see that. Stop wallowing in your insecurity."

"Okay," I said, plastering a smile on my face.

"That looks delicious." Zelda, who was seated next to Walt on the suede sofa, slid forward to get a better glimpse of the cake.

While Aunt Lydia filled two mugs and carried them to the end table next to the sofa, I followed behind her with my tray.

"Anything new with you, Walt?" I asked as I handed him and Zelda each a slice of cake.

"Certainly nothing as interesting as the disappearance of the young lady from Clarion. Have you heard any more about that, Amy?"

"Yes, as a matter of fact . . ." I placed a slice of cake on the end table next to my aunt's favorite chair, then carried the tray over to a tall side table. Setting it next to the coffee items, I shared the information about the footprint Kurt had discovered on the edge of Mary's property. "And I did provide Brad Tucker with some interesting information I found through some Internet sleuthing." I met three expectant stares. "Sorry, he asked me not to share any details until he checks it out."

"Way to dangle the carrot," Zelda said, patting her blonde curls.

"So strange." Aunt Lydia, settled in her favorite armchair, tugged her pale-pink skirt over her knees. "What would compel a young woman not known to be a hiking enthusiast to wander up into the mountains on her own?'

"Bethany claims that Lacey wanted to look for some piece of jewelry she had lost hiking the trail the previous weekend." I refilled my cup and took a sip of coffee. "Of course, now some people are saying she was lured away by the mountain lights."

My aunt waved her hand. "Such nonsense. That mountain lights tale has been circulating longer than the oldest book at the library. I've heard endless variations—UFOs, fairies, and all sorts of other ridiculous notions. Personally, I think those young women simply left town to start a new life elsewhere. I heard from old Mrs. Dinterman that one of them was being forced to marry someone she despised and that's why she and her friend ran off."

Walt crossed one long leg over the other. "I've heard that as well. As for the lights, to me that's a separate story. It's older than the girls' disappearance, you know. I've even read that the lights are linked to Native American folklore about warriors killed in battle. Meanwhile, a lot of people think it's just a natural phenomenon. A form of ball lightning or something. I'm in that camp."

I rested my mug against my other palm. "Have any of you ever actually seen the lights?"

Walt shook his head. "Not me."

"I never have." Zelda patted her brightly tinted lips with her napkin. "But my grandma claimed she saw them once. She said they were glowing orbs that bounced above the treetops. Although"—she winked—"Granny liked a nip of her moonshine, if you know what I mean."

"So, like granny, like grandchild?" Walt's teasing tone took the sting out of his words.

Zelda's crisply permed blonde curls bounced as she tossed her head. "Walter Adams, I don't know why I put up with you."

"Because you love me?"

"I suppose." Zelda turned to me, her merry expression sobering. "I just pray they find that poor child soon."

Walt tapped his fork against the china cake plate. "And I just hope the sheriff's department doesn't target Delbert Frye over this."

"Why would they?" I asked, examining his thoughtful expression.

Aunt Lydia toyed with the handle of her mug. "I know he's a bit of a curmudgeon, but surely they wouldn't suspect him in some girl's disappearance." She looked over at Walt and Zelda. "Everyone have what they need?"

"Yes, it's all perfect, Lydia, as always," Walt said, while Zelda took a large bite of her cake and made an approving noise. "As for Delbert, you must have heard the stories of him chasing hikers and other people off his property with a shotgun. It isn't a lie. He pointed a rifle at me the first time I visited his cabin."

"Really?" I set down my coffee mug. "He didn't take a shot at you, I hope."

"No, not once he realized who I was. But he can be a prickly character. Although he did explain to me that part of his hatred for trespassers comes from what he calls the 'dang fools' who crawl all over his property looking for some mythical treasure."

I studied Walt's calm face. "That's funny, Mary Gardener mentioned something about gold. She seems to think it's like the pot at the end of the rainbow—a tale connected to the 'Folk,' as she calls them."

Walt waved his hand. "That might be an embellishment to the folktale, but it's also mixed up with some story about a valuable cache of coins lost in the mountains during the Civil War. Or so Delbert told me once when I asked what he meant about strangers scouring his property for gold."

"I've never heard that aspect of the story, although I do remember my grandmother's friends gossiping about some treasure hidden on the mountain," Aunt Lydia said.

"Well, who knows? Maybe Delbert just concocted that story to shut me up. He doesn't much care for questions." Walt took a sip of his coffee before continuing. "He builds some beautiful musical instruments, though. I can't play, or I'd have bought one of those dulcimers for myself. But I do admire the craftsmanship."

"And Walt truly appreciates that sort of thing, being a craftsman himself," Zelda said. "In fact, he's got a garage full of some absolutely lovely furniture if you know anyone who's interested."

Walt gave her knee a pat. "Now, no advertising. Amy and Lydia don't want to buy anything from me. It's just a hobby anyway."

"I was thinking more about Richard. He hasn't completely furnished that house of his, has he?"

"Stop it, Zel. If Richard wants any of my pieces, he knows how to find me." Walt shot me an apologetic glance. "Sorry, but at least it seems I'll never need to advertise with Zelda around."

"Now that you're retired, you can use the money," Zelda muttered before taking another bite of her cake.

Walt cleared his throat. "But anyway, Amy, that's how Delbert and I bonded. We both love woodworking. Once he realized that I was more interested in talking about lathes and chisels than in invading his space, he became quite congenial." Walt grinned. "Well, maybe not exactly that. But less gruff, anyway. I've visited with him several times since."

"You don't think he would actually harm anyone?" Aunt Lydia lifted her plate from the end table and settled back in her chair.

Walt wielded his fork with a delicacy at odds with his large hands. "I don't think so, but I'm sure the authorities have other ideas. Delbert does have a temper, and I admit that I have seen him lose it over what I would call minor inconveniences. Of course, there's also that other fellow living in the area now. The one who recently lost his girlfriend in that accident. Some sort of musician, from what I hear. His property is adjacent to Delbert's, so I guess the sheriff will be talking to him as well."

I swallowed another slug of coffee before speaking. "Yeah, Charles Bartos." I twitched my lips into a tight smile. "Aunt Lydia knows Charles, although they only met once or twice."

"Indeed I do." As she raised her mug to her lips, my aunt's eyes asked me a question.

I frowned. "You may not know this, Walt, but Charles and I used to date when I worked at Clarion."

"Ah," said Zelda, with a knowing look at Aunt Lydia. "*That* Charles."

Aunt Lydia's gaze remained focused on me. "Yes." She took a delicate sip of coffee. "Not my favorite person, but it has to be a tough time for him. I understand they still haven't tracked down the driver who struck his girlfriend." She shook her head. "That must be maddening."

"It's an ongoing investigation, or so I hear. Such a shame." Zelda patted her permed curls. "So unfortunate too. Right after they spent all that money renovating the old Patterson place, she goes and dies before she really has a chance to enjoy it."

"It is too bad," Aunt Lydia said. "Although I'm not particularly fond of Charles Bartos, I do sympathize deeply with his loss."

I met her brilliant blue gaze. Of course she did. She'd lost her own first love, my Uncle Andrew, in another tragic accident.

"According to the news, the police are determined to find the driver, but they don't have much to go on. It was dark that morning, and apparently no one else was on the road at the time." Walt shook his head. "You'd think the driver would come forward. Imagine hitting someone and just driving off without even anonymously calling for help. I couldn't live with the guilt, myself."

"Most decent people couldn't," Aunt Lydia said. "But unfortunately, there are many irresponsible and callous individuals in this world."

"It's so sad." Zelda clucked her tongue. "I never actually met the woman, but we did see her once. Remember, Walt? It was at that concert at the Kennedy Center. The one where your coworker's daughter was playing a solo with a chamber orchestra."

"Oh, right." Walt set his empty cake plate on the table beside the sofa. "As I recall, that concert featured a few different performers, including Charles Bartos. He played a couple of piano solos on the program."

"Yes, and when we went backstage to congratulate your friend's daughter, we practically fell over him." Zelda shot me a conspiratorial look. "He was standing backstage, right in the way, not paying any attention to us because this beautiful blonde was draped over him and they were kissing like there was no tomorrow." Zelda fanned her face with her napkin. "His hands were all over her too. About made me blush."

"That sounds like Marlis Dupre," I said.

Zelda bobbed her head. "That's what I figured, especially when I saw her photo in the paper, poor lamb. I didn't get a good look at her face that night, but I remembered that blonde hair and lovely figure."

"I guess she accompanied Charles to some of his concerts even when the trio wasn't playing." I picked up my empty coffee mug and clutched it tight. "I know some people might wonder if I blame her for Charles dumping me, but I really don't, and anyway, I think it's a terrible shame, her dying like that. She'd just turned thirty and had so much talent . . ." I met Aunt Lydia's speculative gaze. "Well, it's always tragic when someone dies so young."

"Yes, it is," my aunt said, giving me an approving smile.

At that point, the conversation turned to other, less interesting topics, so I excused myself and headed into the kitchen, where I loaded the dishwasher and scrubbed the pots and pans Aunt Lydia had used to make dinner.

When Walt and Zelda left, I followed them out onto the porch. Waving goodbye, I glanced over at Richard's house and noticed that his car was in the driveway. Promising Aunt Lydia we'd talk about my parents' upcoming visit later, I bounded up the stairs to my bedroom and flung myself across my bed, cell phone in hand.

Richard answered my call on the third ring.

"Hi there," I said.

"Hey," he replied, in a subdued tone.

Perhaps it was simply exhaustion. "It's good to hear your voice. I know you probably don't feel like leaving the house. Do you want me to come over?"

"Um . . . Maybe not tonight. I just finished unpacking and still need to do laundry. Then I plan to crawl into bed and crash. Honestly, I don't think I'd be very good company."

I lowered my hand and stared at the screen of my cell phone, as shocked as if it had suddenly transformed into a snake. Raising it back to my face, I forced a brightness into my tone that I didn't feel. "If that's what you want, sure. I had a rather long day myself. It's fine."

That was a lie. It wasn't fine. We hadn't seen each other in several days and Richard had never been too tired for my company before. Even when he'd been injured or ill. Even after we'd stumbled over dead bodies and faced murderers with loaded guns.

"Sorry, sweetheart. I really am beat. I'll see you tomorrow sometime, okay?"

"Fine. It will have to be later in the day, though, since we're both working."

"Sounds good. Now I have to wash a few things so I have something decent to wear tomorrow. Catch up with you soon."

"All right. Good-night then." I hung up the phone before he could say anything more. And promptly burst into tears.

I allowed myself a good cry before running to the bathroom to vigorously scrub the dampness from my face with a rough washcloth.

Staring at myself in the mirror, I was glad no one else could see me. My hair was a tangled mess, my nose shone bright as a tomato, and my eyes were rimmed with red.

*But Richard doesn't want to see me anyway . . .* I gulped back a sob and fanned my heated face, telling myself that while I had every right to cry, I now had to clear my head and think things through.

Because no matter how hard I tried to dismiss my concerns, I knew in my heart that something significant had happened to Richard while he was away. As I contemplated the possibilities, my insecurity padded up on its little soft paws and whispered in my ear. *Perhaps he met an old acquaintance in his hometown. Some elegant, beautiful, woman he's always secretly loved. Someone unattainable, until now.*

"Stop it," I told my reflection. "Stop imagining the worst."

I splashed cold water on my face and brushed my hair before I dared to descend the steps and face Aunt Lydia. Hopefully she wouldn't notice any traces of my recent crying jag, or if she did, would assume my appearance was simply due to exhaustion.

Squaring my shoulders, I marched into the sitting room to find my aunt dozing in her chair. I didn't wake her. Instead, I crept back upstairs, brushed my teeth, and crawled into bed. Although sleep, like the answers to the mysteries of Lacey's disappearance and Richard's strange behavior, eluded me.

# Chapter Seven

I put on a brave face at work the next day, but Sunny wasn't fooled. "As the grands would say, you look like something the cat dragged in and refused to eat," she said as I slumped over the circulation desk after lunch.

I waved her off with one limp hand. "It's nothing."

"Sure, tell me another one." Sunny ran her fingers through her silky hair. "You want to talk about it?"

"Nope."

Sunny shook her head. "Well, you know where to find me when you do."

I thanked her and went back to compiling statistics from our integrated library system. It was a part of my job that I hated, which made it a perfect match for my mood.

Not long after I'd completed my task, with my mind still fuzzy with figures, I decided to head out to the archives. Perhaps another dive into the documents referencing the mountain lights story would take my mind off thoughts of Richard's strange behavior.

Flipping through some of the folders I'd pulled for Mona and not yet refiled, I discovered numerous descriptions of the lights, along with a few other related interviews. One in particular caught my eye. It was a transcription of oral recollections of the 1879 disappearance of the two young women.

I leaned over the worktable, scanning the typed report. It contained much of the same details as other material on the topic, except for one difference—it included comments by an elderly woman from a town on the other side of the mountains.

The document was one that I hadn't bothered to look at before, although I was sure Mona and her students had examined it. Within a few pages I realized why Mona hadn't brought it to my attention. The woman who was quoted in the document had been a cousin of Violet Greyson and had met Ada Frye while visiting her cousin's home. She swore that she'd been an ally in the girls' plan to run away after the May Day festival and that she'd even offered to provide them with a place to stay once they made it over the mountain. But the girls had never shown up for their planned reunion, leading the cousin to believe that they had died during their escape. "Violet would never have failed to contact me, one way or the other," the elderly woman had claimed, according to the transcription. "So I knew they was dead, for sure."

I sat back and stared at the document. This was something no one had ever brought into the mountain lights story, and I could see why. It certainly didn't support Mona's or any other storyteller's tales of the fae luring the girls into some mystical realm. If the girls had planned their escape from Taylorsford and their families in such detail, including setting up a safe haven with Violet's cousin in a new town, they hadn't gone out that night simply to chase the "fairy lights." They'd had a destination in mind and an obvious determination to reach it. Somehow I doubted that they would have been distracted, even if they had seen lights or heard mysterious music. The way Mona told the tale, one could picture two young girls running off on a lark and being lured away by the fae.

*Fact is fact, and fiction is fiction, and story is often a blend of both,* I thought as I placed the document back into its folder. Although I found it fascinating, it wasn't up to me to reveal this information. For all I knew, Mona planned to include it in her final research project. I might mention it to her, but I didn't want to expose this truth before she had a chance to do so.

I left the archives and returned to the library, where Sunny remarked that I was finally looking human. Reinvigorated by my discovery, I was able to get through the rest of the workday without too much moping.

On my walk home from the library, the anxiety flooded back. I replayed the previous evening's telephone conversation with Richard several times. Although part of me wanted to confront him, I was conflicted over whether to stop by his house. He'd told me in an earlier text that he'd be home by late afternoon, but I wasn't certain if I was up to seeing him yet. I knew that when I did, I'd feel compelled to demand answers.

*And you're not so sure you really want those answers, are you? Not if they confirm your worst fears.*

My decision was made for me when I reached my destination. Parked on the street in front of Richard's property was a sheriff's department car. Sprinting toward his renovated 1920s farmhouse, I fixed my gaze on the two deputies standing on the covered front porch.

"What's going on?" I called out as I bounded up the cement steps of the porch. "Is he okay?"

"Yes, Mr. Muir is fine," said a petite woman with short dark hair.

It was Alison Frye, a sheriff's deputy who reported to the man standing next to her.

Tall, broad-shouldered, and blond, chief deputy Brad Tucker had been dating Sunny for about a year, so I'd spent considerable time in his company and considered him a friend. But he was also a shrewd and determined law enforcement officer who was devoted to his job. Displaying his stern professional face, he met my concerned gaze. "We just finished questioning him."

I breathed a sigh of relief. *Richard is fine. Perfectly fine.* "About what?"

Brad pushed his hat back and rubbed his forehead. "Amy, you know we can't go into details about things like that."

"Lacey Jacobs? I know she's in his dance studio, but surely that isn't anything . . ."

Alison Frye examined me, her hazel eyes narrowed. "Exactly. And he was apparently the last person on campus to see her before she disappeared. Speaking of which, were you in contact with Mr. Muir this weekend, Ms. Webber?"

*Last person to see her? Wait a minute, what is this all about?* I glared at Alison, biting back a sharp comment about her great-uncle and his guns. "We spoke on the phone on Thursday and Friday evenings. And then again last night when he returned home from a visit with his family."

"You weren't with him Friday or Saturday?"

"No, as I'm certain you're already aware, he was out of town." I met Alison's laser-focused gaze. "He was spending time at his parents' home from late Thursday until yesterday evening. But I'm sure he told you that."

"He did." Alison tapped a stylus against the screen of her cell phone. "But there seems to be some discrepancy . . ."

Brad shot Alison a sharp look. "That's enough. We have Ms. Webber's statement that she didn't see Mr. Muir this weekend. That's all we need."

Alison muttered something under her breath as she slipped her phone back into the jacket pocket of her uniform.

"Any more leads on finding Lacey?" I asked, directing my query at Brad.

He shook his head. "None that I can go into to. Sorry, but this is an open investigation."

I met his steely gaze. "I understand. I'm just worried about the girl."

"As we all are," Alison said, with a quick glance toward Richard's front door. "Well, almost all of us, anyway."

I wondered what she was insinuating. Knowing Richard, I was sure he was deeply concerned about the disappearance of one of his students. "Is that all you need from me? I'd like to go talk to Richard, if you don't mind. As I said, I haven't seen him for several days."

Brad pulled his hat back down over his forehead. "Yes, that's all. Let's go, Deputy Frye. We're done here."

Alison cast me one long, dubious look before she took the stairs. Brad hung back for a moment while she headed for the patrol car.

"Sorry, Amy," he said in a friendlier tone. "I have to follow where the evidence leads. You know that."

"I know." I patted his arm. "It's okay. As long as Lacey comes home safely, nothing else matters."

"I hope that's true," he said, his blue eyes shadowed by something that made my stomach flip. "Anyway, you take care of yourself, okay?"

"Always do," I said, brushing a stray lock of hair from my face.

He smiled, but I noticed that it didn't quite reach his eyes. "See ya," he added with a tip of his hat.

"Sure thing," I said to his broad back as he turned and left.

70

I waited until the patrol car pulled away before I pressed Richard's doorbell.

"Hi," I said when he appeared, wearing a white T-shirt and navy sweatpants. "Can I come in?"

"Of course." He opened the door, but strangely, didn't reach for me.

I swallowed the bubble of bile that had rolled up my throat. Normally Richard would have hugged and kissed me for several minutes after not seeing me for only a day. Now we'd been apart for a week and he was just standing there, showing no interest in even touching me.

*Very well then.* As I slid past him and headed for the center of the room, I noticed his pallor and the shadows, dark as bruises, under his eyes. "Everything okay?"

"Oh sure. Right as rain. Which is a strange phrase, if you think about it. What's right about the rain? I mean, it's necessary, but why would it be right?"

He was babbling. I waited in the middle of the room for him to close the door. "What's going on? I know there's something you're not telling me."

Not bothering to lock the door, Richard flung out both hands. "Please lay off, Amy. First I get the third degree from Brad and that pint-sized harpy, and now you're interrogating me?"

I stared at him, blinking rapidly. "I'm not interrogating anyone. I just asked a simple question."

A string of swear words flew from Richard's lips. He stepped forward, dropping his hands to his sides with his fingers clenched. "I just don't see why you must know every little detail about my movements when I'm out of town. I told you I was busy. That should suffice."

My stomach felt as heavy as if I'd swallowed a handful of stones. "Sorry. I've just been concerned that something was bothering you and thought perhaps I could help. But obviously I was mistaken."

I turned away to stare at the gleaming expanse of wood that covered the other side of the room. Needing a place to rehearse when he wasn't on campus, Richard had turned a large portion of his open front room into a small dance studio, complete with a sprung dance floor, mirrors, and a barre.

"That's not true, it's just"—Richard strode over to stand beside me—"everything's so complicated right now."

"How can anything be that complicated?" I curled my fingers so tightly into my palms that my nails bit into the skin.

"Amy, please . . ." Richard circled around to face me.

"Please what? Look, it's apparent that something has put you in an extremely foul mood. I'm not so sure I want to know what or why at this point."

He furiously massaged his jaw with the back of one hand. "It's all this suspicion, for one thing. First at Clarion, then here, from Brad and that other deputy . . ."

I relaxed by clenched fingers. "What do you mean, at Clarion?"

Richard closed his eyes for a moment. "The campus police also questioned me today. About Lacey Jacobs."

"What about her?"

"Apparently I was the last person on campus to have seen her. Or at least to admit that they had."

When Richard looked directly at me, I was devastated by the pain I read in his gray eyes. I tempered the anger in my voice. "Campus police thought you were somehow involved in her disappearance because of that coincidence?" I stepped closer to him. "That seems like a stretch, especially since you went out of town Thursday right after you saw her. It's been proven that she went up into the mountains on Friday. Bethany Virts actually gave her a ride up to the Twin Falls trail, which means Lacey was fine at that point. So how could her disappearance be connected to you? Weren't you at your parents' the entire time? The authorities could certainly check that out." I stared into his drawn face. "You *were* at your parents' house, right?"

Richard looked away, but not before his face blanched to the color of bone. "I was in that area. But all the errand running meant I was driving around on my own quite a bit. To be honest, no one there can vouch for my whereabouts for hours at a time."

"But you weren't here."

Richard turned back to me. "True, but it's only a ninety-minute drive between Taylorsford and my hometown, so the authorities are still looking closely into my movements over the weekend." He threw up his hands. "Apparently being the last person from Clarion to see Lacey, along with being her teacher, is a big deal."

"Right." I tapped my foot against the hardwood floor. "Strangely, you've never mentioned it, but I understand that she's part of your studio."

"She is." Richard kept his eyes focused on the far wall behind me. "Lacey's a strong dancer and she has a real talent for choreography, but she struggles with academics, among other things." When Richard met my questioning gaze, his typical smile had twisted into a grimace. "Okay, here's the real issue—I didn't just see her in the studio on Thursday. She also stopped by my office after class to talk about her ideas for a piece of choreography. Or so I thought."

"What did she actually want to discuss?"

"That's the problem. I really don't know. She walked into my office already teary-eyed and sniffling. I spent several minutes handing her tissues and trying to calm her down." Richard ran his hand through his short dark hair, making it stand up in spikes. "I guess I wasn't patient enough. I was already running late and still needed to make that drive to Mom and Dad's, so I told Lacey I didn't have time for her problems and she'd have to come back another day to discuss the choreography piece. Then she burst out sobbing and fled my office. I never saw her again after that."

I studied his face, which now had the flushed look of someone battling a fever. "You think she wanted to share some personal problem? I mean, something that might have subsequently made her take a solo hike in the woods?"

Richard took a deep breath before replying. "I do now, which is what I told the campus police as well as the authorities here . . ."

A squeal of tires cut off his words.

I spun around to face the front windows. "Accident?"

"Better check." Richard ran to the front door and flung it open.

I followed on his heels as he dashed out onto the porch, just in time to see a car make a hard U-turn where the paved road ended. The car's tires squealed again as it sped away toward the center of town.

"What the heck?" Richard strode over to the simple white railing that enclosed his front porch. "Wait, do you hear that?"

I stepped up beside him, listening closely. A faint, high-pitched sound rose from the azaleas that lined the stone foundation of the house. "Some kind of animal."

"It could be hurt." Richard took the steps two at a time to reach the ground. He knelt down in the grass and parted several branches to peer into the shrubs.

"Be careful." I leaned over the balustrade. "Injured animals can bite."

"It's just a baby." When Richard drew back his arms, a small ball of black-and-orange fluff was balanced between his palms. "A kitten." He glanced up at me. "I bet someone in that car tossed it out."

"Who would do such a thing?" I raced down the steps to reach his side.

"Thoughtless monsters." Richard gently cradled the kitten against his chest and rose to his feet. "It's breathing hard. Could be hurt. I think I should take it to the vet to have it checked out."

"I'll come with you," I said, meeting his questioning gaze. "I can hold it while you drive."

"Okay." Richard cast me an apologetic smile. "Sorry for being such an ass before," he said, stroking the kitten's back with two fingers.

"Let's forget that for now. We need to work together on this. Give me the kitten while you grab your keys and wallet and lock up." I held out my hands.

Richard carefully passed the tiny creature to me before sprinting toward his house.

The kitten *was* breathing heavily. Its soft sides rose and fell against my palms. I curled in my pinky finger and touched the tip of its little black nose. "It's okay, baby, we're going to help you."

A tiny pink tongue darted out and licked my finger.

And, for the second time in ten months, I fell in love.

# Chapter Eight

Richard drove over the speed limit as we raced toward a veterinary clinic located in a neighboring town, but I didn't ask him to slow down. It was worth a ticket to get the kitten some immediate care.

"You're sure they're open?" he asked for the fifth time.

"I'm sure. I recently had to research the info for a patron at the library. This vet office has emergency services, available twenty-four/seven. Now, you might have to pay more . . ."

"I don't care about that." Richard glanced over at the kitten, who was in my lap, snuggled in a soft throw he'd pulled off one of his armchairs. "Does she seem to be resting more comfortably now?"

"I think so. Her breathing is more regular. Hopefully it was just the shock from being tossed from the car that made it so labored before."

"Jerks." Richard fixed his gaze back on the road, his eyes narrowed and his jaw set. "If I could get my hands on them . . ."

"Me too. But let's just get her some help. That's what really matters."

"Yeah. Now, about before." Richard didn't look at me, but I could sense his tension in the rigidity of his arms. "Sorry I was so testy. Not that it excuses me barking at you, but after all that questioning today, I'd just reached my limit."

That explained some of his behavior, though not all of it. Still, I was willing to let his lack of communication slide, given the pressure he must've been under. Knowing Richard, I was certain that once he'd heard the news about Lacey going missing, he'd spent the past several days feeling guilty about not giving her time to discuss whatever was bothering her. Not to mention he'd probably made himself sick with worry over her disappearance.

"I wouldn't let the questioning bother you too much. You know Brad has to follow every lead even if he doesn't personally see the need for it. And as for the university—well, I'm sure the campus police talked to all of Lacey's instructors and friends at Clarion."

"Yeah, but it was pretty obvious that they were focused on me in particular." Richard's knuckles blanched from his grip on the steering wheel. "I was her primary dance instructor. She was part of my studio. And I was the last one at the university to see her. To admit to seeing her, anyway."

I glanced at him before staring back down at the tortoiseshell kitten. "Surely they don't suspect you of being involved in her disappearance."

Richard peeled one hand from the wheel and massaged his jaw. "I don't know, to be honest. Meredith told me that when they questioned her, they asked some leading questions about my relationship with the girl."

I stroked the kitten's soft fur. I shouldn't have been startled by this reference, although Richard rarely mentioned his former fiancée and partner, Meredith Fox, who was also teaching dance at Clarion this semester. "What sort of questions?"

"She seemed to think that they were trying to uncover any hints that I might've had an inappropriate relationship with Lacey."

"What? Surely no one would believe that."

"To Meredith's credit, she said she set them straight on that score." Richard flashed me a humorless smile. "She told them the idea was ridiculous, among other things."

"Well, good for Meredith," I said, feeling more charitable toward the woman than I had in the past. "But I can see how that line of questioning would be unnerving."

"Yeah." Richard placed his free hand back on the steering wheel. "You know how careful I am. I always have a TA or accompanist or someone else in the studio with me, especially when I'm working on solos with my dancers. And I leave my office door open when I talk to students."

"I know, and that's smart."

"But people are reporting that they saw Lacey flee my office in tears."

"That's all circumstantial." The kitten had curled around my hand, and I took comfort in the warmth of its small body.

"True, yet with the zero-tolerance policy they've instituted at Clarion recently, there's no leeway granted for anything remotely related to improper relations between faculty or staff and students. It means immediate suspension and can be a firing offense." Richard's grip on the steering wheel tightened. "Of course I agree with that, but Lacey running from my office in tears and then disappearing doesn't look good. Not good at all."

"Maybe not, but consider it in context. There's never been a hint of any indiscretions on your part toward your dancers, at Clarion or elsewhere, has there?"

"No, but you have to understand"—Richard cast me a troubled glance—"such behavior is so rampant that it's easy for people to jump to conclusions."

"I know. I remember all the gossip and rumors swirling around certain professors and staff when I worked at Clarion." I shook my head. "It's a shame."

"It's disgusting is what it is. When you're in a position of authority, like a teacher or a mentor or choreographer, you should never abuse the power you've been given. No one should be made to feel like they're being harassed or that they have to offer up . . . anything just to get ahead or keep a job." Richard said this with such vehemence that I turned to him with raised eyebrows.

He looked away, focusing on the road. "You have to understand—I know the damage it can do. I've been on the other side of it as a dancer."

"Oh," was all I could manage to say as I stared at his handsome profile.

*Of course he had*. I shook my head. "I know you'd never do something like that to someone else. Abuse your authority, I mean."

"Good. Because you may hear all sorts of sordid speculation until this whole Lacey Jacobs situation is cleared up. It's the way these things go, sadly."

"I'll just follow Meredith's example and set them straight."

Richard offered me the first real smile I'd seen from him that day. "As only you can."

"I'll certainly shut them down. Probably not as elegantly as Aunt Lydia, but I'll do my best. Okay, there's the clinic. Time to get this little one checked out."

After we parked in the surprisingly full parking lot, Richard insisted that he carry in the kitten. "If she makes it, I'm going to keep her, so I'd like to register her under my name." He held out his hands. "If you don't mind."

"Of course not." I handed over the bundled ball of fur with reluctance. I would've liked to adopt her, but that was something that would have to be cleared with Aunt Lydia, and I wasn't sure how she'd react. She'd never shown any interest in having a pet. It was probably best to allow Richard to take in the kitten. It wasn't like I wouldn't see her all the time, anyway.

I hoped. I cast a surreptitious glance at Richard as he filled out the paperwork. His words in the car had relieved my anxiety, at least in terms of his odd behavior toward me. No doubt a combination of guilt, concern, and exhaustion had taken a serious toll on him, temporarily altering his behavior. But I was still concerned that he hadn't told me everything.

*There is still something to do with a station. I don't understand why Richard was standing in a bus or train station during our phone call Friday evening.* No, I couldn't think about that right now. I had to file away that question for another day.

After Richard and the kitten were ushered into an exam room, I sank down on one of the plastic benches that lined the waiting room and allowed my attention to drift to the television monitor. Although the sound was muted, it displayed the latest news via a text crawl.

"Amy, is that you?" asked a masculine voice.

Ethan Payne, the young firefighter who'd once rescued me from an abandoned well, approached me. He was a good-looking young man in his late twenties, with a physique that spoke of hours spent at the gym.

"Hi, Ethan. What brings you here?"

"My dog, Cassie. She was injured when we were out hiking today." Ethan sat down beside me. "They're checking her over now. X-rays and all that, so I have to wait out here. What brings you in so late?"

"Someone tossed a kitten out of a car in front of my boyfriend's house. She seemed to be breathing irregularly, so we're getting her checked out."

"Well, talk about scum." Ethan unzipped his lightweight camouflage jacket to reveal a plain navy T-shirt. "Sometimes I just don't understand people."

"Me either." I looked him over. "How are you? We haven't spoken in quite some time." As Ethan leaned back against the painted concrete block wall, I couldn't help but notice the red mud discoloring his hiking boots and jeans. "Looks like you took a tumble."

He glanced down and flicked some caked dirt off one knee. "Yeah. Cassie fell into a hole. I had to pull her out."

"Seems like something you have to do far too often," I said with a smile.

Ethan stretched his legs out across the tiled floor. "This wasn't quite as difficult as your rescue but just as unexpected. Cassie and I have hiked that trail plenty of times, and I never realized there were any deep pits right off the path. But I guess it makes sense, being in the mountains and all. Lots of rock falls and fissures up there. Even a few caverns."

"I'm sorry that Cassie was injured," I said, realizing that I hadn't expressed that sentiment yet.

Ethan cast me a warm smile. "Thanks. Vet says she'll be okay. They just need to make sure she didn't break any bones." He slid off his jacket and draped it, inside out, across his lap. "She was chasing a rabbit."

I noticed the bullets tucked into a specially designed pocket inside his jacket. "Were you out hunting?"

"Um, no." Ethan swiftly folded the jacket so that the bullets were hidden. "Not hunting season."

I made an *aha* face and pressed my finger to my lips. "I see. Anyway, I'm glad to hear that the vet thinks your dog will recover. I hope we hear the same about the kitten."

"Yeah, me too." Ethan stirred beside me on the hard bench. "By the way, you probably don't know this, but Chris Garver is my boyfriend. We met this past fall when I was taking some continuing ed courses at the university. You're going to laugh, 'cause we actually met in the library. We were both reaching for books from opposite sides of those double-faced shelves, and our eyes met . . ." Ethan's smile made me suspect he was reliving the memory.

"A definite 'meet cute,'" I said.

"It was. Anyway, I wanted to thank you for helping Chris and the other students with their research. That professor of his has been such a taskmaster. It's tough for him to complete all of her assignments, not to mention the extra-credit work. And it's not like that's the only course he's taking."

Ethan spoke these words in such a disgusted tone that I turned to look at him more closely. "Doesn't sound as if you like Professor Raymond much."

He raised and dropped his broad shoulders in an exaggerated shrug. "I've never been able to stand the woman. Not just because she's always piled too much work on her students. She also . . ." He shook his head. "Never mind. She's just made some unfortunate comments in the past. Things I haven't appreciated, especially when it comes to Chris."

"Are you saying she's a bit of a bigot?"

"More than a bit." Ethan grimaced. "It's hard enough for Chris as it is, what with his family not being very accepting, so when one of his teachers kept dropping little comments too . . ." Ethan squeezed a wadded section of his jacket between his fingers. "She always acted like she was something special, with all her stories and other talk, but tell you the truth I think shutting Mona Raymond up permanently could be called a community service."

These last words were spoken with such passion that I couldn't think of an appropriate reply. Fortunately, the vet tech walked out and called for Ethan.

"See ya," Ethan said as he headed back toward the exam rooms with a wave goodbye.

I pressed the back of my head against the hard wall behind me and stared at the television monitor. Reading the news scroll without any real interest, I suddenly leapt to my feet.

"Well, how about that," I said under my breath, before crossing the room to stand closer to the screen.

"Something happening?" asked the receptionist.

"The authorities think they might have a new lead on the Jacobs girl." Seeing the young woman's confusion, I continued, "Haven't you heard about that case?"

"Oh, right." The receptionist stepped out from behind the desk to get a better look at the monitor. "Looks like her friends are asking for help too."

I stared at the screen, reading the information scrolling below the faces of Chris and Hope. Chris was apparently mentioning a hat that Lacey loved and suggesting she might have worn it into the woods.

"White, with neon blue snowflakes around the edge," the closed captioning read. "Lacey's grandmother knitted the hat and gave it to Lacey right before she passed away, so Lacey treasured it. It's fairly bright and so should be something you could easily spot."

I knew that hat. Lacey had seemed excessively attached to it, sometimes even keeping it on indoors. Although, come to think of it, I hadn't seen her wearing it the last couple of times she'd been in the archives. Of course, the weather was much warmer than when the semester had begun.

"But," the receptionist said, shaking her head, "even with the nights still turning cool, would she wear a knitted hat in late April?"

"I don't know. She did love that hat." I met the other woman's inquisitive gaze. "I've helped the girl with some research at the Taylorsford library."

"Ah, okay. Well, I sure hope they find her soon. It gets pretty cold up in the mountains at night, even this time of year." The receptionist crossed back behind the desk to greet Richard. He'd walked out from the exam area with the kitten wrapped in the soft throw and snuggled against his chest.

"What's up?" he asked.

I examined the kitten, but all I could see was her slightly comical face, with its splash of black fur framing one eye and corresponding orange patch encircling the other, and her oversized black ears. "Just some more news about the search for Lacey. Her friends are making a plea for information, that's all." I reached out to stroke the kitten's head. "Is she okay?"

"Perfectly fine. No internal injuries or broken bones. It was apparently just the shock of being tossed out of the car that had her breathing hard. But she's going to be okay." Richard bent his head to address the kitten in a soothing voice. "Aren't you, Loie?"

I lifted my eyebrows. "Loie?"

Richard looked up at me with a smile. "I named her after Loie Fuller, a famous modern dancer from the early twentieth century. I thought it was appropriate because Loie the dancer was flamboyant, rather like this kitten's coat. And cats move like dancers, you know."

"If you say so." I touched the kitten's nose. "Hello, Loie. You do realize what a lucky cat you are, I hope? Because I can already tell that your new dad is going to spoil you rotten."

Loie just licked my finger again and stared at me with a smug look in her wide green eyes that told me—yes, she knew.

# Chapter Nine

When we finally arrived back at Richard's house, all I wanted to do was hurry home and fall into bed. After working all day, the unpleasant argument with Richard, and the adventure with the kitten, I couldn't face anything but my pillow. Also, it was late. When we'd left the veterinary office, we'd had to drive to another town to find the closest pet store. Because, according to Richard, Loie immediately needed not only kitten chow, water and food bowls, and a litter pan; she also required toys and a cat bed.

I'd eyed the last item and made some remark about the kitten ending up on Richard's bed. He'd replied that he didn't intend for that to happen.

Of course, as soon as we set the cat bed in a corner of his bedroom, Loie jumped out of it and headed for Richard's king-size sleigh bed. Using her tiny claws like pitons, she crawled almost all the way up before Richard saw her and peeled her away from the coverlet. He placed her in the cat bed, where she glared up at him, her eyes slitted into emerald slivers.

"Now, where were we?" Richard asked, before kissing me again.

Richard had pulled me into a close embrace and passionately

kissed me as soon as we'd set up everything for Loie. It was like he wanted to make up for his previous lapse. While I enjoyed it, I was too tired to consider anything else. Sneaking a glance over his shoulder, I glimpsed Loie once again clawing her way up the bedspread. "Look—she's at it again."

Richard swore and released me. "Stop this," he told the kitten as he carefully detached her claws from the quilted material. He held her up before his face. "You have a perfectly good cat bed. You should use that."

Loie just stared at him without blinking before licking his nose with her raspy pink tongue.

I laughed, which was probably not the best choice in that moment. Richard's expression instantly sobered me and also brought to mind the other less-than-welcome news I had to share.

"By the way, Mom and Dad are coming for a visit this weekend."

"What?" Richard placed Loie in her bed. She arched her back and jumped out again with a swish of her black tail. "Coming here, as in staying with you and Lydia?"

"Of course. So prepare yourself to meet the parents."

He let out a guffaw, but there was a definite edge to his laughter. "That's rich. I meant to tell you sooner, but with everything that's happened . . ." He sank down onto the bed as he met my questioning gaze. "My parents are visiting me this weekend as well. So not only will you and I be introduced to each other's parents—they will also undoubtedly meet."

"Oh joy. Oh rapture," I said, my tone conveying no trace of those sentiments.

"Yeah, this could be an interesting weekend. As in the old Chinese curse . . ."

"'May you live in interesting times.' Exactly."

Richard flopped back on the bed and stared at the ceiling. "It's a good thing I don't have to work Friday. It'll give me time to thoroughly stock my liquor cabinet and wine rack."

"Are your parents big drinkers?" I asked, smoothing down my rumpled blouse.

He grinned. "No. It's for me."

"On that note, I should head home. Don't get up. I'll just let myself out and make sure that the front door locks behind me."

Richard sighed. "You're not staying?"

"No. I'm too tired, and so are you, judging by the way your eyelids keep drooping."

"Okay. But come over tomorrow night. If nothing else, we need to discuss our battle plans for the weekend."

"Sorry, I doubt that I can. Not with all the cleaning that needs to be done. I don't want Aunt Lydia doing too much of it on her own. But I promise I will call you. By the way, I'm taking Friday off as well, but will be working in the garden most of the day. The weeds have taken over recently. It looks like a jungle out there."

"I should do the same in my yard, I suppose. But need to clean the house too . . ." Richard's voice trailed off and his dark eyelashes fluttered.

As his eyes closed, I didn't have the heart to tell him that Loie had finally grappled her way to the summit of the spread and now sat on top of the bed, victorious. She gave me one long, speculative look before delicately padding over to the spot where Richard's bent arm created a perfect nestling spot. She spun around twice and then plopped down, her head resting against his arm.

I left them both there, sleeping peacefully, and made my way downstairs.

Stepping through my own front door, I was met by the jangle of the landline phone. "I'll get it," I said as Aunt Lydia appeared in the hall, muttering about *idiots who call at all hours*.

"Hello, Amy," said the last voice I'd expected to hear.

"Charles? What are you doing, calling me so late?"

"Sorry. I don't seem to have much sense of time these days." There was a pause as Charles cleared his throat. "Anyway, I wondered if you'd be willing to do me a great favor. Not that you have any reason to do so, but I simply hoped . . ."

"What is it?" I said, more sharply than I intended. In my defense, I was irritated over being kept from the comfort of my bed.

"Come see me at my mountain house tomorrow. Say, over lunch? If you can get away. I just want to talk to you again. Somewhere private."

My exhausted brain registered this as odd, but I was so tired I decided to agree just to wrap up the call. "All right. Sunny will be at work tomorrow, along with some volunteers, so I should be able to take a longer lunch. Give me the directions. No, wait, I need to write this down." I clamped the receiver between my jaw and shoulder as I grabbed a pen and paper from the drawer of the hall side table.

Charles rattled off the directions, and I scribbled them across the notepad.

"I'll look for you around noon then. And Amy—thanks so much for agreeing to do this. I know you have no reason to be nice to me."

"Hmmm . . ." I said, not daring to say what I really thought. "I'll see you then. Night." I hung up before he could reply, silently acknowledging that this visit was probably a bad idea. But what the heck, maybe I would finally get my apology.

Anyway, I didn't want to worry about it. All I wanted to do was sleep.

\*  \*  \*

The following morning, Sunny almost blew a gasket when I told her why I needed extra time off at lunch.

"Charles freaking Bartos? Are you out of your mind?" Sunny raked her hands through her hair, destroying the elegant upswept twist she'd obviously spent time creating that morning. "I seem to remember weeks of frantic texts and phone calls, not to mention all-night therapy sessions, to get you through that breakup."

"I know, and trust me—I have no romantic interest in the guy. It's just that I feel a little sorry for him right now. A brief conversation seemed like the acceptable thing to do. I mean, what's the harm?"

Sunny's blue eyes blazed as she yanked at her hair and allowed it to tumble free of its pins. "Yeah, because there's no possibility that he might make a move on you again. Now that he's lost his main squeeze . . ."

"Really, Sunny, the woman just died a few months ago. I doubt Charles is on the prowl already."

"I don't," Sunny muttered. She tossed her hair behind her shoulders. "But go on—talk to the jerk. Just don't come crying to me if he mistreats you again."

"Be fair. He's a bit selfish, but he's not a monster." I tugged down the sleeves of the copper-colored silk blouse I'd worn that day. Not to impress Charles, of course, even if the color and cut did flatter me.

"If you say so." Sunny sniffed and turned away. "Anyway, I have things covered here, and we have extra volunteers today, so you don't have to worry about the time."

"Thanks," I said, patting her arm. "You're a peach."

"I'm an idiot is what I am. I should tie you up and stash you in the workroom before I allow you to see that man again. But"—Sunny pulled her arm away—"Go ahead. Listen to his nonsense. See if I care."

Of course she cared. I could tell that by the concern wrinkling her brow. "Don't worry. I won't be fooled again. I plan to see what he wants and provide a little help if it's something I think is reasonable. Only then," I added, offering my friend a reassuring smile.

"Are you going to tell Richard about this little expedition?"

"Not that it's any of your business, but yes." I plucked a tiny speck of lint from my blouse. "Eventually."

Sunny made a face and turned away. "I'm going to shelf-read now. The Nightingale was here earlier, so I'd better check for misshelved books."

I let her go without replying. I knew that she was only concerned because she'd experienced all the painful aftereffects of my breakup with Charles.

Later that morning, when Sunny had returned to the desk, I slipped away to work in the archives.

"We never refiled some of those folders we pulled for Mona," I told her before I headed out. "I thought maybe I'd better get on that." What I didn't say was that I was also seeking a task that could take my mind off my upcoming meeting with Charles.

The pile of acid-free folders on one of the archive's shelves *did* need to be placed back into their appropriate boxes. I carried the folders over to the worktable and sorted through them, arranging them in archival number order. Unlike books, archival materials were not cataloged by Dewey decimal numbers. Instead, they were assigned to subject and date groupings, creating specific collections. Most of these folders referenced town folklore, so there were only two boxes that I had to pull in order to refile them.

Flipping through one of the folders, I noticed that the contents were dated much later than 1879. The disappearance of the two young women had been used by folklorists to add an air of truth to the "mountain lights" story, although such information obviously couldn't validate the legend.

But Ada Frye and Violet Greyson had been real women, even if their part in the mountain lights story had been fabricated. I shuffled the folders. Finding none that dealt with town history from the proper time period, I stepped away from the table and scanned the metal shelves that held the rest of our archival collections.

Mentally kicking myself, I realized that when I'd assisted Mona with her research, I'd pulled items that she'd specifically requested without ever suggesting a deeper dive into the actual historical record. Mona might have rejected my suggestion, but I still should've considered that angle.

*Bad researcher*, I told myself as I pulled a slender gray box from one of the shelves. At Mona's request, I had scoured any digitized newspaper archives covering the time period, but had only turned up a two-sentence mention of the missing girls. Faced with this lack of coverage, Mona had surmised that the families had hushed up the story, only allowing the bare bones of it to live on in folklore. The newspapers had proved a legitimate dead end, but not checking other sources at that point had been a failure on my part. As a professional researcher, I should have been more diligent.

Since it was a repository of information for a town founded before the Revolutionary War, the Taylorsford library stored an abundance of material from the nineteenth century. Fortunately, one of my predecessors had carefully cataloged most of it, at least by year. I fiddled with the elastic tie that closed the acid-free box holding materials from 1879. Maybe I'd find something that would add the final flourish to Mona's project. Sliding the elastic loop off the button closure on the front of the box, I popped open the lid.

I slipped on a pair of white cotton gloves before removing any papers from the stack of acid-free plastic sleeves that filled the box. Most of the materials were legal documents, such as wills or deeds, but there were also one or two letters, a few postcards, and an assortment of notes.

Holding up the fragile paper so that I could decipher the elegant cursive script, I realized that the majority of the correspondence also touched on legal matters—requests for assistance from the town in land disputes and similar things. But then I noticed that one of the letters had been clumsily stuffed into its clear envelope. No archivist or librarian would've filed an old document in such a manner.

That meant that someone else had hastily returned this item—someone who'd apparently looked at the letter in secret, as I hadn't pulled these folders for anyone recently.

I removed the letter from its sleeve and gently unfolded it. The first thing I noticed was the date—May 1879. The salutation was to a "Cousin Maud." Intrigued, I flipped the paper over to read the signature and immediately sank down onto the wooden chair behind the table.

The letter was signed by a Delbert Frye. I whistled. The writer had to have been the current Delbert's ancestor.

If there was any factual basis to the Frye girl's connection to the mountain lights legend, I was certain I'd find it in this document. Surely the nineteenth-century Delbert Frye wouldn't have omitted a mention of such a traumatic event from a personal letter to another family member.

It took some effort to decipher old Delbert Frye's scrawl, and I glanced at only the first paragraph or two, but it was clear that I'd hit the research jackpot. Frye wrote of the family's "great loss," as well as the need to keep the details of Ada's disappearance a secret, since "it could bring shame upon us all, but Ada most of all, if she ever returns."

Glancing at my watch, I realized that it was almost time to leave for my visit with Charles. I hurriedly filed the other folders in their respective boxes but set the letter aside, planning to carry it into the library with me and share it with Mona at the earliest opportunity. After shelving the boxes, I returned to the table and picked up the letter. Preparing to fold it properly and insert it back into its sleeve, I stopped and stared at a word scrawled on the bottom of the first page—"gold."

I peered at the surrounding text, finally making out: "She took all the gold coins Father had so judiciously hidden as well. Our family's secret fortune and our protection against the vagaries of life, now lost, unless Ada can be found."

*Gold coins.* I laid the letter back on the table. *So there is a kernel of truth to the rumors about a treasure lost in the nearby mountains.*

Of course, the obvious conclusion was that Ada had used the coins to finance her new life in another town, far from Taylorsford. In that case, no trace of the gold would ever be found. But if the other account I'd read was true—if she and Violet had died in the mountains—had that fortune been buried with their unrecovered bodies? Or had they hidden it somewhere before their untimely deaths?

I took a deep breath and picked up the letter again, folded it along its set-in creases, and slid it back into the thin plastic sleeve. Slipping it into an empty acid-free folder that I tucked under one arm, I left the archives.

As I crossed the parking lot, another thought surfaced—a theory I might need to share with Brad Tucker rather than Mona.

The archives were not heavily used, except by Sunny and me, and had been thoroughly inventoried following the events of the past summer. By process of elimination, that meant that the person most likely to have discovered the 1879 Delbert Frye letter, and to have shoved it back into its envelope inappropriately, was Mona or one of her students.

Which might put an entirely new spin on why Lacey Jacobs had decided to hike the Twin Falls trail on her own.

# Chapter Ten

I shared my discovery of the letter with Sunny, who swore to keep it safely stashed in the workroom until we could show it to Mona. Before, of course, she once again warned me to watch myself around Charles.

The letter had effectively pushed thoughts of my upcoming meeting out of my head. *It's possible*, I thought as I drove along, *that Lacey saw the information about lost gold coins and was determined to find them for herself. Or maybe Hope was the one to discover the secret, along with Lacey, and that's why she was so upset over the dancer's disappearance. Maybe she was concerned that Lacey had found the treasure and decided to run off with it.*

I gnawed on my lower lip. *Of course, if Chris made the discovery, he could've confessed his find to his boyfriend. Perhaps that was why Ethan was out tromping through the woods on the evening we took Loie to the vet.*

Preoccupied with analyzing these theories, I made several wrong turns despite Charles's clear directions. I finally found his property by spotting the distinctive Swiss chalet–style house, which was located close to the road. Pulling up in front of the house, I sat in my parked car for a few minutes, working up the courage to approach the crimson front door.

Our conversation at the bonfire had felt even more odd after I'd replayed it in my mind several times. Unsure of what Charles wanted from me, I couldn't help but feel nervous about this meeting. Would he truly apologize, or even bring up the past?

Swallowing my anxiety, I crawled out of the car and crossed the neatly trimmed front yard. Looking out over the property, I noticed a weathered shed that seemed at odds with the pristine appearance of the rest of the property, then realized that the shed actually sat behind a wire fence that separated the neatly trimmed yard from a field of orchard grass.

*That building probably belongs to Delbert Frye*, I thought as I climbed the stairs to the rough-timbered front porch. *Brad did say Delbert's land was adjacent to Charles's property.* I narrowed my eyes and studied the contrast between Charles's perfectly maintained property and the derelict condition of the shed. *I bet that drives Charles mad. He never did like a mess.*

I turned my attention back to the brightly painted door. As my fingers hovered over the brass acorn knocker, the door opened.

"Hello, Amy. I heard your car. Please come in." Charles motioned for me to slide past him before he closed the door behind us.

My gaze swept over the interior of the chalet. It was a large, open space, with a cathedral ceiling supported by exposed timbers. The opposite end of the room was comprised of floor-to-ceiling windows that looked out over a large deck and the pine woods beyond. The flanking tall walls, painted a soft beige, were bare except for two framed posters and a large photograph. I recognized the posters—they advertised some of Charles's older solo concerts—but the photograph was new.

It was a blowup of the cover of the Alma Viva Trio's first album. A grand piano floated on a raft adrift on an obviously CGI-enhanced pond. Water lilies filled the pond, their platelike green pads reminiscent of the raft. Seated at the piano was a barefoot Charles, wearing worn jeans and a blue T-shirt that highlighted the color of his eyes. Behind him the cellist, also wearing casual clothes, leaned on his instrument. And perched on top of the piano, cradling a violin . . .

Marlis Dupre.

I sucked in a deep breath as my gaze swept over the flowing mane of blonde hair that appeared to have been swept away from her gorgeous face by a breeze.

*Probably a wind machine*, I thought, before I composed myself and turned to face Charles.

"I do want to express my condolences again," I said, examining him. Although I still thought he was far too thin, today his slender frame matched the Romantic poet theme of his loose white shirt and tight black trousers.

*But he's no Byron*, I thought, contemplating his pale skin and light hair. *More of a Shelley.*

He had followed my earlier gaze and stared at the photo of Marlis for a moment before dropping his head. "Thank you. It's getting a little easier, but still . . ." When he looked up at me, his eyes glistened with tears. "It's the little things that are the hardest. Marlis used to go out jogging so early. She said she liked to get an active start on her day. Half the time she'd dress in the dark and just grab a hat or gloves or whatever out of a basket in the hall closet. So when she came home I'd catch her wearing one blue mitten and one brown one, or my knit cap, or a scarf that clashed with her jacket. We'd often get a good laugh out of that." He wiped his eyes with his index finger.

My chest tightened. I hadn't expected him to display such

obvious emotion. "I really am sorry," I said, with more sincerity than I'd mustered on my first attempt.

"It's all right. I know I didn't treat you well, Amy. You had no reason to agree to meet with me, much less sympathize with me."

I shrugged. "But I do. You two were together for a couple of years. I know it has to be difficult to deal with such a loss."

Charles looked me over. "There you go, being nice again. Anyway, please have a seat." He motioned toward a white leather sofa anchored to a central seating area by a brightly patterned wool rug.

I sank down into the buttery soft cushions, mentally calculating the cost of the sofa, as well as the coffee table created from a single slice of a tree trunk. "You know, if you ever need any other handcrafted pieces, I have a friend who builds furniture."

"You mean Walter Adams?" Charles paused beside the marble-topped wooden island that separated the seating area from an extravagantly appointed kitchen. "I've heard he does good work."

"Yeah, that's him."

"I'll have to check out his pieces sometime. Now—what would you like to drink?" Charles headed for his stainless-steel refrigerator, which looked like it could store enough food to feed a household for an entire winter. "I'm having a glass of wine. Would you like one?"

"No thanks." I did want some wine. It might take the edge off this visit. But . . . "I have to drive back and work this afternoon. I don't think drinking alcohol is my best option. Just some water will be fine."

Charles returned with a glass of water for me as well as his goblet of white wine. Settling into a rocker that looked like it had been constructed from carefully bent and polished tree branches, he took a long swallow from his glass before staring at me. "You look good, Amy."

"Do I? Nice of you to say so, but I think I look just the same as I did when you unceremoniously dumped me. Now—tell me why you wanted to talk with me so urgently."

Charles laughed. "Same old Amy. Straight to the point. Very well—I would like your help in tamping down some ridiculous rumors."

I circled the rim of my glass with one finger. "About *Moon and Thistle*?"

"So you've already heard that gossip? Yes, that."

"Mona Raymond claims that you plagiarized her research." As I swiped the rim again, a delicate ringing sound rose from the glass.

"That bi . . ." Charles swallowed the end of the epithet along with a gulp of his wine. "She was always looking for a cut of my profits off that composition. As if I would entertain such a notion. I stole nothing from her, as you very well know."

"Actually, I don't," I said, meeting Charles's intense blue gaze with a lift of my chin. "You'd already composed that piece before we started dating, if you recall."

Charles set his empty wine glass on a matching end table next to the rocker. "I didn't steal anyone's research." He widened his eyes and fixed me with a gaze that would've melted me in the past. "You must know I would never do such a thing."

I leaned forward to set my glass on the coffee table. "To be honest, Charles, there were a lot of things I didn't believe you would ever do—until you did them."

He threw up his hands. "Are we going to delve into the whole breakup thing now? I really thought we could move past that, especially after our conversation the other night."

"Why? Just because you want to? And because you need my help?" I tilted my head and examined him with a critical eye. "You aren't *that* charming, I'm afraid."

"So why did you come, if you dislike me so much?"

"I didn't say that I disliked you. I simply no longer trust you. As for Mona's claims—I can't prove or disprove them. Sadly, I suppose I'm of no use to you. Once again." I stood, tugging the hem of my blouse down over my hips.

Charles leapt to his feet. "Wait. If what you want is an apology . . ."

"That would make a good start. But honestly, Charles, I still couldn't help you, apology or no apology. Because I don't know if you stole Mona's research or not. I wasn't there when that piece was composed, and as for whether I believe you're capable of using someone else's work without acknowledgment or compensation"—I lifted and dropped my shoulders in an exaggerated shrug—"the jury is still out."

"Surely you know me better than that." Charles covered the distance between us in two long strides. "You of all people should understand that I'm not the sort of person who'd do such a thing. You who always believed in me." He hung his head to stare at his expensive leather loafers. "Amy, I am sorry. I know you truly loved me, and I abused that love. But I do sincerely apologize for how badly I treated you. Can't we be friends again, at least?" As he lifted his head to gaze into my eyes, he reached out and took hold of both of my wrists. "I can't believe you no longer feel anything for me."

I stepped to the side, yanking free of his grip. "Don't touch me again without my permission or you'll see exactly how I feel."

There it was—the anger that I'd attempted to bury under a bushel basket of sympathy and basic human kindness. I glared up into Charles's bemused face. "Your apology is accepted, but that doesn't mean we're friends. Honestly, we never were, and we're not going to be now. I can be civil to you, and even muster sympathy for your current situation, but don't think for a minute that means you'll have free rein to manipulate me. You may believe you know me, but I'm not quite the pushover you think, Mr. Bartos."

Passion flared in his blue eyes. "Very well. Although I confess that seeing you now, ablaze with all this fire and confidence . . . well, I regret I never saw this side of you before."

"You might have," I said, crossing my arms over my chest, "if you'd ever bothered to really get to know me instead of trying to change me all the time. And news flash—I am no longer available, even if I were still interested in you. Which I am not."

"So this thing with Richard Muir is serious?"

I stared at Charles, refusing to look away despite the intensity of his gaze. *He believes he could lure you back.*

I choked back a bitter laugh. It was true. He really seemed to think that such a thing was possible. As I shifted my weight from one foot to the other, it I struck me that, while I could remember spending nights in his arms, such memories evoked no emotion. It was like remembering a movie I'd watched once. It didn't ring with the resonance of something that had actually happened to me.

"Yes, Richard and I are very serious. To the point that we aren't seeing other people and are not likely do so. And on that note, I think I'll leave." I turned away, heading for the door. "You do have my condolences on the death of your girlfriend, Charles, but I'm afraid you'll have to deal with Mona on your own."

"And I will." Charles, who'd followed on my heels, gazed down at me with an expression I'd never seen on his face before.

It was a repressed fury, and something else. Something calculated. Something dangerous.

I grabbed the doorknob and twisted it, cracking open the front door. "Are you planning to slap her with a defamation suit? Be careful with that. She claims she has some dirt on you . . ."

"What? What did she tell you?" Charles made an attempt to grab my arm again, but I was too quick for him.

I crossed to the edge of the porch but stopped short as sirens wailed through the clear mountain air. The sirens trailed off, as if moving in the opposite direction. I gripped the top rail of the balustrade as a sheriff's department car roared up the short driveway and spun around in the parking circle, spitting gravel. I glanced at Charles over my shoulder and noticed that he had gone as still as if he'd been encased in ice.

*Of course*, I thought, my anger fading to a hollowness in my chest, *this is probably exactly what happened when they came to tell him about Marlis. No wonder he looks like he's in shock.*

Brad Tucker jumped out of the vehicle and strode over to the porch. "What are you doing here?" he asked, his eyes searching my face.

"Just expressing my sympathy over Mr. Bartos's recent loss." I tightened my lips when Brad waved me aside and headed straight for Charles.

"Charles Bartos," he said in a tone of command, "I need to ask you some questions, so if we could move inside . . ."

Charles stretched out one arm, barring entry through the open front door. "Not until I know what this is all about. Does it have anything to do with Marlis?"

"No." Brad motioned for the other man in the car, whom I recognized as Deputy Coleman, to join him on the porch. "An unrelated case."

"Pertaining to what?"

Brad shot me a swift glance before leveling his sharp gaze on Charles. "The discovery of a young woman—lost, injured, and incoherent—on property adjacent to yours."

"Lacey?" I sprang forward. Deputy Coleman blocked my path to Brad but gave me an almost imperceptible nod.

"And the dead body we found near her," Brad said, his gaze never leaving Charles's expressionless face. "Someone I think you might know, Mr. Bartos. Are you familiar with a professor named Ramona Raymond?"

# Chapter Eleven

B rad sent me on my way as soon as Deputy Coleman made one or two more inquiries into my visit with Charles. It was clear from both deputies' disinterest in my presence, as well as Brad's swift ushering of Charles inside for further questioning, that they suspected that Mona had died some time before I'd arrived at the house. Realizing this was not the time to share anything about my theories concerning Delbert Frye and his family's gold, I simply filed that information away until I could call Brad later.

As I drove away, I kept my speed slow while my mind raced.

*Mona Raymond is dead, but how? Was it an accident or murder?* Of course, neither Brad nor Deputy Coleman had shared their thoughts about that with me.

As I approached the town, I flipped my car radio to a local station and caught the tail end of a special report detailing Lacey's rescue and Mona's death. The mention of a gun confirmed my suspicion that it had been a murder.

*Don't jump to conclusions, Amy. It could've been an unfortunate hunting accident.* I mulled over Ethan's words from our recent encounter. It wasn't hunting season, but that didn't always stop people from taking a shot at wildlife. And if someone had done so, without a license and out of season . . .

I listened intently as the reporter described the sheriff's department's discovery of Mona's car abandoned at the Twin Falls trailhead. It appeared that she had parked there and walked into the woods. Possibly searching for her missing student, one commentator remarked, although that action seemed like something best left to the authorities. "But," they continued, "sometimes concern can make people take peculiar actions."

The only indisputable facts were that Mona had been shot by someone wielding a rifle and that Lacey couldn't have been the shooter. No gun was found anywhere in the area, and that, along with Lacey's poor physical condition, seemed to rule her out. But why Mona's body had been discovered near the girl was still a mystery and unfortunately seemed destined to remain so for some time. The authorities couldn't question Lacey, as she was suffering from a serious head injury, and the doctors had induced a coma to give her brain time to heal.

*Rifle*, I thought, remembering Walt's comments about Delbert Frye. Perhaps that was why Brad had been so insistent on speaking with Charles—he might have hoped that Charles could provide some information on the recent comings and goings of his eccentric neighbor.

I gnawed on the inside of my cheek for a second. Mona *had* hinted that she had some information on Delbert's family that she hoped to use to force the old man to speak with her. Perhaps she had parked at the trailhead to hide her car, then had taken one of the woodland trails that connected with Delbert's property to walk to his cabin. If she had appeared on his doorstep threatening to expose a Frye family scandal, it was possible, given Walt's mention of his volatile personality, that Delbert had lost his temper. Knowing how Mona could provoke even the most mild-mannered individuals with her tenacity and impolite demands, I wouldn't have been surprised if someone like Delbert had shot her.

But I knew that the existence of that old letter in the archives, and its mention of gold, also pointed to other suspects. One of her students, or in Chris's case, a romantic partner, could have followed Mona and killed her to keep a valuable discovery to themselves.

*Or to keep her from turning it over to the authorities.* I flexed one cramped hand and then the other as this possibility occurred to me. Anyone obsessed with obtaining a fortune might kill an individual standing in their way, and knowing Mona, I was positive she'd have turned over any old gold coins to a museum or historical society. She would've been more interested in the research possibilities associated with such a find than in hiding its discovery.

Maybe one, or two, or even all of her students had disagreed with that plan.

Still shaking slightly when I reached the library, I parked in the back lot and entered through the rear door. As I approached the circulation desk, I realized that Lacey's discovery and Mona's death were already hot topics of conversation. Several of our older patrons stood in front of the desk, asking Sunny to read information off the computer, while some younger patrons stared intently at their cell phones and chatted excitedly with each other.

"You heard?" Sunny sent me a raised-eyebrow glance as I slipped behind the desk.

"Yeah, actually . . ." I surveyed the interest on the faces of the patrons clustered before the desk. "Never mind, I'll fill you in later."

Fielding continuing questions over the latest unexplained death in Taylorsford took up most of the afternoon. I had to wait until we closed the library before I could share any more information with Sunny.

"Charles wanted your help and support? That's rich." Sunny frowned as she locked the back door and we headed for our respective vehicles. "You don't think he had anything to do with Mona's death, do you?"

I made a disbelieving sound. "Who, Charles? Heavens, no. I can't imagine him even owning a gun, much less firing one." I bit my lower lip as the image of Charles's furious face rose in my mind. *But no, it couldn't be. I lived with him. Surely I would've picked up on something like that.* "Besides, I think I'd know if someone I had dated for over a year could be a killer. I mean, we were intimately involved . . ." I shook my head. "Honestly, I just can't imagine such a thing."

Sunny unlocked her canary-yellow Volkswagen Beetle and paused, holding on to the door. "How about for now we make a pact—I won't suggest that I think Charles is capable of anything, and you won't go running off and meeting him alone."

"Oh, come on. We're talking about Charles here," I said, unlocking my own car. "I know he's a self-obsessed jerk, but a murderer? I sincerely doubt it." I flashed a grin. "It might muss his hair."

"There is that." Sunny returned my grin. "Anyway, enjoy your day off tomorrow, and tell your parents hi from me."

"You should stop by. I'm sure they'd love to see you."

"And have to navigate the churning whitewater of parents meeting parents? No, thank you."

"Why did you have to remind me?" I dramatically pressed the back of my hand to my forehead. "I may develop the vapors."

Sunny laughed. "You? I doubt it. Just don't drink too much."

"Not promising that." I waved goodbye as I climbed into my car.

But as I drove slowly past her still parked Bug, Sunny leaned out her rolled-down window and called out, "And tell Richard about today's visit, or I will."

I groaned and drove off—and spent the short distance between the library and my aunt's house rehearsing how I should best confess today's events to Richard. Because I knew Sunny. If I didn't tell him, she would follow through on her threat.

I sighed. Sometimes friends who cared too much were as difficult to manage as family members who noticed too much.

* * *

I set my alarm to wake me early on Friday. Despite having the day off, I knew I needed to start my work in the garden as soon as possible. I'd ignored the overgrown vines and burgeoning weeds for far too long.

The day was warm enough to allow me to wear a light pair of pull-on cotton pants and a T-shirt. Both were faded and full of holes, although—as I'd informed Aunt Lydia when she'd cast a disparaging gaze over my ensemble—that was for the best. I needed to prune some roses, among other things, and with their thorns . . .

"No use wearing something nice that will just get ripped up," I'd said, while she'd narrowed her eyes and tapped one finger against the kitchen table.

"As long as you change before your parents arrive."

"Of course. I'll want to get a shower too," I'd replied, pulling on my floppy straw hat. "Never fear—I will look presentable this evening, I promise."

Aunt Lydia had muttered something about "promises being like pie crusts" as I'd dashed out of the kitchen and across the back porch before racing down the steps that led outside.

Aunt Lydia's entire backyard was a garden, comprised of square beds set in a grid marked out by gravel paths. The white pea gravel contrasted beautifully with the greenery and the rainbow colors of flowers and vegetables and also kept the underlying red clay from soiling our shoes. But it did require constant maintenance, especially in the rainy spring months. Having neglected this chore for far too long, I knew it might take me all morning to simply clean up the paths.

I was right. By early afternoon I'd finished yanking the weeds from the gravel but still had to tackle the flower and vegetable beds. I straightened and pulled my hat off my head, using it to fan my flushed face as I surveyed the garden. Wiping my damp upper lip with a crumpled tissue, I stretched out my legs, one at a time, before slamming the hat back over my tangled hair. I couldn't possibly clean up everything and decided to focus on the most visible areas, like the front row of beds.

Aunt Lydia called to me from the back porch about a half hour later. I thought she intended to scold me for ignoring lunch, but when I jogged over to the back steps, she informed me that I had a phone call.

"From someone named Adele Tourneau," my aunt said, rolling a dust rag between her hands. "She said she called the library and Sunny told her you were at home."

"Adele? I wonder why she'd be calling me." I bounded up the steps, slid past Aunt Lydia, and made a run for the hall phone.

Aunt Lydia trailed after me. "So you know this woman?"

"Yes, from my trip to New York. She's one of Richard's former teachers." I lifted the phone receiver from the side table and shooed away my aunt with a wave of my hand.

Aunt Lydia snapped the dust cloth through the air before walking into the dining room.

"Hi, Adele, sorry to put you on hold, but I was working in the garden . . ."

"Hello, Amy, and it isn't a problem. I have no pressing engagements." Adele Tourneau's cultured voice took me back to a night from the previous fall, and a party given in honor of the Ad Astra Dance Company. Richard had choreographed the company's latest contemporary piece and danced the lead role for a series of charity performances. The reception held following the final performance, at a gallery owned by Kurt Kendrick, had been the first time I'd met Adele Tourneau.

And the last time I'd spoken with her, until now. "What can I do for you, Adele?"

"Actually, it's what you can do for Richard. I'm sure you've heard about his recent encounter with Karla Dunmore."

I pulled the phone receiver away from my ear and stared at it for a second. No, I hadn't heard anything, but I wasn't about to tell Adele that. "Um, sure."

"I assume he's rather broken up about it, poor boy. I just wanted to let you know that I spoke with someone who's in touch with Karla, and she apparently feels terrible about how that situation played out." Adele delicately cleared her throat. "I thought you might share that information with Richard. Perhaps you could even suggest that he try to approach Karla again. I would call him directly, but I thought it would be better coming from you. I was so involved with both of them back in the day, he may believe I'm interfering more on Karla's behalf than his. If the news comes from you, a neutral party, it might seem less like a directive and more like a suggestion."

"I guess that makes sense," I said, although nothing about this conversation made any sense to me. "I'll certainly talk with him about it."

*And chastise him for not telling me the truth.* Sweat slicked the fingers that gripped the receiver, while the nails of my other hand bit into my palm.

"Thank you, dear. I just hope the two of them can work out their differences. It seems such a shame that they can't be friends, after all this time."

"Definitely a shame," I replied, fighting to prevent my anger from vibrating through my voice. "Anyway, thanks for keeping me in the loop, Adele."

"Thank you, Amy. And give Richard my best, would you?"

"I will." *Along with a piece of my mind.*

I was able to maintain my pleasant tone while we said our good-byes, but after Adele hung up, I slammed my phone receiver back into the cradle and immediately flew out the front door.

My hat sailed off my head as I ran toward Richard's house, but I didn't bother to stop and pick it up. It could decorate the front lawn for days for all I cared.

I was on a mission to find answers, and I would get them, one way or the other.

# Chapter Twelve

Allowing anger to fuel my progress, I dashed up the steps and across Richard's front porch and leaned heavily on the doorbell.

Richard stepped back as soon as he opened the door. "Hey, what's up?"

"Maybe you should tell me." I marched over to the sofa.

After closing and locking the door, Richard strode across the room and stood in front of me. "Tell you what?"

I squared my shoulders and glared up into his face, not allowing the tension I spied there to weaken my resolve. "Oh, I don't know. About some mysterious meeting with Karla, perhaps?" I tapped his chest with one finger. "I'm thinking that this little encounter may have been the reason you were in a bus or train station that Friday night, despite your ambiguous statements to the contrary. And it might also explain why you stayed out of touch while you were visiting your parents. It wasn't just the party. You were also tracking down your old dance partner."

Richard expelled a gusty sigh and slumped onto the sofa, scaring away Loie, who darted under the coffee table. "Who told you about that?"

"Well, not *you*." I sat down as well, but immediately scooted to the opposite end of the sofa. "Adele Tourneau just called me. She assumed I'd know all about your meeting with Karla and wanted me to tell you that she'd heard something . . ."

"Heard what?" Richard turned to me, his gray eyes blazing.

He seemed so intent on learning the answer to this question. Almost like it mattered to him more than anything.

*Maybe more than me . . .* I sucked in a sharp breath. I'd always taken Richard at his word and believed his assertions that he'd never entertained any romantic feelings for his former dance partner. But what if that had been another evasion on his part?

I fixed my gaze on him, hoping his reactions would reveal the truth. "If you must know, Adele said she'd been told that Karla regretted her behavior at your meeting or something like that. Anyway, Adele thinks you should try to contact Karla again. There, you have her message." I clutched my upper arms with both hands to still their trembling.

"Did she really say that?" Richard's focus shifted. He stared at the wall behind me as if its shelving held the Holy Grail.

Out of the corner of my eye, I spotted what had captured his attention—Loie was climbing up the shelves with her usual determination to conquer any tall object. "She did. Now"—I released my grip on my arms and snapped my fingers—"you'd better explain why this is the first time I've heard about this."

Richard's gaze slid back to me. "It was extremely personal. I didn't want to involve you, that's all."

"Oh, is that right?" I sat up so I could stare straight in his eyes. "It was too *personal* to share with me? How interesting. I guess that tells me where I stand."

"Now look, sweetheart"—my heart lurched at the endearment as Richard lifted his hands in a conciliatory gesture—"don't twist this into something it isn't."

"I'm not doing anything of the kind. Last night on the phone I told you about meeting Charles at his house, and you seemed none too pleased. But I told you anyway. Because Sunny was right—it was the proper thing to do. Two people who are as close as we're supposed to be shouldn't keep important things from one another. But then I find out that you've been hiding a gigantic secret from me." I swallowed back a sob. "Did you ever intend to tell me?"

"No . . . yes . . . I don't know." Richard raked his hands through his dark hair. "It was all so sudden and unexpected. There was no calculation involved—I simply acted on impulse."

"You just happened to fall over Karla when you went home?"

Richard lowered his head and stared at his hands. "No. On Friday morning I ran into a mutual friend from our old dance studio. He told me that Karla was in town for some family event of her own."

"Which sent you on a quest to try to track her down."

"Yes." Richard lifted his head and met my furious gaze. "I honestly did run errands for the party. It's just that I spent time trying to locate Karla as well."

"So you didn't lie to me, you just didn't share the entire truth. And also neglected to mention the real reason you didn't stay in touch. Okay." I swatted away the hand he'd attempted to place on my knee.

"You have to understand . . ."

"No, I don't. The one thing I am not required to do is understand. At least not without more information." I took a deep breath to silence my desire to shout. "Okay, so tell me what happened when you did meet up with Karla. From what Adele said, I assume it didn't go well."

"It did not." Richard stood and crossed to the shelves. He lifted

Loie off one of the top shelves and gently placed her on the floor. "I tracked Karla to the bus station because, based on something our mutual friend had told me, I knew she'd taken a bus into town. And I'd also tracked down one of her cousins, who told me that their family event was over and that Karla had already snagged a taxi and headed to the station. I hoped I might find her there, but I didn't spot her until after I talked with you that evening. I ran over to speak with her, but . . ."

I leaned over to pet Loie, who'd sidled up to my foot. "I take it she wasn't happy to see you."

When Richard turned to face me, I was shocked to see tears welling in his eyes. "She was almost as furious with me as you are now. I tried to talk to her, but she just shouted me down and strode away." He absently wiped away the tear sliding down his cheek. "I didn't follow. Not after what she said. Which was all true but still very hard to hear."

"Why would she be so angry?" As I rose to my feet, Loie scooted under the coffee table again. "It sounds like you believe she had some cause to be mad at you. But from what you've told me, you weren't the reason she abandoned her dancing career. I thought she left because she couldn't secure a position in any major company, despite her talent, just because she was so large-boned and tall."

"That's true, but . . ." Richard stood quietly, his hands at his sides. He would've appeared relaxed if I hadn't spied the anxiety in his eyes. "The truth is, there are aspects about Karla's disappearance that don't reflect well on me. When I told you that story early in our relationship, I didn't share all the details." His lips briefly curved into a sad smile. "I wanted to make a good impression on you and doubted that sharing those details would accomplish that goal."

I crossed to stand before him. "What do you mean?"

"I didn't tell you everything that happened the night before Karla fled the conservatory and disappeared from the dance world, and my life." Richard closed his eyes for a second before continuing. "Karla and I had a fight that evening because I was angry with her for not wanting to celebrate with me. I'd just received a letter inviting me to join a prestigious dance company after graduation. I felt like celebrating and wanted my best friend to go out on the town with me. Oh, I knew she was suffering because she'd been rejected everywhere she'd auditioned, but I still thought she should be willing to put that aside and celebrate *my* success. I believed it was what true friends would do. I mean, why shouldn't she be able to get over her own hurt to make me happy?" Richard stepped closer to me. "Anyway, it's what I thought at the time—selfish, arrogant, self-centered jerk that I was."

We were standing toe-to-toe. I reached out and clasped his hands in mine. "And that's why it's always remained such a painful wound? And why you've wanted to find Karla so desperately after all these years—to apologize?"

*Not because he wanted her as more than a friend. You can put that foolish notion out of your head. He never lied to you about his true feelings for Karla, or for you. Anyone could see that from the way he's looking at you now.*

"Yes." Richard pulled me close. "Now I have to also apologize to you, sweetheart. I shouldn't have kept all this from you, but I really thought . . ."

I tilted my head so I could look up into his face. "That I would think less of you? Me, with all my faults?"

Richard leaned in so he could whisper in my ear. "You don't have that many faults."

"Not that many? So not none, it seems," I said sternly, but smiled when he tipped my chin up with one finger.

"Just enough to make you interesting."

"Hmmm, good recovery," I murmured as his lips met mine.

We didn't speak for some time after that, until the chime of the grandfather clock in the hall brought me back to my senses.

I jumped up, dislodging Loie, who'd snuggled on the cushions beside me when Richard and I had ended up back on the sofa. "My goodness, is that the time? I definitely have to go. My parents will be here any minute and I haven't taken a shower or changed . . ."

My words were cut off by Loie's loud meow echoing the doorbell.

Richard swiftly stood and crossed to my side. "My parents," he said, casting me a panicked glance.

"No, no, they can't see me like this." I yanked on the hem of my tattered T-shirt with one hand and brushed my tangled hair behind my ears with the other. "I'm sneaking out the back."

"Good plan," Richard said, confirming my suspicion that his parents wouldn't approve of my current outfit, or the grime embedded under my fingernails.

I dashed down the hall and into the kitchen as I heard him open the front door, then kept running—across the back porch and out into his backyard. Circling around the side of the house, I hid behind a forsythia bush until the two people on the porch walked inside the house.

Expelling a loud sigh of relief, I made my way to Aunt Lydia's front porch, stepping back when the door opened before I'd even laid my hand on the latch.

"Hello, Amy," said my mother, while my father looked me up and down from over her shoulder. "We wondered where you'd gone."

"Been gardening, it looks like," my dad said.

Aunt Lydia appeared beside him. "As you can see, your parents are here." Her disapproving gaze swept over me. "I assume you'll want a shower and change of clothes after all that . . . gardening."

"Um, yeah," I said, offering my parents an apologetic smile. "In fact, maybe we'd better save the real welcomes for later. I'm kind of a mess."

"Don't be silly," my dad said, before wrapping me in a bear hug. "Good to see you again, baby girl."

"Same," I said, breathing in the familiar scent of his aftershave. "And you too, Mom," I added when Dad released me.

"I'll wait until after your shower," my mom said, wrinkling her nose. But she gave me a grin. "Not that I smell like a flower after work sometimes."

Since she was a biologist whose expertise lay in the study of the Maryland blue crab, this was all too true. I followed my parents into the front hall, where Aunt Lydia had paused beside the side table.

"Found your hat," she said, handing it to me. "Now go shower and change. Dinner isn't going to be anything fancy, but I'd rather not serve it cold."

I nodded and made it halfway up the stairs before Aunt Lydia's following words stopped me in my tracks.

"Oh, and by the way, Amy—I received a call right after yours. It seems Kurt Kendrick has invited us all to his home tomorrow night for a special dinner. Your parents think it a lovely idea." She looked up at me, her blue eyes sparkling. "Especially since he's also invited Richard and his parents. Anyway, I just thought you'd like to know."

I forced a smile and ran upstairs, where I allowed myself one scream in the shower before sending a text to Richard warning him of our impending doom.

# Chapter Thirteen

I called Brad on Saturday morning to inform him of my discovery of the 1879 letter. He was intrigued but warned me that it wasn't actual evidence.

"Except I found it improperly stuffed in its protective sleeve," I said. "Neither Sunny nor I would do such a thing, and I doubt the previous library director would have either. So it looks like someone may have discovered it more recently. Maybe Mona or one of her students?"

"I'll see what I can find out when I talk to the students again, but I doubt it's connected to the Ramona Raymond case. Still, thanks for telling me. We need all the information we can get." He cleared his throat. "By the way, you'll hear about this on the news, but there's a new wrinkle in the Lacey Jacobs case. Something that makes it somewhat more difficult to explain. And since we still can't speak with the girl to clear it up . . . Well, I just wondered if you'd ever heard her mention knowing anyone in the area. Anyone she could've stayed with for a few days, I mean."

"Wait, I thought she went hiking and got lost and that was that."

"Apparently not. The doctors who first checked her over don't think she exhibited signs of having been out in the wild since Friday evening. For one thing, her head injury seems to have occurred just a day or so before she was found."

"That's easily explained. If she was lost and wandering aimlessly through the woods, she could've fallen at any time."

"Sure, but Friday to Thursday is over five days, and according to the experts, she didn't appear dehydrated enough or some such thing. Anyway, I just wondered if you'd ever heard of any family or friend connections she had in Taylorsford."

"No, I never heard anything like that. I'd have thought if she knew someone, she'd have stayed with them while she was working on Mona's project instead of doubling up with Hope Hodgson in a room at the local motel."

"Okay, just thought I'd ask. Any information helps, as you know."

As I prepared to say goodbye, a question rose in my mind. "By the way, Brad, when Lacey Jacobs was found, was she barefoot?"

"What? No, no she wasn't." Brad expelled a gusty sigh. "And now that's another mystery you've brought to my attention. Just when I thought I was getting a handle on things, I have to figure out whose footprint was at Mary Gardener's house."

"Who indeed?" I said, adding in a lighthearted tone, "Maybe it was one of the fae. I can imagine them visiting Mary from time to time, can't you?"

"No, and please don't spread that idea around. I have enough problems sorting fact from fiction these days."

I laughed. "I promise not to say a word, but I can't vouch for Kurt Kendrick's silence. Or Mary's, for that matter."

Brad mumbled something about "blasted fairy tales" before wishing me a good day.

After we hung up, I sat on my bed and unrolled a spool of ideas through my mind. Why had Mona been in the woods—to track down Delbert Frye, or look for Lacey, or to make sure the girl didn't run off with a historical treasure? It was certainly possible that Mona had spied that letter along with one or more of her students, although it would've been odd for her to refile it improperly. But if she'd been sneaking a look, and someone had surprised her . . . I ran my fingers through my hair, untangling a knot that had formed while I'd tossed and turned overnight. Although I didn't want to believe it, I couldn't rule out Chris or Hope, or even Trish, as Mona's killer. Or Ethan, who certainly knew how to handle a rifle and obviously often hiked or hunted in the mountains.

Of course, it was also possible that Mona had decided to track down Delbert Frye and question him about his family history. If she had threatened to expose a scandalous family secret unless he spoke with her, I could certainly imagine a volatile hermit gunning her down. Or perhaps it had been some out-of-season hunter, who'd accidentally shot Mona as she'd attempted to locate Delbert's house.

I sighed, knowing I couldn't solve any of those mysteries at the moment. I had offered to show my parents around town before we headed off to the dinner at Kurt Kendrick's historic home.

"We won't be meeting Richard until this evening?" asked my mother, after we'd made a quick tour of the library.

"No. He drove his parents over to Clarion University to show them around. You know, letting them see where he works." I motioned toward the circulation desk. "Just like I am."

"Beautiful structure," my dad said, his gaze lingering over the deeply set windows and hand-carved wooden trim of the 1919 Carnegie library building.

"Yes, it is. A little limited in some areas, like electrical lines and outlets, but it is lovely." I glanced up at the high ceilings. "This fall the town did shell out the money to fix the roof, so at least it no longer leaks. That's certainly been an improvement."

Mom smiled and said hello to the volunteer manning the circulation desk. "Sunny isn't here?"

"She's at lunch, unfortunately. But I told her to stop by the house tomorrow so she can visit with you guys. She said she would."

What she'd actually said was that she'd show up as long as Richard's parents weren't there. I'd told her I'd text when the coast was clear, which I expected would be the entire day. Somehow, I didn't get the feeling that the Muirs would want to spend more than an evening in my company.

"Call it a hunch," I'd told Sunny when she'd questioned this belief. "Based on the fact that they refused Aunt Lydia's offer to stop by for drinks last night. And not too politely either. It just seems to me like they want to spend as little time with me and my family as possible."

Sunny had absently spun one of her bangle bracelets around her wrist. "You've been warned that they aren't the most congenial people on the planet. Richard's former dance teacher made that pretty clear."

"Yep. Which just makes me anticipate the dinner at Kurt Kendrick's house like a turkey anticipates Thanksgiving."

"Oh, you'll do great. They're sure to love you, and if they don't," Sunny had said, flipping her braid over her shoulder for emphasis, "Richard does, so that's all that matters."

"Hadn't we better head back to Lydia's?" My mom asked, jolting me out of my reverie. "I know the dinner isn't until seven o'clock but I'd like to kick back and relax before we have to go out again."

I agreed and ushered my parents back to the car. "I'm glad staying in the old family home doesn't bother you now, Mom," I said as I drove down Taylorsford's main street.

"Strangely, it really doesn't make me anxious anymore." Mom

cast me a sidelong look out of her dark eyes. She and I resembled each other to the extent that I'd warned Richard he'd be able to see what I'd look like in the future. He'd gallantly replied that my mom must be beautiful then, which had earned him some serious brownie points. Not that I'd told him so. I was still a bit peeved with him over his reluctance to trust me with the truth about Karla, as well as his evasiveness over his efforts to find her.

"Lydia believes it's because the spirit of Grandma Rose has been laid to rest, but you know how I feel about such things." Mom smoothed down her short cap of brown hair. Unlike Aunt Lydia, she hadn't grayed much yet, although white wings streaked the hair above her ears.

I nodded and pulled into the driveway. "If it can't be proven scientifically . . ."

"It's nonsense," my mom said, completing her oft-repeated aphorism.

My dad, sitting in the back seat, leaned forward. "That's my girl." He patted Mom's shoulder before shooting me a quick glance as I removed the keys from the ignition. "Surely you aren't becoming a believer in ghosts and foolishness like that, Ames."

I smiled at the old nickname. Climbing out of the car, I waited until Dad and Mom did the same before I answered him. "I remain skeptical, although I've experienced some events over the past year . . . Well, let's just say I'm just trying to keep an open mind."

"But not so open that your brains fall out," my dad said, moving to stand beside me.

That was another saying I'd heard a lot as a child. Nicholas Webber, whom everyone called Nick, was a computer programmer. Although we were alike in our preference for jeans and T-shirts, his casual appearance was much more calculated than mine. I always suspected that it was intended to confuse his business rivals, who didn't understand that his tendency to dress down and keep his opinions to himself didn't negate the sharpness of his mind.

"I just hope Richard's parents aren't so stuffy that they expect us to dress up for this dinner." Looking up at my dad, who at five feet eleven topped me and Mom by several inches, I wondered what the Muirs would make of his silver-threaded dark hair, which was pulled back into a short ponytail.

Dad shook his head. "I'll go as far as khakis and a polo shirt, but no further." He widened his brown eyes, giving me the "puppy-dog look" that my mom claimed he used to get what he wanted.

Not that he really needed to work so hard in that area. Generally quiet and cheerful, he was an easy man to live with. Which was good, since my hyper mother contributed enough excitement to the household. Although a logical and pragmatic scientist, she possessed enough internal energy to fuel a small town's electrical grid.

As we climbed the porch steps, Mom slid her hand through Dad's crooked arm. "Too bad Scott couldn't come along, but he's off on one of his mysterious trips again."

Dad tapped her wrist with his other hand. "Now Debbie, you know we shouldn't talk about that." He glanced back at me. "More of that government high-security-clearance stuff, so we have to stay hush-hush about where he's traveling."

"Scott the spy, who'd have thought?" I called up a mental image of my younger brother. With his short dark hair and tortoiseshell-framed glasses, he was the most unassuming-looking guy on the planet, but I suspected that was why he was so successful at infiltrating organizations to assess and analyze their cybersecurity. Not to mention his missions to stop malicious hacking into the national infrastructure.

Because, although neither he nor my parents would admit it, I knew that's what he did.

My mother said something about Scott "not actually being a spy, you know," while my dad just grinned and escorted her into the front hall.

"I set out some drinks in the sunroom," Aunt Lydia called out.

My parents headed toward the back of the house as I joined my aunt at the kitchen door, noting the joy that sparkled in her blue eyes. "You're thrilled they're here, aren't you?"

"I am. Now we can finally all be together in the family home. Well, except for Scott, but I'm going to make sure he comes at Christmas, you wait and see."

"If anyone could compel him to drop his work for a few days, it would be you." I slid my arm around her slender waist and gave her a hug. "Let's join the others. I hope you brought out the wine. I could use a little afternoon buzz before I face tonight's lions."

Aunt Lydia hugged me in return. "They can't be that bad. And just remember, Richard and your parents and I will have your back." She tapped her lips with two fingers. "And Kurt too. I believe he's very fond of you."

"Strangely, so do I, but that may be due to my connection to Richard." I dropped my arm and headed for the sunroom.

Aunt Lydia murmured something like "it's not just about Richard" as she followed me.

My parents had opted for the glider, so I chose the wicker chair with its rose-and-vine-patterned cushions.

"I'd forgotten how beautiful the view was from this porch," my mom said. "You can just see the mountain ridge peeking over the treetops."

"Nice garden too," Dad observed.

"Amy really helps out with that." Aunt Lydia crossed to the tall side table positioned on the exterior wall. "I couldn't manage without her."

"As long as she earns her keep." My dad gave me a wink.

"She does, and then some," said my aunt. "Now, what can I get you?" She motioned toward the bottles of wine, soda, and water nestled in an ice-filled bucket.

"Wine for me," I said.

"Of course." Aunt Lydia rolled her eyes. "But you need to go easy if you want to remain coherent at the dinner party tonight."

"Who says I want that?" I leapt up and took the glass from my aunt and set it on the table next to my chair. "Mom and Dad, what's your poison?"

"Water is fine for me," Mom said.

"I think I saw a bottle of lemonade—that will do," said my dad.

"I'm the only lush?" I motioned for Aunt Lydia to sit in the rocker near the table while I handed out the drinks.

My mom pointed toward her sister. "Apparently not."

Aunt Lydia lifted her wine glass in a little salute. "I know how to pace myself," she said, before taking a sip.

"Tell me about this new rash of criminal activity in Taylorsford," Mom said as I took my seat. "It seems odd to have yet another murder."

"I know. It's almost like Mona Raymond's fanciful fae creatures have cursed the town."

Mom leaned back against the glider cushions. "You don't really believe that."

"No, although you have to admit that a girl disappearing followed by her professor getting killed is a peculiar turn of events." I took a long swallow of my wine. "Then there's that recent hit-and-run death too, although it was near the university rather than in Taylorsford."

"I heard about that on the news." Mom eyed me with interest. "The victim was a girlfriend of Charles Bartos, right?"

"Yeah, Marlis Dupre." I met my mom's gaze with narrowed eyes. "So yes, he's available again, and no, I'm not interested."

"I wouldn't think so," Mom said, tapping her water bottle against her palm. "Not after the way he treated you."

"Oh, is this *that* Charles?" Dad asked.

"It is," Aunt Lydia said, "but I wouldn't worry. I don't think Amy intends to run back to him."

"Hardly." I finished off my wine and set the empty glass on the end table. "I do feel sorry for him, though. Not only did he lose his lover; he also lost one-third of his trio."

Dad tapped his chin with one finger. "What exactly happened to the girlfriend?"

"She was hit by a car while out jogging." I slumped into the chair cushions. "The authorities haven't located the car or the driver yet, and apparently no one saw anything."

"Sounds like whoever hit her wasn't too concerned with her survival," Dad said thoughtfully. "I mean, usually in an accident like that, the driver would've at least notified 911, if only anonymously."

"That's what I keep wondering—why did they just leave her there, without even calling for any help?" I pursed my lips as another thought popped into my mind. "It's almost like the driver was happy to let her to die, or even hit her deliberately."

My mom wrinkled her brow. "If you look at it that way, wouldn't it logically follow that the investigation should focus on the person or persons who'd have a motive for such a thing? Which means you'd need to figure out who could possibly want the young woman out of the way. Or, thinking about the other case, who'd benefit from the professor's death. How either act was done seems less important than the why."

Both Aunt Lydia and I slid forward on our seats and focused our attention on Mom.

"You're absolutely right, Debbie," my aunt said. "Why indeed."

"When it comes to the professor, I can think of a couple of reasons," I said. "One would be her homophobic attitude ticking off Ethan Payne, the boyfriend of one of her students. A guy who does own at least one gun and knows how to shoot."

"Is that type of slight enough to kill over?" Dad asked.

"Hard to say. You know what happened last summer, with our cousin Sylvia. I didn't think her motives were that compelling, but apparently she did."

"True." Mom took a sip of water. "Okay, so there's one suspect. Are there more?"

"Sure," I replied. "Either of her students, Chris Garver or Hope Hodgson, or even her graduate assistant, Trisha Alexander. I mean, I'm not sure what the motives would be for any of them, other than maybe they thought there was the possibility of finding a treasure."

With my parents gazing at me expectantly, I detailed the contents of the 1879 letter.

"But to kill someone over a mythical cache of gold coins? Especially since it seems just as likely that the young women made off with it to start a new life." Dad leaned forward, gripping his knees with both hands. "Logically, to imagine any of those coins remaining hidden in this area seems like a stretch."

"Stranger things have happened. Besides, it appears that the girls probably did die in mountains. And there is another, unrelated, angle. Trish hates the girl who disappeared because she blames Lacey's dad for a false accusation that forced her to leave her first-choice university. Who's to say she didn't follow Lacey into the mountains and then conk her on the head or something? Maybe Mona found out about it somehow, confronted Trish, and Trish killed her."

"But does this Trish know how to shoot a gun?" my aunt asked.

"She does," I said, and mentioned my discovery of the skeet club photo.

"But you told me she doesn't have a car. That would limit her actions, wouldn't it?" Aunt Lydia finished off her drink before speaking again. "How would she have gotten up to the trail without anyone knowing about it?"

"True." I sat back in my chair.

"Also, if this Trish person shot Mona, wouldn't she have high-tailed it out of town? She's still around, from what I've heard," my aunt said.

"You'd think, but who knows? Maybe she's trying to play it cool."

"The other case seems unrelated," my dad said. "The hit-and-run, I mean. What's your theory on that, Ames?"

I frowned. "Not sure. It seems like that was just a tragic accident, although someone just leaving the poor woman to die is pretty cold." I tapped the arms of my chair with my fingers. "Of course, getting back to the Mona Raymond case, there's old Delbert Frye too. He's been known to chase strangers off his land with a gun. He could've shot Mona in a fit of temper." I tapped my lips with one finger before continuing. "Mona told me she'd uncovered some scandal involving the two girls who went missing back in 1879 and intended to confront Mr. Frye about that. So he'd be more inclined to talk to her, she said."

My mom made a face. "Blackmail? Not a very nice way to collect information for your research."

"And a very good motive for old Delbert to shoot her, in my opinion," Dad said.

"Now in terms of the hit-and-run, there's always Charles," my aunt said thoughtfully.

I turned to stare at her. "What do you mean?"

Aunt Lydia shrugged. "Isn't if often the significant other who's to blame in these cases? Maybe he decided, for whatever reason, that he wanted to break off the relationship and chose a rather dramatic way to do so. He would've known his girlfriend's schedule and where she normally went jogging and that sort of thing."

"Yeah, but . . ." I could feel the questioning looks of the three people in the room land on me. "I just don't believe he'd kill someone. At least, not for that reason. All right, I admit he's vain and full of himself, but that's exactly why I doubt he'd feel it necessary to murder someone to dump them. He'd probably just start up something with a new woman and flaunt it, like he did with me. I can't imagine Marlis would've fought to stay with him in that case."

I gripped the arms of the chair. Charles might also have had a reason to harm Mona, especially if she had carried through on her threat to confront him with some unspecified wrongdoing, but I decided not to raise that specter. After all, just like her comments concerning a scandal in the Frye family, I only had Mona's word that she had any dirt on him. She could've just as easily been lying to persuade me to take her side.

"It seems like there's a missing piece or two in all this," my mom said. "But I don't think we're going to solve these mysteries today, so let's change the subject. I don't want to discuss murder and death any longer, but one thing I certainly do want to hear more about is this Hugh Chen that you've been dating, Lydia."

A faint blush tinted my aunt's cheeks. "He's a good friend."

I snorted. "Friend with benefits, you mean."

"Amy!" Aunt Lydia shot me a fierce look.

My mom just laughed. "Good for you, Lydia. Please tell me more."

My dad stood up. "I think I'll check out the garden, if you don't mind."

I shared a smile with him and excused myself as well, claiming I needed to catch up on emails and texts before the activities of the evening. It was obvious that the sisters wanted some time to dish about personal matters. Following Dad's lead, I decided to give them an opportunity to do so.

But despite my attempts to quiet my thoughts, the points my parents had raised about recent events set my brain working overtime throughout my shower and my futile attempt to blow-dry my straight hair into a more glamorous style. Finally opting for simple barrettes to hold my shoulder-length bob away from my face, I then pulled at least ten outfits from my closet before settling on a cotton dress with short sleeves and a full skirt. *The perfect choice*, I thought as I twirled in front of my standing mirror. The print fabric, a deep coral sprigged with turquoise-and-white flowers, provided a bright contrast to my dark hair and eyes.

But the bare legs . . . I pointed one foot and then the other, admiring my jaunty rope espadrilles. Unfortunately, my legs were frog's-belly pale. I knew I should tug on some pantyhose but resisted the temptation to give in to conformity. Comfort trumped style. The Muirs would simply have to deal with my bare legs, along with my dad's ponytail.

True to his word, Dad wore a pair of khaki trousers with an ivory polo shirt while my mom had opted for chestnut-brown slacks and an amber silk blouse. Only Aunt Lydia had chosen to dress more formally for the occasion, donning an elegant linen suit the color of purple hyacinths. She'd even worn her best pearls.

I shook my head. "You've outclassed us, I'm afraid."

My aunt lifted her fine-boned hands. "We've all obviously chosen to wear what makes us feel comfortable. I don't see the problem."

"Because there isn't one," said my dad, offering Aunt Lydia his arm. "Now, shall we go? I'm anxious to meet the young man who's taken up so much of my daughter's time over the past year."

"Ten months," I said, earning a sharp look from both my mom and my aunt. "I know how you like me to be accurate, Mom."

"And if I ask you how in love you are with him, are you likely to tell me that with pinpoint accuracy?" my mom asked as we stepped out onto the front porch.

Aunt Lydia, locking the front door, cast a glance over at my parents. "Don't worry, Debbie, you'll know. All you have to do is wait until they're in the same room and look at them."

# Chapter Fourteen

At dinner I was seated between Richard and my dad, facing Richard's parents across the table.

The evening had begun with strained introductions, with Richard's burly, sandy-haired father loudly announcing that he was "James Muir, but please call me Jim," while Richard's mother, Fiona, had stared pointedly at my dad's ponytail and casual attire.

For my father's sake, I was glad to see that Kurt had opted for light-gray trousers and a cerulean-blue sweater over a pale-yellow shirt, especially since Richard was dressed more formally than usual, in gray slacks and a navy linen jacket over an ivory shirt. His father was even more severely attired in a charcoal-gray pinstriped suit, white button-down shirt, and a tie.

With his short hair and pewter-framed glasses, Jim Muir looked every inch the investment banker that Richard had informed me he was. *He could pose for an advertisement featuring a successful business-man*, I thought, *especially with his wife by his side.* A slender woman whose head barely reached her husband's shoulder, Fiona Muir was the picture of understated elegance in her midnight-blue silk sheath, navy pumps, and draped silver rope necklaces.

Richard looked nothing like his dad, which didn't surprise me, since I knew from old photos that he bore a striking resemblance to Fiona's uncle—the man who'd once owned his house, Paul Dassin.

Fiona, still eyeing my parents with barely concealed disapproval, didn't meet my gaze. In fact, since our introduction, which had offered all the warmth of a plunge into a frozen pond, she'd studiously ignored me. But her rose-tinted lips did twitch upward when she turned to her left to address my aunt. "Lydia, I do hope we'll have a chance to get to know one another better. Richard has mentioned you quite often. As did Uncle Paul."

*Aunt Lydia's appearance and demeanor are obviously more to Fiona's taste*, I thought as I leaned into Richard and whispered, "How did it go earlier today?"

"As expected," he said under his breath. "Meaning that we've almost reached critical mass and an explosion is imminent."

Kurt took a silver basket filled with rolls from the hands of a young woman dressed in a traditional black-and-white maid's uniform. "I'm so delighted that you could all join me tonight, but please, relax. No one needs to stand on ceremony in my house. With that said, I'll start the bread around." Kurt handed his basket to my father, while the maid passed another to Aunt Lydia.

"Is this Haviland?" Fiona Muir held up a bread plate. The china was so fine that I could see her fingers outlined behind the plate by the light from the chandelier.

"No, Limoges. Early nineteenth century. I do have some Haviland at my townhouse, but I picked up this set in France a few years ago." Kurt flashed one of his brilliant, toothy smiles. "I thought this particular pattern matched this residence better."

"Indeed," said Richard's mother, laying down the plate as Aunt Lydia handed her one of the bread baskets. "By the way, Kurt, I want to apologize for not realizing that my uncle had a foster son, but honestly, he never mentioned it." She passed the bread, as well as a butter dish, directly to her husband. "No thanks, I never eat bread. So many carbs."

Taking the other basket from my mom, Richard plucked out two rolls and placed them on his bread plate.

"Not to worry, Fiona." Kurt slid a pat of butter onto his plate. "I fled Paul's house rather unceremoniously at age eighteen. Since I never contacted him after that, I certainly don't blame him for neglecting to mention my existence to his family."

"I just feel bad that you didn't inherit any mementos or anything from Uncle Paul," Fiona said, before taking a sip of her lemon-infused water. "If you'd like, I could send you something . . ."

"No, no." Kurt waved aside her suggestion as if it were a gnat. "I don't need more things. Just getting to know you and Jim, along with Richard, is gift enough."

Fiona narrowed her gray eyes and stared at him over the rim of her crystal goblet.

*She isn't stupid*, I thought. *She's a bit skeptical of Kurt's effusive gallantry. As well she should be, judging by the cutting looks he's been casting her and her husband.*

Fiona turned her attention to my mother. "I understand that you have two children, Mrs. Webber?"

My mom swallowed the last bit of her roll before answering. "Please call me Debbie. And yes. You've met Amy, of course, and then there's our son, Scott. He's two years younger than Amy and is a computer security specialist."

"Really?" Jim Muir looked up from his plate. "Following in the old man's footsteps. That's nice."

I wasn't surprised by his interest in this conversation. He'd quizzed my dad about his job within minutes of meeting him and had also shown at least a modicum of interest in my mom's scientific career.

"Not exactly," Dad said. "I'm a programmer. He's in cybersecurity. Somewhat different."

"Still, both respectable fields and similar enough that you can probably talk shop. It must be gratifying to have that connection." Jim Muir dabbed a trace of butter from his lips with his linen napkin.

Richard's extra roll tumbled onto the white linen tablecloth as his hand came down hard on the edge of the plate.

"Of course, Richard has achieved great success in his field." Kurt leaned to one side, allowing the maid to ladle soup from a tureen into his bowl.

"Yes, you must be very proud," my mom said.

Fiona Muir cast a quick glance at her husband. "We're definitely pleased that he finally has a steady income. I mean, the teaching thing is nice. Before . . . well, you know how unpredictable the arts can be." She looked up at the maid, who was hovering at her shoulder. "Is there any cream or butter in the soup?"

The maid dipped her ladle into the tureen. "Yes, ma'am, It's cream of broccoli."

Fiona laid her hand over her empty bowl. "Then never mind."

Richard's spoon tapped against his plate. I didn't dare look at him.

"Being a creative person can mean feast or famine, I suppose." My mom narrowed her brown eyes as she stared at Fiona. "But Richard has achieved quite a bit of fame, from what I understand. Based on some videos Amy has shared with us, I can certainly see why."

Richard offered my mom a warm smile. "Thank you, Mrs. Webber."

"It's only the truth. Isn't it, Nick?"

"It certainly is," my dad replied. "Frankly, I was amazed. No way could I ever make my body do anything like that."

"And his choreography is so brilliant too," Aunt Lydia said.

"That's all very well, I suppose," Jim Muir said, after polishing off a spoonful of soup. "But you know it's not a career that lasts forever. The body will give out eventually, and then where are you? I suppose one can always continue to teach, although that by itself seems hardly lucrative enough to support oneself, much less a family."

Richard coughed so hard that he had to press his napkin to his lips. "Hot spot," he said, as Aunt Lydia and Mom eyed him with concern.

I swirled my spoon through my soup and fixed my gaze on his parents. "Have you ever seen Richard dance?"

Fiona twisted one strand of her long silver necklace around her hand. "When he was younger. Not lately."

"I never have," Jim said, digging back into his soup. "Not really into that sort of thing."

"How curious." Kurt tipped his shaggy white head to one side as he examined Richard's parents. "I would have thought you'd want to celebrate his work, splendid as it is."

Jim waved his spoon through the air as he pushed away his now empty bowl. "I'd have fallen asleep anyway. Always do at those artsy things."

"Well, except at the opera, dear." Fiona's overly bright voice was rimmed with anxiety. She looked over at my parents with a smile as brittle as dried leaves. "We went once, but Jim couldn't make it past the first act. Too much yelling, he said."

My parents shared a conspiratorial glance.

*They'll have so much to talk about later.* I straightened in my chair and gazed directly at Richard's parents. "Allow me to say that you've missed out."

Jim and Fiona Muir's gazes both snapped to me. I took a deep breath before continuing. "I was fortunate enough to see Richard dance one of his own pieces not long ago, and it was absolutely one of the most amazing evenings of my life. So I can't imagine why you wouldn't have attended every one of his performances that you possibly could. Frankly, I find that extremely odd."

My aunt's sharp intake of breath was matched by my mom's short burst of laughter as Richard's hand slid over to my lap to grasp my clenched fingers.

"Amy's one of my biggest fans," he said, giving his parents a look that dared them to say anything more.

"No doubt," murmured Fiona, while Jim looked me over as if he couldn't decide whether I was stupid or simply rude.

"Ah, here comes the main course," Kurt said as the maid and a male waiter entered the room bearing trays. "Perhaps you'll eat something now, Fiona? It's trout, so I promise—no carbs."

My mother buried her face in her napkin to muffle her giggles.

"Just watch out for the bones," my dad said, shooting me a grin.

"Thank you, I'm sure I can manage." Fiona lifted her fork with a great show of dignity.

We somehow managed to make it through the main course without incident, but as the maid cleared away the dinner plates, Fiona mentioned something about being grateful that at least we hadn't been pestered at dinner by "that awful cat."

Aunt Lydia tapped her buffed fingernails against the tablecloth. "Oh now, I may not have any pets, but even I think Loie is adorable."

"My wife doesn't believe in keeping animals in the house," Jim said. "I can't really argue with her about that."

Dad glanced at Richard. "So you never had a pet growing up?"

"No." Richard crossed his arms over his chest and stared at his parents. "It wasn't allowed."

"What a shame," my mom said. "We always had a dog or a cat, or both, didn't we, Amy?"

"Yeah, and Scott's fish. He went crazy over fish for a while. We had two enormous aquariums in the basement. One saltwater and one fresh."

"Then there were your hamsters," Dad said. "What were their names?"

"Cathy and Heathcliff," I said. "I was a very literary child," I added, meeting Kurt's amused gaze.

"And did they yearn for the freedom of the moors?" he asked, with a lift of his bushy white eyebrows.

"More like the wilds of the carpeting," I said, raising my wine glass in a little salute.

"Did you always want to be a librarian, Amy?" Fiona asked after a brief moment of silence.

"No, I started out in art history. That was my undergraduate major. But when I decided to go to graduate school, I switched gears and got a library science degree. It seemed more marketable, for one thing."

"Definitely a plus," Jim said.

I ignored him. "And I've always loved books and reading, so it was a natural fit."

Fiona examined my face with the first hint of interest she'd shown in me all evening. "Do you enjoy it? I would think so. It sounds like such a nice, quiet profession."

I opened my mouth and shut it again, unsure how to respond.

"Amy is the director of the local public library," Richard said. "As I think I have mentioned numerous times. Her job isn't really that peaceful or relaxing. She has to manage the building, the staff and volunteers, and the budget, among other things. As well as assist a wide variety of patrons, including some challenging individuals. It can be quite stressful and demanding."

"Is that right?" His mother wrinkled her nose and pursed her lips.

"It's a respectable profession, at least," Jim Muir said, his pale-blue gaze raking over me and his son.

Richard tapped his dessert spoon against the table. "Unlike mine?"

"Well . . ." Jim tipped up the front legs of his chair and leaned back. "You know how I feel about that."

Richard rolled his eyes. "I certainly do."

Fiona toyed with the edge of her napkin. "Now, Jim, not at dinner."

My dad made a great show of patting his stomach. "Such an excellent meal, Kurt. Please thank your chef."

Kurt smiled. "You're quite welcome, Nick. I'll be sure to convey your compliments to her."

Fiona Muir was still studying me. I squirmed until Richard draped his arm around my shoulders.

"Speaking of research, and in keeping with all the news about that poor folklorist," Fiona said, turning to Aunt Lydia. "Did you know that Uncle Paul planned to write a book about the mountain lights, focusing on the disappearance of those two unfortunate young ladies? I remember him talking about it during one of my visits. I used to try to get to see him at least two or three times a year. He often talked with me about his writing, although he only mentioned that particular book project once. Honestly, I hadn't thought about that for years. Not until the recent news brought it to mind."

"No, I never heard him mention it," Aunt Lydia said.

"Neither did I, but I suppose it might have been after I moved out." Kurt pushed his chair away from the table and stretched out his long legs.

"Yes, it was late in his life. He'd collected quite a bit of research on the topic, but for some reason he abandoned that book. Or at least I never found any evidence of it when we went through his papers after his death. Of course, I know Richard uncovered some additional materials in the attic during renovations, so perhaps some evidence still exists, although I doubt it's anything more than notes. Not enough to complete the book, I'm sure." Fiona met Kurt's inquisitive gaze with a lift of her sharp chin. "But Paul talked about the concept extensively during one of our visits. He was over eighty at that point, so perhaps he eventually realized that he no longer had the energy to pursue something that complex. It was too bad, because it sounded fascinating when he discussed it with me. That was not long before the one time we took Richard to visit him."

Richard lifted his arm off my shoulder and stretched it across the back of my chair. "Right, I only met him once, when I was four. I didn't spend a lot of time with him."

"Just long enough for him to leave all that money for your dance training," Jim Muir muttered, before taking another gulp from his wine glass.

I shot him a sharp look, but he was too focused on his drink to notice.

"What was his take on the mystery?" Richard asked.

Fiona shrugged her slender shoulders. "Naturally, he didn't believe in fairy creatures or any of that nonsense. He was a journalist by training, so he was a stickler for the facts," she added, addressing my parents.

Dad leaned forward. "Did he think the girls just ran off, or was there more to it?"

I could practically hear the gears clicking in his head. Give my dad a puzzle and he'd jump in to solve it. I smiled as I studied his eager face. *Like father, like daughter.* "Some people claim the Frye girl ran away to escape her parents' plan to marry her to an unwelcome suitor," I said.

Fiona's cool gaze flickered over my face. "Yes, that was the angle Uncle Paul was pursuing. But he also felt there was more to the story than the tale of two runaways. His other theory would've been the premise of his book, from what I gathered."

"Really? What did he think happened to the girls?" Aunt Lydia asked.

"Oh," Fiona said, waving her hand in a flourish worthy of a queen, "he thought they were murdered."

# Chapter Fifteen

"Great-Uncle Paul truly thought the girls were the victims of foul play?" Richard pulled his arm away from my chair and leaned forward.

"He seemed to believe it was a possibility." Fiona smoothed back a strand of hair that had slipped free of her chignon. "He based his theory on some of the interviews he'd conducted with family members whose parents were alive at the time of the disappearance. He said that his journalistic sense told him that they were lying."

"About anything in particular?" Aunt Lydia asked.

Fiona fiddled with her necklace, twisting one strand between her slender fingers. "He didn't go into detail, although he mentioned something about the family covering up for someone's rash actions. His working theory was that a parent or uncle tracked down the girls and killed them in a rage when they refused to return." She released her grip on the necklace with a flick of her wrist. "It would've been considered unpremeditated murder, or perhaps even manslaughter, I suppose, but still . . . It was something the family wanted to conceal."

*A family member tracking down the girls makes sense, but not simply to avert a scandal. They would've also wanted the girls to return the coins, or at least confess where they'd been hidden.* I glanced over at Aunt Lydia. "The gold," I mouthed at her.

She gave an almost imperceptible nod.

Kurt leaned forward, resting his forearms on the table. "He thought the girls never made it over the mountain?"

"Perhaps," Fiona replied, eyeing Kurt with a look I recognized from Aunt Lydia—*elbows never belong on the table.*

"Ah, here comes dessert." Kurt sat back as the maid entered the room bearing a tray laden with crystal bowls. "I hope you enjoy ice cream. My chef is a master at whipping up unusual but delicious flavors." He focused on the maid as she placed the bowls in front of all the guests. "What do we have this evening, Cheryl?"

"A coffee ice cream laced with black walnuts and a hint of spices, Mr. Kendrick." The maid gave him a pert smile.

He winked at her. "Make sure you get some before it's all gone."

"Oh, I already had a bowl, and it's delicious," she replied, leaving the room with a flounce of her full, crinoline-enhanced skirt.

Aunt Lydia widened her blue eyes as she met my amused gaze.

"So, Amy," Fiona said, staring intently at me as I sucked in my upper lip to silence a burst of laughter. "I understand that you knew the girl who disappeared as well as the woman who was killed."

"Only superficially," I said, my spoon hovering between my bowl and my mouth.

"Amy was helping the professor with some research," Richard said. "And the girl was a student working on the professor's project."

"How unfortunate for you. Was that related to the professor's studies on the mountain lights?" Fiona absently stirred her spoon through her ice cream, turning it into slush.

I tasted some of my own ice cream. It was delicious, and I intended to enjoy it, even if Fiona Muir was examining me in a way that indicated she'd like to offer up an impromptu lecture on calories and carbs. "That's right. I had to be involved because the Taylorsford town council funded Ramona Raymond's research. The mayor's trying to increase tourism and asked Mona to offer a special presentation as part of a May Day event."

Aunt Lydia daintily scooped up a spoonful of ice cream. "I wonder if they plan to go forward with the celebration."

"They do," Richard said.

I turned to look at him. "You know this for a fact?"

"Yeah, because . . . Well, you'll see."

I wrinkled my nose at him. "More secrets?"

He shrugged. "If you must know, Mayor Blackstone asked me to coordinate the dance portion of the festival. The maypole dance in particular. I recruited some of my female students, who were happy to participate."

"Really? A dance around the maypole?" Fiona eyed Richard, her dark eyebrows arched. "That's quite the pagan custom, you know."

"It is, but supposedly it was a traditional event in Taylorsford until about fifty years ago."

"That's right," my aunt said. "I remember the festival from when I was a child. They held it at the elementary school, and one of the older girls played the May Queen. They also had a court of princesses chosen from each grade. I was selected one year but wasn't allowed to participate."

Mom sighed. "Grandma Rose didn't approve."

This didn't surprise me, given the stories I'd heard about my great-grandmother. "But your parents were still alive then, weren't they? Wouldn't they have made that decision?"

"Grandma Rose always had the final word," Aunt Lydia said, sharing a look with my mom.

"If what my friend Mary tells me is right, Ada Frye and Violet Greyson disappeared immediately after the 1879 May Day celebration," Kurt said. "I tend to believe her, as Mary's an expert on the folktales associated with Taylorsford. Storytelling is her avocation, and she's collected quite a bit of local folklore over the years."

I finished off my ice cream before replying. "I think that's why Ada and Violet's story got tangled up with the tale of the mountain lights, along with fables about fairies and that sort of thing. The festival, with its pagan and folklore roots, bled into the story of their disappearance."

My dad tapped his chin with one finger. "And it would've been convenient for the family to encourage that idea if they wanted to hide the truth."

*Bingo*, I thought. *Score one for Dad.*

"You know, Richard," Kurt said, setting aside his empty ice cream bowl. "The fae luring people into their underground kingdom sounds like a great concept for a piece of choreography. You could use folk music from the region for the score."

Richard smiled. "That is a good idea. I may have to explore that."

Jim Muir muttered something under his breath that sounded like "a whole lot of nonsense."

"We should discuss it. I might be interested in underwriting such a work." Kurt turned his laser-sharp gaze on Jim Muir. "That's how these things get done in the arts, Jim. A little different from your work, but it's still business."

"Don't waste your breath. You'll never convince my dad that dancing is anything but a ridiculous waste of time." Richard crumpled his napkin in his fist before tossing it onto the white linen tablecloth. "Trust me, I've tried."

Fiona clutched her necklace again. "Now, dear, don't go getting all dramatic on us."

"I'd consider investing in such a production a risk, Kurt, but perhaps you have enough money to take the chance." Jim's spoon clanged as he dropped it into his empty bowl.

Kurt shrugged. "It would simply be good business. As I mentioned before, Richard is a master in his field. I'm sure any money I invested would be repaid and then some."

"If you say so." Jim Muir shot Richard a sharp look before focusing on Kurt. "But I have to wonder how such sporadic opportunities will keep my son in his old age. Don't get me wrong—I know some people can make big money in the arts, but I don't see that happening with a dance career." He leaned back, crossing his arms behind his head. "You know, I would've been happy to give Richard every advantage, if only he'd decided to pursue a field that made use of his intelligence. He could've been a scholar, or a financial expert, or any number of things. But he decided that he'd rather play pretend for the rest of his life. Flitting around with a bunch of . . . well, irresponsible types like himself."

"A bunch of what?" Richard shoved back his chair and leapt to his feet. "Go ahead and say it, Dad. A bunch of gay boys, is what you mean. So say it. You might as well own your bigotry if you're going to think it."

Richard's chest heaved as he faced off with his father. I cast a desperate glance at our host, who'd also risen to his feet.

"Perhaps we need more ice cream to cool off." Kurt said.

As my gaze flitted around the table, I noticed that my aunt's face was scrunched up like she'd just smelled something spoiled, while my parents' faces were frozen in expressions of dismay.

*And disapproval.* My brother Scott was openly gay and had been since high school. I was sure my mom and dad, already taken aback by Richard's father's rude dismissal of his own son, were appalled by his display of open bigotry.

"Don't worry, Kurt, I'm not going to cause a scene." Jim dropped his arms as he fixed Richard with a cold glare. "As my wife said, my son tends to be a bit overdramatic at times. I'm sure he'll apologize to both of us presently."

"I'll apologize to Kurt, but as for you . . ." Richard rubbed at his jaw with the back of one fist before lowering his hands to his sides. "That will be a cold day in hell."

Aunt Lydia rose gracefully to her feel. "Kurt, I expect Debbie and Nick would love a tour of your home. And Jim and Fiona as well." She turned to Richard's parents. "Kurt has the most amazing art collection. You simply must see it."

Fiona cast my aunt a grateful smile. "Oh yes, that sounds delightful. Would you do us that honor, Mr. Kendrick?"

"Of course," he said, inclining his head. "Just follow me." He strode toward the hall, followed in quick succession by my aunt, Mom, Dad, and Fiona.

Jim Muir didn't move from his chair. "I think I'll pass."

"Dad doesn't have much use for art," Richard said in a tone sharp enough to etch diamonds.

Fiona lingered in the doorway until Kurt took her arm and led her away.

"You should probably join the others, Amy," Jim said. "It seems my son and I have once again revived a tired old argument."

I stood and moved next to Richard. "No, I don't think I will."

Jim Muir rose to his feet with great deliberation. "No offense, young lady, but this really isn't any of your business."

As I pressed closer to Richard, his barely contained rage vibrated through his arm and into mine.

"Now let's get one thing straight," he told his father. "You can talk to me however you want, but never speak to Amy that way again."

"I mean no offense to your girlfriend, son. I just think this is something that needs to be ironed out between us. It doesn't involve her."

Jim Muir rolled his broad shoulders and flexed his large hands. I stared at him, struck by the knowledge that his polished appearance couldn't hide his true nature. He was obviously someone who always had to be right, who'd always demand blind obedience from his family and friends. In short, he was a bully, and no amount of tailoring and expensive haircuts or handcrafted shoes could hide that truth. Not for long, anyway.

You couldn't bend to the will of a bully. Richard obviously understood that. And so did I.

"I do have every right to be here, Mr. Muir, and I will tell you why," I said, reaching for Richard's hand.

"Really?" Jim looked me up and down. "We've just met, and so far, I'm not impressed. The best I can say is that at least you're female."

"For heaven's sake, Dad . . ." Richard tightened his grip on my fingers.

I was not about to be silenced by some man in a suit, no matter how much older he was or how much more money he had, or even how much he might end up disliking me.

"Mr. Muir, just so I'm clear on this"—I gave Richard's hand a final squeeze before pulling away and stepping up to the table—"you've truly never seen Richard dance?"

Jim shoved his hands in the pockets of his trousers and rocked back on his heels. "No, I haven't. Well, other than watching him swoop around the living room when he was a kid."

"Or watched any piece he's choreographed?"

Richard's father shook his head. "I'm just not interested . . ."

"In what? Your own child? You've never been interested in his accomplishments, in what matters to him, in the very essence of who he is?"

"Amy, don't bother." Richard moved up behind me and laid a hand on my right hip. "It's a lost cause. Let's just go join the others."

"No." I crossed my left arm over my body and covered Richard's hand with my trembling fingers. "I want to tell your father how I really feel."

Jim Muir snorted. "I know—you think my son is fantastically talented and oh-so-charming and I should be happy with that, despite the fact that he's squandered his life on senseless pursuits."

"No, that isn't it." I leaned back against Richard, drawing strength from the warmth of his body. "I don't care what you think about Richard's career in dance or how little you appreciate his many accomplishments. That's all on you, no matter how wrongheaded it is. No, here's what I really feel for you, Mr. Muir—sad. That's right, I feel sorry for you. Because you've been blessed with one of the best men in the world as your son and you can't see past your own prejudices to enjoy that gift." I met Jim Muir's openmouthed stare without flinching. "So go ahead—wallow in your own anger and disappointment. The rest of us will happily enjoy your son's company and talent for as long as he chooses to share it with us."

"Quite a speech," Jim Muir said with a bravado that I didn't see reflected in his eyes. "I suppose I should admire your loyalty to Richard. Although I doubt I'll have to put up with such talk from you for much longer. My son's relationships never seem to make it past the two-year mark."

Richard's arms wrapped around me. "You're wrong there, Dad.

You'd better get used to her talk, and the rest of her too. She isn't going anywhere, and if she ever does—I'm going with her."

* * *

Shortly after the others returned from their tour, Fiona claimed exhaustion and asked Richard to drive her and Jim back to his house.

"Wish I could see you later," I told Richard when he leaned in to kiss me goodbye.

He stroked the side of my face. "Hang out in the sunroom around eleven. My parents will be in bed by then."

I nodded and kissed him again, right as Jim Muir strode past us on his way to the front door.

"Already gave my thanks to the host, so let's go if we're going," Jim said, cutting his eyes at me.

"As you wish," Richard called out, but tapped my nose before stepping away. "Eleven."

Aunt Lydia and my parents and I stayed and chatted with Kurt a little longer, but I kept close tabs on my watch and made sure that we left in time to get home around ten thirty.

True to my prediction, Mom, Dad, and Aunt Lydia headed into the sitting room to discuss and dissect the evening's events. I joined them for a few minutes but slipped away as soon as I could to wait in the sunroom.

At eleven, a pebble hit the back porch door.

I peeked out and motioned for Richard to sneak inside.

"Hey, you," he said, after wrapping me in his arms.

I tipped my head to look up into his face. "How do you stand it?"

"By keeping my distance. I plan infrequent visits which include numerous excursions for various, unspecified reasons." He gave me a grim smile. "I find that limited interaction works best."

I caressed the side of his face with my fingers. "It must be tough, though."

*Tough enough to explain why he latched on to a friend like Karla so tightly when he was young. And why it's so hard for him to let go of her.*

"It is, but I can manage. Especially since I have a new family now." He lifted my hand and kissed my fingers, one by one, as he recited names. "You and Lydia and Sunny, and even Kurt. And your parents, I hope." He smiled, genuinely this time, as he lowered our clasped hands. "I like them."

"And they like you. I can tell."

"Good. Now I just have to win over your brother."

"Well, despite being a bit younger than me, he is very protective." I grinned at the touch of concern that creased Richard's brow. "But he will love you, I'm sure."

Richard took a step back and looked me over. "By the way, I forgot to tell you how much I like that dress."

I quirked my eyebrows at him. "Thanks, but your mother seemed very dismayed by my bare legs. I don't think she approved."

"I wouldn't let that worry you. She doesn't approve of much." Richard rested one hand on my waist. "I, on the other hand, think your legs are stunning. Just like the rest of you." He pulled me close. "Thanks for standing up for me back there."

"Of course," I said, resting my head against his chest. "But I suspect that your dad now despises me."

"More like a mild dislike. He never allows his feelings to rise above a tepid disinterest, except where I'm concerned. Sadly, despite his reaction tonight, he's not likely to spare you much thought."

"Which is fine by me, only"—I gazed up at him—"I wonder what will happen in the future. I mean, if we're still together . . ."

"We will be."

"Okay, but how will we deal with your parents? They may never like me very much."

"Then you're in good company, because they don't like me much either. They love me in their own way, I guess. But they definitely don't like me." Richard slid his hands down to rest at my waist. "Again, very infrequent visits will help. Also, I'd advise you to continue to stand up for yourself. My dad may admire that, eventually."

"I hope so." I tipped my head back and studied his stoic expression for a moment. "I've been thinking . . ."

"As you always do," Richard said with a grin.

"As I always will. Anyway, I think you should follow Adele's advice and contact Karla again."

"I just might. If only to please you and Adele. Now, the important stuff—my parents are leaving tomorrow morning, so if you want to come over sometime later in the day, after your parents take off . . ."

"That sounds like a good idea." I flashed him a wicked grin. "I do miss Loie."

"Oh, is *that* what you miss?" Richard pulled me closer and whispered in my ear. "Nothing else?"

"Can't think of anything," I said, then gasped when he spun me around and plopped me down onto the glider.

"Let's see if I can refresh your memory," he said, before kissing me again.

I didn't bother to come up with a snappy reply.

# Chapter Sixteen

At the library on Monday, Sunny listened patiently while I repeated my litany of complaints about Richard's parents.

"You know you're going to have to come to terms with them, sooner or later," she said. "Like it or not, they'll always be a part of Richard's life, if only peripherally."

I glumly removed sticky notes from a returned book. "I know."

"I bet they'll end up thinking you're great. Especially"—Sunny winked at me—"if you give them a grandchild."

"Whoa, cart miles before the horse." I dumped the bits of colored paper into the recycling bin.

"I'm just saying it could happen."

"So could a comet striking the earth, but I'm not anticipating either one of those things at the moment."

"Now, tell me more about this May Day dance event. Is the mayor really having someone construct a maypole?"

"Yep, and some of Richard's students are going to do the ribbon-winding thing. He researched the traditional dance and got some additional help from another folklorist at Clarion. Should be interesting."

"I did hear they're setting up everything in that empty field near the town hall," Sunny said. "With craft vendors and food, and a small stage for some musical acts. Bethany told me she's planning to have a booth selling stuff from the Heapin' Plate."

"It's just the one day, though. Not quite as big an event as the Heritage Festival in the fall."

"Not yet, but it could be in the future, I suppose. I mean, if someone really put some effort into it." Sunny jangled the enameled bracelets encircling her slender wrist. "You know I'm still planning on running for mayor, right?"

"Sure, because Zelda never stops talking about it. When's the election, again?"

"Not until November, but we're planning to start campaigning by August."

"Well, I'm glad to help. Not just because it's you, but also to get that weasel Bob Blackstone out of office."

"I can't believe the council let him stay on after he confessed to his part in that mess last summer. But it seems like some people get a pass on everything."

I shrugged. "His family has held power in Taylorsford for decades. It's difficult to shake loose that sort of grip, I guess."

"But I will. Watch me." Sunny whipped her glasses off the top of her head, popped them on, and struck a "thinking" pose. "Do I look appropriately official?"

I poked her with the edge of a book. "No, you look darling, as usual. Now you'd better stop goofing around. Here comes Brad, and he definitely has his serious face on."

By the time Brad reached the circulation desk, Sunny had removed her glasses and run her fingers through her long hair to smooth out any tangles. "Hi there, here on official business or what?"

"Partially." Brad took off his hat.

Sunny toyed with one strand of her golden hair, twirling it around her finger. "Before you get into all that, how's Lacey? Any updates on her condition?"

"She's still in the induced coma, so—no. The doctors did tell me that she's improving, though." Brad twisted the brim of his hat between his hands.

"That's good, but I guess it means you have to wait a while longer to question her."

"Yes, and that's a problem. The trail is growing cold pretty fast. Speaking of which, I need to ask you a few follow-up questions, Amy."

"Let's head to the back, then," I said, turning away.

Brad circled around the desk and followed me into the workroom. Without, I noticed, actually making eye contact with Sunny.

"What do you need to know?" I asked as I perched on the large table in the center of the room.

"For one thing, I just want to confirm that you didn't arrive at Charles Bartos's house until around noon on Thursday."

"That's right. Why? Did he tell you something different?"

"No, but Delbert Frye swears someone was stomping around in the woods near his property earlier than that. He was out walking and heard something but says he didn't see anything."

"Hunters? I know it's out of season, but still . . ."

Brad scratched at the back of his neck. "Not likely. Delbert said whoever it was made too much noise for any hunter worth their salt."

"Maybe it was Lacey? If she was disoriented, she could've been stumbling around."

"Possibly, although I don't know if the girl was still on her feet at that point. Of course, some of my team were out searching the general area, so perhaps Delbert heard one of them from a distance.

Sound bounces off rocks and trees strangely in the mountains. Sometimes determining the origin of a noise can be next to impossible."

*Or perhaps Delbert was being deliberately misleading to cover his own actions.* "Did you ever find the gun that shot Mona?" I swung my legs to dispel some nervous energy.

"Not yet. We checked all of Delbert's weapons, but none matched the bullet casings we found. Bartos has a pistol registered in his name, but that's all."

I leaned forward and gripped my knees with both hands. "Charles owns a gun? I would've never expected that."

"He does. But since Ms. Raymond was killed with a rifle, not a handgun, and he has a legal permit, we didn't bother to investigate that angle any further."

"But I bet you questioned Delbert Frye thoroughly. He must be the most likely suspect, since he's been known to warn people off his property with a gun."

"He's definitely on the list, but we can't tie anything to him directly yet, so we've just questioned him at his cabin and left it at that. Now, if we do locate the murder weapon . . ." Brad slapped the brim of his hat against his other palm. "Anyway, the other thing I wanted to check with you is related to your research work with Professor Raymond. I wonder if you ever heard anything from her about some sort of feud with Charles Bartos."

I slid off the table to face Brad standing. "I think that's pretty common knowledge, isn't it?"

"At Clarion, maybe. Not around here." Brad looked me up and down. "I was just curious if she'd shared any particulars of that story with you."

"She did mention it once, after I'd heard something of it from her graduate student Trisha Alexander—the one who I told you might have it in for Lacey, remember? Anyway, all Mona told me was that she thought Charles had plagiarized some of her research when he composed a successful song cycle. She was angry and seemed determined to demand compensation, or at least some acknowledgment of her contribution to the work."

*That isn't all.* I gnawed the inside of my cheek, wondering if I should mention Mona's warning about the "dirt" she had on Charles. But I didn't know what she had been referring to, and it was only hearsay, and . . . *Despite everything, you loved Charles once, and throwing him to the wolves while he's still reeling from Marlis's death, especially on the word of a woman who bore a grudge, seems wrong.*

"I've heard the same from others; I just wanted additional confirmation from someone I trusted," Brad said. "It seems she had a serious beef with him, although he doesn't appear to have been too troubled by it. At least not from what I can tell from talking to him and to others at the university."

"You may have noticed that Charles possesses plenty of self-confidence." I gave Brad a wan smile. "I doubt he cared much what someone like Mona thought of him. I do think her constant badgering over that song cycle infuriated him, but I don't think he'd waste a lot of time plotting revenge. He's more the type to get angry and tell her off and then move on."

"That's my impression too." Brad stared at me with a searching look. "Sure there's nothing else? I sense there's something else you want to say."

"Should've known I couldn't put anything past you. Yes, there is something. Two things, actually, although I heard them from the same person." I took a deep breath before continuing. "Mona Raymond pulled me into the archives that Monday before she was shot.

She wanted me to corroborate some information she'd apparently uncovered, but I couldn't."

"What information?"

I clutched my hands together in my lap. "She hinted around at some old scandal involving the Frye family, and some 'dirt,' as she called it, that she said she had on Charles. It was all very vague, which is why I didn't share it before. Frankly, I was very put off by the way she was talking. It was like she was planning to use this information to not only force Charles to admit that he'd plagiarized her work, but also to try to blackmail old Delbert Frye into providing her with information on his family."

"And you're just telling me this now?" Brad tapped his booted foot against the wooden floor. "Really, Amy, I wish you'd shared this sooner."

"I know. I should have. I just didn't know if I believed Mona, and honestly didn't want to cast suspicion on either Charles or Mr. Frye based on Mona's cryptic hints."

"I understand, but trust me next time, okay? You should know I'm not one to overreact." Brad fixed me with a stern gaze. "I would never harass or arrest someone based on that type of limited information. But it might've helped me develop a better picture of the overall situation."

I ducked my head. "I'm sorry. I promise I won't do that again." I looked up at him, widening my eyes as I'd often seen Sunny do when she was attempting to get out of a jam.

Brad snorted. Obviously I wasn't quite as adept at the innocent routine as Sunny. "I accept your apology. And, just as an aside, the doe-eyed thing doesn't really work for you, Amy."

"Really? Thanks for sharing." I shot him a cheeky grin.

"Okay, well . . ." Brad's face tensed and he twisted his hat brim to the point where I thought he might permanently crease it. "That's all I needed from you, I guess. But I did want to tell Sunny something."

"I'll ask her to come in. You need me to go?"

"No, that's okay. You both can hear this, I guess. I mean, you'll find out soon enough, so you might as well."

My curiosity piqued, I called Sunny away from the desk.

"What's up?" she asked, looking from me to Brad.

He lowered his head and stared at the mangled hat in his hands. "I just wanted to tell you, before you heard it somewhere else, that Alison Frye asked for a transfer and it's been granted."

"Oh, where's she going?" I asked, absently rearranging the pens and pencils shoved into a repurposed tin can.

"To another sheriff's department. Neighboring county, so she isn't actually moving away from Taylorsford, just changing jobs."

"Is it because of her great-uncle being under such suspicion and scrutiny?" Sunny's expression displayed sincere concern.

"No. Well, as it turns out, it's good for that reason too, but she asked for the transfer a while back." When Brad looked up and met Sunny's sympathetic gaze, his face was flushed as red as a tomato. "But the truth is—we're dating. I mean, we will be, once her transfer is complete. We haven't up to now. In all honesty, we didn't want to get involved before, what with me being her supervisor, so . . ."

Sunny cut off his rambling words with a bright smile. "I think that's splendid."

Brad's audible sigh filled the room. "Good to hear. I know we'd agreed we could date other people, but I didn't want you to hear about this through the grapevine. Or even for Amy to hear it that way," he added, casting me a swift glance.

"As long as you're happy, I'm happy." Sunny flipped her shining fall of hair behind her shoulders with both hands.

"Thanks." Brad stared at Sunny for a moment, but when her cheery smile never faltered, he shoved his hat back over his short blond hair. "Guess I'll be going then. Just promise me that if either of you hears anything even vaguely related to the Lacey Jacobs or Ramona Raymond cases, you'll keep me informed."

"We will."

"See ya," Sunny said as Brad strode away.

I waited for a moment before circling around to look her in the face. "Are you really okay?"

"Oh sure." She waved me away with one hand—the one that wasn't wiping away tears from her eyes. "I am happy for him, you know."

"I know," I said, wrapping my arms around her.

Sunny allowed me to hug her for a moment before she pulled away. "I'm just sad that I couldn't be what he wanted. It would've been so perfect if I could have been."

"You'll be exactly what someone wants someday. Just as you are."

"I hope so." Sunny fanned her flushed face with one hand. "But I have to be me, whatever happens. Even if I end up alone."

I made a *pfft* sound. "Alone? Who's going to be alone? Not you. Not while I'm alive."

Sunny burst into sobs at that point. I handed her a box of tissues, told her to take the rest of the day off, and headed out to cover the circulation desk.

# Chapter Seventeen

Fortunately, the rest of the day was quiet, with few patrons and even fewer problems. I was even able to send a few funny texts to Sunny, hoping to cheer her up, until she finally responded: "Don't worry, I have wine and the grands are looking after me. Put down the phone and get back to work!"

It would be a long day for me, since we closed at eight on Mondays and I'd arrived at seven that morning. Usually whoever was scheduled to stay late arrived midmorning, but today that had been Sunny. When I'd called Aunt Lydia to inform her of the schedule change, she'd said she'd stop by around six to drop off something for my dinner, then hang out in the library until eight so she could drive me home.

"That's not really necessary," I'd told her, but she'd insisted. Since I'd walked to work so she could have the car, I'd relented without much fuss. There was still the possibility that a murderer was lurking in the area. I didn't think I was in danger but preferred not to walk home in the dark.

Around three o'clock, when one of our volunteers showed up to cover the circulation desk, I decided to satisfy my curiosity over Fiona Muir's statements concerning Paul Dassin's research into the disappearance of Ada Frye and Violet Greyson. After the events of the past summer, Richard had donated all the papers he'd uncovered in his great-uncle's attic, in addition to his mother's collection, to the archives, so if any of Paul's information on the missing girls existed, I should be able to find it. Of course, Paul might not have saved any of that research if he'd decided not to write the book, but it certainly wouldn't hurt for me to take a look at his collected papers.

In the archives building, I surveyed the Paul Dassin file boxes with a practiced eye. Neither Sunny nor I had yet created detailed finding aids for the collection, but I knew that the material was at least arranged by years. Based on Fiona's comments, I assumed that anything related to a book on the missing girls would have been from a later period in Paul's life and retrieved the three file boxes that spanned the ten years before his death in 1985.

After pulling on a pair of white cotton gloves, I began flipping through the file boxes, sliding out the materials just far enough to check for any mention of the 1879 incident. I spied no references until I reached the box covering 1981–1985.

Fiona was right—it was a project Paul Dassin had only embarked on late in his life. He must've already been in his eighties before he started gathering any research on the subject. I lifted several acid-free folders from the box and sat down at the table to peruse their contents.

The material consisted of handwritten notes, which made reading it quickly a little more difficult. I knew that I'd probably end up carrying the boxes into the library to look through them more closely later. But curiosity drove me to continue to skim over the notes, hoping to at least narrow down my search. If I could find any references to foul play in the disappearance of the girls . . .

"There it is," I said aloud as my eyes focused on a page that appeared to be transcripts of interviews Paul Dassin had conducted with older members of the Frye clan. One of the speakers, identified only as "C. F.," mentioned long-held, secretive rumors that had circulated at family gatherings when she was a child.

"Didn't understand it at the time," the speaker had told Paul. "I was too young to catch the innuendoes. But now that I've lived through so much, all the changes in society and all, I think I can make sense of it. I can see why all the old folks were so anxious to keep it hushed up, especially back then."

I leaned in, peering at the scrawled script with a frown. That was odd. Even a child should've been able to understand rumors that concerned possible murders. Flipping over the page to read more of the interview, I sucked in a quick breath. There was a sticky note pasted to the paper. That was disconcerting. No one should have marked these pages in any way.

*Another secretive search*, I thought. *Because if Sunny or I had approved it and then refiled these documents, that sticky note would've been removed.* I examined the note. "Important!" it said in a broad scrawl. I was not entirely surprised to discover that it matched what I'd seen of Mona Raymond's handwriting.

So she'd rifled through these papers without asking, as well as the other historical files. I made a huffing noise and pulled away the note to read the text beneath it.

"I didn't grasp what my grandmother and great-aunts meant when they said that Ada and Violet were 'far too close,'" C. F. had told Paul. "And at the time I had no idea what 'Sapphic' meant either."

I sat back in my chair, staring at the page lying flat on the table in front of me.

So that's what Mona had been referencing when she'd talked about a scandal. Considering Ethan's words about her biases, I supposed in her mind such a thing *would* appear scandalous, although the notion that two young women in the late nineteenth century had fallen in love was not something that seemed particularly salacious to me.

*But think about how a conservative family member might feel if such information was shared.* I slid the document back into its folder and refiled it in its proper box. I didn't know enough about Delbert Frye to guess his reaction to such news, but given his age and hermitlike ways, it was entirely possible that he would do something drastic to keep this type of information buried.

*And perhaps "bury" anyone who threatened to expose the truth.*

I stood, cradling the box in my arms. I'd carry it inside and read through the documents more thoroughly, but even this quick perusal had turned up an additional reason for Delbert Frye to want to silence Mona Raymond.

After closing up the archives, I walked back into the library, still considering this angle. To me, old gossip wasn't enough to consider killing anyone, but I knew that wasn't true for everyone. If a decades-old scandal in my own family had been enough to drive one of my older cousins to kill several people, a forbidden relationship between Ada and Violet, along with their possible murders by someone in their family, might be enough of a motive for Delbert Frye.

It was another bit of information to tell Brad Tucker, at any rate. I set the archival box on a shelf in the workroom and called him to share this latest revelation.

\* \* \*

"I would've asked Richard to come and get me this evening," I told Aunt Lydia when she showed up with sandwiches, two bags of baby carrots, and bottled water, "but he has a late rehearsal at school."

"It's no problem," my aunt replied, spreading some paper towels over the worktable. "I needed to pick up some books anyway." She glanced over at me as she unwrapped the sandwiches. "How's Sunny doing?"

"Like I told you, she's pretty upset. Not really because of Brad, though." I hovered near the workroom door so I could keep an eye on the desk. "It's more about not ever finding anyone who can love her just as she is. It seems crazy to me, because I think she's so amazing, but it seems her being herself is not what most men want."

"That's a tricky thing." Aunt Lydia unscrewed the lid on one of the bottles and took a long swallow of water. "I thought Andrew and I loved each other just as we were, but it turns out that wasn't exactly the case. Well, the error was more on my part than his, I suppose." She set the bottle on the table and laid out the two packages of carrots. "Sometimes I think finding the right companion is really more luck than anything else. Meeting your best match seems so difficult, and yet it often happens by chance. Who would've thought I would find my best partner so late in life, and in such an unexpected way?"

"You and Hugh *are* perfect for one another."

"But you have to admit that it was just luck that we met. Like you and Richard." Aunt Lydia looked up at me from under her lowered lashes. "I like to think Sunny will experience the same good fortune one day. But it might take a while."

"Not too long, I hope," I said as the bell at the desk rang. "Hold on, let me handle this."

I spied a tall figure with white hair as soon as I stepped behind the desk. "Hello, Kurt, what brings you here?"

"I had a little business in town and thought I'd pop in and see if you were working this evening." He spread his hands wide. "I would've called you later in any case, but since you're here—how would you like to visit Mary Gardener tomorrow afternoon? She's been talking about you ever since our last visit, so I'm sure she'd be delighted to see you again. Oh hello, Lydia," he added, as my aunt stepped out of the workroom. "Volunteering tonight?"

"No, just bringing Amy something to eat and then driving her home after work. Sunny had to leave suddenly, so Amy needed to stay later than she'd planned."

Kurt frowned. "I hope everything's all right with Ms. Fields."

"She's fine," I said. "She just needed an afternoon off for . . . reasons. As for tomorrow, I think I can swing that. We close at five on Tuesdays now, and I'm sure Sunny will agree to handle things if I leave early. If you want to go in the afternoon like we did before, that is."

"That would be perfect. And Lydia, if you're free, perhaps you'd like to join us? I think you might enjoy the visit. Mary is a wonderful storyteller and knows a great deal about local history. She may even have some tales to tell about your parents that you've never heard."

"I'd be delighted," my aunt said. "Should we just meet you out front, say around three?"

"That will work." Kurt's gaze swept over Aunt Lydia before coming to rest on me. "I hope you didn't have too painful a time at my dinner party the other night."

"Oh no, it was lovely," I said. "I mean, you're not to blame if . . ."

"Some of my guests behave like boors?" Kurt flashed a grin. "I would be inclined to believe that Richard was adopted if it weren't for the fact that he bears such a strong resemblance to Paul Dassin."

Aunt Lydia sniffed loudly. "That only proves that Fiona is his biological mother. I think I might've sought out someone else to father my child if I were her, so who knows?"

"Aunt Lydia, the things you say sometimes . . ." I shook my head as Kurt burst out in a loud guffaw.

The Nightingale, perusing the "New Books" rack, shushed him, but he simply offered her a gallant bow and left the building, still chuckling to himself.

# Chapter Eighteen

When we arrived at Mary Gardener's house the following afternoon, I was surprised to see a battered pickup truck parked in the driveway.

"It looks like Mary already has a visitor. I hope we aren't intruding," Aunt Lydia said as Kurt opened her car door and offered his assistance to help her climb out of the low-slung front seat.

"It's fine; she's expecting us." Kurt cast a glance at the truck, which had obviously seen a lot of hard use. It's bright-red paint had faded into patches of pink, and dents dimpled its chrome bumper. "That's Delbert Frye's vehicle. He sometimes stops by to play music for Mary."

I jumped out of the back seat while Kurt held the door open. "What? I thought he was a hermit who didn't mix with other people." I pressed my lips together before I could say more. The thought of spending time with another murderer . . . *No, possible murderer*, I told myself. *You have no proof that he killed Mona, and obviously neither do the authorities, since he hasn't been arrested yet.*

"Really?" Aunt Lydia said as we made our way to the front porch. "I knew he built instruments, but I didn't know he played."

"And sings too. He's actually quite good," Kurt said. "And yes,

Amy, he doesn't get out much. But he and Mary have been friends for some time. Really, it's a shame he's such a loner. He only shares his talents with a few people, Mary being one."

As we entered the house, a rich baritone voice, accompanied by what sounded like the soft strum of a dulcimer, wafted through the air.

"O mother, mother, make my bed!
O make it saft and narrow!
Since my love died for me to-day,
I'll die for him to-morrow."

"I know that song. 'Barbara Allen'—an old Scotch-Irish folk tune," Aunt Lydia said as we crossed the living room. "My great-uncle used to sing it with a piano accompaniment."

"Yes, it's quite a classic, often adapted by Appalachian musicians and others," I said as I followed Kurt and my aunt into the kitchen.

Delbert Frye, a short, wiry man who looked to be in his eighties, sat in a wooden ladder-back chair that he'd pulled up beside Mary's rocker. The cinnamon streaks in his bushy gray beard bore witness to its original color, while only a few sprigs of white hair fringed his bald head. That, and the loose white shirt he wore over a pair of faded jeans, lent him the appearance of a medieval monk. Although, loner that he was, I doubted that Delbert Frye had much use for organized religion.

He didn't look like a killer, but then, neither did the other murderers that I'd encountered over the past year. I gritted my teeth and forced a smile. I knew I had to be careful and watch my words. Brad had asked me to keep the information I'd recently uncovered a secret while the sheriff's office continued to build their case. I couldn't betray my suspicions, no matter how uneasy I felt.

As Kurt pulled up chairs for Aunt Lydia and me, Delbert stared at us with a mixture of embarrassment and suspicion. "Didn't know you were expecting visitors today, Mary," he said in a voice more gravelly than his singing would've led me to expect.

"Oh laws, I'm sorry, Del." Mary reached over and patted the arm he'd stretched protectively over the instrument in his lap. "But these aren't strangers. You've met my friend, Karl Klass, and this is a local girl, Lydia Talbot, and her niece. Lydia was a Litton, a granddaughter of the Bakers who lived in that big stone house at the end of Main Street."

"I still live there," Aunt Lydia said, extending her hand first to Delbert and then Mary. "So nice to meet you both."

Delbert Frye reluctantly brushed my aunt's fingertips with his. "Hello," he muttered, not meeting her eyes.

In contrast, Mary gave her hand a firm clasp. "Pleasure. I almost feel I know you, since Karl has mentioned you so often. You were married to his best friend, as I recall."

"Yes, Andrew Talbot, but he died many years ago. Now I live in the family home with my niece." She motioned for me to step forward. "You know Amy, I believe. Her mother is my younger sister, Deborah."

"I'm glad for the chance to make your acquaintance, Lydia." Mary looked us over. "Now I remember—I sometimes saw you and your sister around town when you were small. You were so different— one so blonde and one very dark. Like that old story . . ." Mary pursed her thin lips. "What was that? Oh yes, Rose White and Rose Red. You two girls always reminded me of that fairy tale."

Aunt Lydia blinked rapidly. "Funny, my father used to call us that. Rosie White and Rosie Red," she said softly, brushing at her eyes with her fingertips.

Mary tipped her head as she examined my aunt, her eyes bright as a sparrow's. "Yes, the Littons. I remember them. Your grandmother may have been as ornery as an old biddy hen, but your daddy was a sweet man. He was the only one to ask after my health when those people at the orphanage fell sick. I'd left, along with Karl there, before any of those poor folks died, but Randy Litton still took time to stop by and make sure I was all right." Mary's gaze rested on my aunt with compassion. "I was so heartsick when I heard about him and your momma dying in that accident. As I recall, you were still a child at the time."

"Fourteen," my aunt said, slipping a lace handkerchief from her purse and dabbing at her eyes. "And thank you for your kind words, Mary. He was a special man."

Seeing her distress, I thought it was time to change the subject. I shifted my focus to the beautiful instrument cradled in Delbert's arms. Crafted of fine-grained cherry, its buffed surface and sinuous curves called to mind an elegant piece of sculpture. "Is that one of your dulcimers, Mr. Frye? Walt Adams has told me about your musical creations. He's often said they were as beautiful as works of art. I can see that he wasn't exaggerating." I sat back in my chair, pleased that I'd found a way to engage with the man without betraying my suspicions over his possible crime.

*Yes, keep the conversation on music. That's a safe subject.* I examined Delbert, hoping his weathered face would betray something of his true character.

His hazel eyes, flecked with green, studied me in return. Bright and unblinking, they reminded me of the hidden, sly gaze of a fox. And just as wary.

"Yes, this is one of mine."

"It's gorgeous," I said. "Just like your voice."

Delbert's cheeks turned the color of the russet streaks in his whiskers. "Thank you, but I'm not much for singing in public."

"I keep telling Del he should perform for the folks in town during one of those festivals they hold in the fall, but he won't hear of it." Mary patted her gray topknot with one knobby-knuckled hand. "Won't sing for anyone but a doddering old lady like me."

"You feel the music," Delbert said. "Not like them people in town. They'd say it was all too old and strange." What I suspected was a rare smile flitted over his face. "Like me."

"Oh, pshaw, the things you say." Mary gave Delbert's arm a surprisingly strong slap. "You're only a few years older than Karl over there, and he acts like time don't matter. Which it don't, really." Mary settled back in her rocker, her bright gaze sweeping over the rest of us. "That's the thing you young'uns need to learn. Time don't change who you are, just what you look like. If you don't pay no mind to that, you don't need to worry about the rest either."

Delbert snorted. "I was already running the farm when that fellow was knee-high to a grasshopper." He stared at Kurt, his eyes narrowing. "Though you were more like a hornet, from what I've heard. Ran some scams and stung a few folks before being thrown out of that orphanage. Lucky that Paul Dassin fellow took you in, or who knows where you would've ended up."

Kurt leaned back against the kitchen counter and studied Delbert with interest. "Not here, certainly. Now Delbert, I don't remember you ever mentioning that you knew anything about me. Did we meet when I was young? I'm afraid I don't recall that."

"No, never did, and I didn't really know you. Just heard stuff. I mean, it's Taylorsford and, well . . . word got around."

"That hasn't changed." Aunt Lydia primly crossed her hands in her lap. "I do want to apologize, Mr. Frye, for so many people leaping to conclusions lately. It seems the location of your property has drawn some unwanted scrutiny, due to the disappearance of that girl and the professor's death."

I squirmed on my chair, but Delbert simply shrugged. "I've got nothing to hide. It's true I own guns, but the sheriff's office has already checked them over and figured out that none of them was used to shoot that teacher. Of course, I'd already told them that. They could've skipped all the bother, but they aren't much for listening to folks like me."

I scooted to the edge of my chair. Here was my opportunity to question him without betraying that I knew anything more than the rest of the people in the room. "You didn't see or hear anything, Mr. Frye? I mean, about that girl that was lost as well as the professor?"

"Not a thing, just like I told those deputies. I was farther up the mountain around the time they seem to think that woman was killed." He shot me a sharp look. "I collect wood for my instruments off state land, close to where they put in those trails. Limbs and branches are naturally gonna break off, so I never saw no harm in it. 'Course I have to cut down trees on my property for larger pieces, but for trim and stuff, well . . . it's just litter lying there, and I only grab an armful at a time. No one seems to mind."

"I'm sure they don't," I said, lifting my hand to stave off more of his outburst. It was a taste of that quick temper Walt had mentioned. Perhaps Delbert's volatility really could drive him to violence. I tempered my tone before speaking again. "I just thought if you'd noticed anything . . ."

"I would've told the deputies, like I did after I heard all that thrashing about in the woods last Thursday morning. Couldn't exactly tell where the noise was coming from, but I thought maybe it was that fellow who moved into the old Patterson place."

"Charles Bartos?" Kurt asked, shooting me a raised-eyebrow glance.

"That's the one." Delbert turned to Mary. "Remember, I told you about him and his fancy ways. Toted a camera that looked like it cost more than any sensible person would pay, then stomped through the woods loud enough to scare away every bird or critter for miles."

"He wanted to photograph wildlife?" The incredulous note in my voice made everyone's gaze swivel to me. "Sorry, but I know Charles, and that doesn't sound like him."

Delbert scowled. "That's what he told me, not that we talked much. I only saw him a couple of times. It's not like we socialized."

I brushed a bit of lint from my chocolate-brown slacks. "Did you ever meet his girlfriend, Marlis Dupre?"

"Once. I was driving up the old farm road and she was out by the fence, near my shed, yelling her fool head off. I jumped out of my truck and ran over and spied this big blacksnake near her feet. She begged me to kill it, but I refused. Told her it was harmless and would keep the mice and rats off her property. She got real quiet then and stayed still while I shooed the snake off." Delbert rubbed at his temples, as if this memory pained him. "I mean, I could've shot the thing, because I keep a loaded rifle in the shed for protection against rats and copperheads that sometimes crawl in there, but I don't see no point in killing something that isn't a danger." Delbert's bright eyes clouded over. "The girl was nice about it once she calmed down. Thanked me and even invited me to join them for dinner sometime. Which I never did, and then she was killed." Delbert frowned. "I can't say I'm fond of Bartos. Too much of a city slicker for these parts. But I do feel sorry for him, losing his lady like that."

I stared at Delbert. His compassion over Marlis's death added a new brushstroke to my picture of him. Of course, I knew that didn't eliminate him as a suspect. I had learned the hard way that you couldn't assume that someone was innocent—or guilty—based on just a few character traits.

"It is a shame, losing someone like that," Mary said, gently laying her hand on Delbert's arm. "I know you sympathize, Del, having suffered through your own troubles. Just like Lydia over there, poor dear." She tightened the grip of her gnarled fingers on his sinewy arm. "Not only did her parents die when she was young, she also lost her husband in an accident not long after they were married. Just like your wife."

Delbert lifted his lowered head and gazed at my aunt. "Is that right?"

"Yes, it's true." Aunt Lydia offered him a sympathetic smile. "I'm sorry, I didn't know you'd lost your wife, Mr. Frye."

"Wife and child," he said gruffly.

Kurt straightened and stepped away from the counter. "My sympathies."

"It was a long time ago," Delbert said. "Wasn't living here at the time. I'd gone off to the city because I was sick and tired of scraping by on the farm and wanted to make more money. I met Claire there, while I was apprenticed to a furniture maker. It was all good at first—seemed I had a knack for woodworking, and Claire and I got hitched and she was expecting soon after. But then Claire was hit by one of them city buses when she was trying to cross the street. Right before the baby was due, so I lost both of them at once. That was the end of living in the city for me."

Mary cleared her throat. "Pretty much the end of living for you."

I saw this arrow hit home as Delbert stood and clutched his

dulcimer to his chest. "Now look here, Mary Gardener. We're friends, but that don't give you the right to say such things to me."

"Just speaking truth, as only we old ladies can do," she replied without batting an eyelash. "I only bring it up, Del, because I know Lydia has lost as much or more, and yet she doesn't hide herself away, burying her talents in a mountain cabin and chasing everyone off with a gun."

I gnawed at the inside of my cheek. Delbert Frye was under suspicion for both Lacey's disappearance and Mona's death. On the surface it seemed reasonable, and I had to admit that the information I'd uncovered, along with Mona's remarks about using an old family scandal to force him to talk to her, lent credence to that theory. But would this man really take a shot at an unarmed woman? My thoughts circled around the question as Delbert, urged by Mary, sat back down and played an instrumental folk tune.

*It could've been a hunter, shooting out of season. Someone like Ethan*, I thought, recalling our encounter at the vet's office. Or perhaps even one of the students, like Trish. Despite her small stature, she could obviously wield a rifle. I didn't know if Chris or Hope could handle guns, but it wasn't outside the realm of possibility. And there was the matter of the treasure. I was fairly certain that one or even all of the students had seen that letter in the archives. If they'd decided to search for the missing gold coins, no matter how hypothetical the quest, would any of them have gunned down Mona if she stood in their way?

I studied Delbert Frye as his fingers plucked and strummed the dulcimer. There was the problem—I still couldn't rule him out. Not only might he have reacted violently to Mona's threat of blackmail, but there was a strong possibility that he also knew about the gold. It was information he could've easily learned from his family. Perhaps

Mona *had* known about the missing coins and threatened to expose that family secret as well. It would have given Delbert another reason to silence her. I knew only too well what the search for treasure could drive even the most unlikely person to do, and Delbert, with his temper, secretive nature, and tendency to use guns as a threat, was a more likely killer than most.

*Although he didn't want to shoot a creature he felt was harmless, even though he had a gun handy . . .*

I jumped up so quickly that my chair toppled over behind me.

Aunt Lydia turned to stare at me.

Delbert Frye did own another gun—a rifle stored in a shed some distance from his house. He'd mentioned that the authorities had checked all the guns in his cabin, but I wondered if he'd revealed that additional weapon to them. He might easily have omitted that information—whether through an innocent lapse of memory or a more sinister motive.

"Are you all right, Amy?" Kurt asked, striding to my side and righting the chair.

"Yeah, I'm fine. Sorry." I turned to Mary and Delbert. "And forgive me, but I just remembered something I promised to do. There's a call I have to make. Will you excuse me?"

"Of course," Mary said, while Aunt Lydia eyed me with suspicion. "Go on, dear. We'll have some snacks and tea when you get back. Karl, could you help me up?"

"You stay seated and just tell me what to do," Kurt said as my aunt rose to her feet. "Go ahead, Amy. Lydia and I can handle this."

"Okay," I said, forcing a smile. "Back in a minute."

I rushed out of the house and onto the front porch. Pulling out my cell phone, I punched in Brad Tucker's number. I would tell him to bring a few deputies and search the building near Charles's property line. They had to investigate the shed belonging to the old man still playing the haunting music wafting out from the kitchen.

Pocketing my phone after my call, I took several deep breaths to slow my racing heart. I wasn't looking forward to facing Delbert Frye again, but I knew I had to go back inside and make small talk and smile and not betray what I had done.

No matter how difficult it would be, I couldn't allow Delbert, or anyone in that kitchen, to know that I'd just made a call that might end in his arrest.

# Chapter Nineteen

At work the next day, I heard the news that Delbert Frye had been taken in for questioning from at least five patrons before I told Sunny that I needed to go straighten the shelves.

"I just did that yesterday," she said, but I mumbled something about the Nightingale having made the rounds as soon as we opened and headed for the stacks. I knew I'd done the right thing but still felt conflicted. Running my finger along a row of books and silently reading off call numbers didn't entirely block the image of an old man delicately plucking the strings of a dulcimer, but at least it was a distraction.

"Ms. Webber, could I talk to you for a moment?"

I turned, a book I'd discovered shoved behind the others on its shelf clutched in my hand. "Oh hello, Hope. What can I do for you?"

"I just wanted . . ." Hope stared down at her bright-red high-top sneakers. "I need to tell you something is all."

"Okay." I placed the book on the cart I'd rolled over to collect misshelved items and motioned toward the reading area. "There's a free table by the windows. Let's head over there."

Hope followed me, glancing around. "It's a little personal. I mean, I don't want anyone overhearing us."

I paused to survey the area. There was only one patron and he was seated at one of the sturdy oak tables on the other side of the room. "Don't worry, Mr. Dinterman won't be a problem. He isn't much of a snoop, and anyway, his hearing isn't that good." I sat down, pushing aside the bronze library table lamp with its green glass shade.

"I wouldn't bring this up, except that no one knows when they can bring Lacey out of the coma"—Hope took a seat across from me—"or even how aware she'll be after they do. Her parents told me she might suffer lasting effects."

"You mean brain damage? I certainly hope not." I used my finger to trace the faded outline of a heart and arrow etched into the table-top—"B and W forever." I had no idea who "B" or "W" might have been, or how long their forever had lasted, but when I'd taken over as library director, I'd resisted the suggestion that the etched memory be sanded away. Which just proved I was as much a romantic as anyone, I supposed.

"They can't be sure." Hope drummed her fingers against the table. "Sorry, but this is difficult. I just thought you should know, because . . ."

"Because?" I asked, as Hope chewed on her lower lip. "What is it? Something to do with Lacey?" I leaned forward, wondering if Hope was about to reveal the truth about Lacey's real purpose in hiking the Twin Falls trail alone.

*If she knows about the gold coins and thinks Lacey was searching for the treasure . . .* I gave Hope an encouraging smile. "It's all right. I won't judge, whatever it is. I promise."

"Okay." Hope drew in an audible breath. "It's just that I've spent a good bit of time talking to Lacey's parents at the hospital. There's a lot of sitting around doing nothing under those circumstances."

"Yes, I know that quite well," I said, recalling the events of the past summer and fall.

"Well"—Hope tugged at one of her tight braids—"they mentioned something about Lacey dating a mysterious guy for some time now. Apparently, they'd had words about it because it was an older man. Considerably older. That's the one thing her parents could figure out even though Lacey always refused to introduce him to them. She said that she couldn't. So I thought that perhaps there was something to that idea that she and Mr. Muir . . ."

"What?" I sat bolt upright in my chair. "No. That's ridiculous."

"I'm sorry, it just seems to fit. According to her mom, this relationship started up around the time that Lacey first worked with Mr. Muir two summers ago, when she danced in some one-off collaborative performance sponsored by the music and dance departments."

"But that was before . . ." I tightened my lips over my gritted teeth.

Soon after Richard and I had met, he'd told me about a short-term program he'd participated in at Clarion—something related to the university wanting to foster cross-discipline events. I remembered this because he'd also mentioned how much he'd disliked Charles, who'd provided the music for a piece that Richard had choreographed. Richard had claimed that Charles had been rude to his dancers, even bringing some of them to tears. Which was why Richard had refused to ever work with Charles going forward and had never again allowed him to play for any of his dance studio performances.

*No, it couldn't be.* I crossed my arms over my chest, hugging my upper arms. Although I could picture Richard comforting a distraught dancer, especially if someone as acerbic as Charles had cut them down . . .

"That's impossible," I said, meeting Hope's questioning gaze with a lift of my chin. "You can't imagine that they were involved all this time, or that Richard had anything to do with Lacey's disappearance."

"I don't know. It does seem strange, but her parents were so sure that she was seeing someone, and in secret. So when I heard about Lacey running out of Mr. Muir's office in tears . . ."

"He explained that to me. It had nothing to do with her disappearance."

Hope narrowed her brown eyes. "That's what he told you, anyway."

I shoved back my chair and leapt to my feet. "This is all supposition and innuendo. There are plenty of older men on and off campus who could've been involved with Lacey."

Out of the corner of my eye, I caught Mr. Dinterman looking up from his magazine.

"Maybe," Hope said, standing up to face me. "But there's talk on campus. And with what Lacey's parents said . . . well, I just wanted to put you on your guard. I may be young, but I've hooked up with a few people and I know sometimes you don't see things clearly when you're in love with someone. It's easy to fool yourself and pretend someone is something they're not." She shrugged. "Done that myself a couple of times."

"This is totally different."

"Probably. But I thought I should tell you what Lacey's parents said, mainly because I didn't want you to be blindsided if there was any truth to it. Sure, just because it was an older man doesn't mean it's Mr. Muir, but he does fit the profile, and Lacey does interact with him on a regular basis. She always talked about how much she likes him too, which is the other thing that made me wonder. You know how people like to mention someone they're involved with, even if they have to keep the true depth of the relationship a secret.

Anyway, it just seemed like something you should know." Hope looked me over. "I like you, Ms. Webber. That's the only reason I came here today. If there's any truth to the rumors, I don't want you to be the last to know."

I thrust my hands into the pockets of my slacks to hide their trembling. "Thank you for your concern, Hope. But if that's all, I need to get back to work."

"Sure. You just take care of yourself, okay?"

"I will. Now, excuse me." I turned away and practically ran back to the circulation desk.

Sunny poked her head out of the workroom. "Was that Hope Hodgson?"

"Yeah." I shifted a stack of books from one end of the desk to the other.

"What did she want?"

"Nothing, really. She was just updating me on Lacey's condition," I said without looking at Sunny.

"Which is?"

"Same." I turned to her. "Do you mind if I take the afternoon off? I'm not really feeling too well." I pressed my palm against my forehead. "Headache."

Sunny examined me with a critical eye. "Okay. I took off the other day, so it's only fair."

"You already paid me back by covering yesterday afternoon, but thanks. I really need the break. I'm just going to check something on the staff computer and then I'm heading out." I slid past Sunny and dashed into the workroom before she could say anything else.

Firing up the computer, I typed in a search, then peered at the screen, half hoping I'd get no results.

But there they were—photos of Richard with members of his

dance studio. Mostly group shots, but there was one of him with his arm draped around the shoulders of a blonde girl. True, the information linked to the photo said it had been taken when Lacey won some sort of prize for her junior year choreography project, but . . .

I clicked away from the images and slumped in my chair. The idea that Richard could have been involved with one of his students went against everything I thought I knew about him, everything I believed in my heart. It wasn't possible.

Yet I'd been wrong before. A little over two years ago, when I had still been involved with Charles, I would've never imagined that he would cheat on me with the violinist in his new trio.

I could write that off as Charles being fundamentally unable to be faithful to anyone. Except . . . as far as I knew, Charles and Marlis had lived together as a couple until her death, so it seemed he was capable of maintaining a longer-term relationship. Just not with me. Maybe Richard wasn't capable of monogamy either, despite all the evidence to the contrary. Perhaps he also needed more than I could offer—with someone who could truly share his love of dance.

I stared blankly at the screen saver for a moment, then leapt up and grabbed my jacket and purse. "Taking off," I called out to Sunny before shoving my way through the workroom's exterior door.

I needed clean air and quiet. I had to escape, and to someplace where I wouldn't run into anyone I knew. Thankful that I'd driven to work, I circled around the building to reach the parking lot and jumped into my car. I took off, not certain where I was going until I drove outside of town and onto the road that led to the Twin Falls trail.

* * *

When I reached the small parking lot at the trailhead, I slipped my keys and phone in my pockets and locked my purse in the trunk. I was dressed for work, not hiking, but decided that it made no difference. *It isn't important*, I thought. *I won't walk far.*

I also didn't care that my leather loafers were getting scuffed by the rocks and twigs under my feet, or that the sweat dampening the armpits of my ivory cotton blouse would probably leave stains.

*It doesn't matter*, I thought as I stormed down the trail. *It just doesn't matter.*

I was so wrapped up in my own anxiety that I didn't hear the man walking up behind me.

"Amy," he said, "what are you doing out here?"

I wheeled around and stared up into Ethan Payne's handsome face.

"Oh hello." I tugged my rumpled blouse down over the waistband of my black slacks. "Just taking a walk."

Ethan's gaze swept over me. "Not really dressed for it, are you?"

"No, I guess not. I came out here on a whim."

"Well, be careful," Ethan said, pointing at my feet with the butt of his rifle. "Those shoes aren't suitable for this trail."

He was wearing camouflage pants and a tan shirt, with a fluorescent orange vest and hiking boots.

"You look ready to stalk some game. But I thought you said it wasn't hunting season."

"It isn't. I just bring the gun along in case I run into any copperheads or rattlers. Or bears," he added, giving me a significant look. "There are some up here, you know. Bobcats too, although they usually aren't prowling around in the middle of the day."

"So you're just taking a hike as well? Without your dog this time, I see. And . . . how did you get here exactly? I saw another vehicle parked at the trailhead but didn't notice you behind me until you suddenly appeared."

"I left Callie at home today. Didn't want her chasing off after critters again. As to your other question, there's another path that intersects with this one a little farther up the trail. It comes out on that road near Delbert Frye's property. I parked at the trailhead and circled around to that path and then cut through the woods." As Ethan shifted his gun to his other shoulder, he opened his clenched fist.

A gold coin glinted against his calloused palm.

"Where'd you find that?" I blurted out before thinking. *That was foolish, Amy. If Ethan was searching for the treasure, he might not appreciate your interest. And he has a rifle. The type of gun that killed Mona Raymond.*

Ethan closed his fingers over the coin. "In a gulley in the woods." He gazed up and over my shoulder. "Looks old, so it was probably dropped by someone crossing the mountains long ago."

I studied his profile. He was tall and well-muscled. He could easily overwhelm me if he wanted, and just as easily dispose of my body.

But that was foolishness. Surely this young firefighter wasn't a killer. I decide to test my theory of his true mission. "Out treasure hunting then?"

Ethan dropped his gaze and stared intently at me. "What? No, I just saw something glinting in the dirt and checked it out."

As I met his piercing stare, I noticed his clenched jaw and realized that he wasn't going to admit that Chris had told him about the old letter, even though I was convinced that's what had happened. I wanted to question him further, but his glower silenced my curiosity. "I imagine that happened more than once. There must've been a lot of people who crossed these mountains toting all their worldly goods."

"Right," Ethan said sharply as he pocketed the coin. "Why'd you say you were up here again?"

"I just needed some fresh air."

"And you couldn't get that in town? Taylorsford might be a little too built-up on the edges for my taste, but it still has clean air, as far as I can tell."

He wasn't buying my story. Maybe he suspected I was another treasure hunter, searching for those gold coins. If Chris had told him about discovering the letter in the archives, Ethan could easily have surmised that I'd also seen it. I inched backward as the wind picked up, circling dead leaves around my ankles.

"You really shouldn't be up here right now," Ethan said, shouldering his rifle. "It isn't safe." He made a grab for my arm. "Come on, I'll walk you back to your car."

"No, I'm fine," I said, sliding my cell phone from my trouser pocket.

Ethan reached for me again. "I really think you should come with me. I can't be responsible for what happens if you don't."

I backed away and held up my phone. "I said I'll be fine. As a matter of fact, I have the sheriff's office on speed dial."

Ethan stared at my cell phone as if it were one of those rattlesnakes he'd mentioned earlier. "Have it your way. But there's a storm brewing. Don't say I didn't warn you."

"Just making that call," I said, punching in numbers before holding the phone to my ear.

Ethan swore under his breath and strode off in the direction of the trailhead.

After he'd disappeared from view, I hit the "end" button on my call, but not until after hearing the weather service alert. There *was* a storm coming. I looked up through the canopy of leaves over my head and noticed that the sky had darkened to an ominous purple.

I considered making a run for my car, but Ethan had headed off in that direction and I didn't want to encounter him again. Maybe he had no intention of harming me, but I wasn't willing to take that chance. People had tried to shoot me before. People I'd never have expected to be killers before they'd turned on me.

Ethan had mentioned a cutoff from the main trail. I hurried on, searching for it, but before I found the intersecting path, the wind had risen to a dull roar and raindrops pelted my bare head.

*If this trail ends at Delbert's property, it's also close to Charles's house*, I thought, dodging flying leaves and twigs ripped from the trees as I jogged down the path. Even if he wasn't home, Charles had a covered porch, which had to be a better spot to wait out the storm than the middle of a forest.

# Chapter Twenty

By the time I reached Charles's property, I was soaked to the skin. After banging the front door knocker, I plucked my blouse away from my body. The light fabric was plastered to my skin, outlining everything down to the lace trim of my bra. Taking additional inventory of my condition, I noticed that not only were my black slacks clinging to my legs like baggy tights, but they were also splashed with bits of dead leaves and mud. I sighed. I probably looked like a drowned rat, but I knew I couldn't allow that to deter me. I banged the knocker again.

Charles cracked the door open and peered out, his blue eyes widening with surprise.

"Thank goodness you're home. Could you give me a ride to the start of the Twin Falls trail? I left my car there before I foolishly took off on a walk."

Charles looked me over. "Of course, but first come inside and dry off."

"No, no, I don't want to bother you."

"It's no bother, and"—Charles offered me a smile—"if you need more motivation, I really don't want you dripping all over my leather seats."

"Right," I said as I slid by him and stood on the rectangle of ceramic tile that separated the front door from a shining expanse of hardwood flooring. "I guess the first thing I should do is take off these shoes."

"Good idea. You do that while I grab a towel." Charles sprinted off toward what I assumed was a bathroom.

I slipped my feet out of my squelchy loafers before balancing on one foot and then the other to peel off my dripping socks.

"Just leave those on the tile and wrap up in this," Charles said, handing me a white towel so large and fluffy I was sure he must've stolen it from a luxury hotel.

*Nonsense*, I thought as I vigorously rubbed my head. *He has the money to buy such things.* After blotting some of the water from my hair, and no doubt turning it into a tangle resembling Medusa's serpent locks, I wrapped the towel around my upper body.

"You should change out of those things before you catch a chill. Follow me." Charles strode away again.

I trailed him with trepidation, suspecting the only clothes he could offer would have once belonged to Marlis. Definitely not what I wanted to wear.

Charles led me into a large, airy bedroom. One wall held built-in closets and cabinets. Crafted from pale wood, the various doors and drawers were fitted together with the precision of storage space in a yacht. The opposite wall consisted of floor-to-ceiling windows that provided a view of a well-tended flower garden bordered at the back edge by a thick grove of trees.

"Here, let me give you some privacy." Charles pulled a set of vertical blinds across the lower level of windows. "Not that anyone's around, but I don't want you to feel exposed." He crossed to one of the built-in drawers and pulled out a pair of sweat pants and a sweatshirt. "Some of my workout gear. Hope you don't mind," he added as he laid the items on the bed.

"No, that's fine." I eyed the sweatshirt, wondering whether something that would fit Charles's slim torso would actually accommodate my more curvaceous figure.

"Very well, I'll let you change. Just bring those wet things out with you and I'll give them a quick spin in the dryer." Charles turned in the doorway to glance back at me. "Would you like some tea or coffee? I can easily brew some."

"Coffee, please, and if you have any brandy, I wouldn't mind a shot of that thrown in."

Charles smiled and inclined his head in a gesture not unlike a bow. "Your wish is my command."

After he left the room, I crossed over to the door and locked it. Not that I thought Charles would try to take advantage of me, but because . . .

*Because it feels odd to be in his house, changing into his clothes, with him just beyond that door. Even though he's seen you dress and undress plenty of times in the past, this isn't the same.*

It felt different because I was different, I realized, as I pulled the sweatshirt over my head. I wasn't the same girl who'd fallen in love with some renowned musician eight years her senior. No longer the naïve young woman who'd idolized Charles and put up with his controlling behavior, I now felt immune to his charms. Honestly, I couldn't even imagine why I'd ever thought he was justified in demanding that I change everything about myself to better fit into his life. Which hadn't worked, of course.

*It would never have worked because I was never what he wanted. Not then.* I yanked on the sweat pants, which were tight but fortunately stretchy enough to fit. *No, he never really wanted me,* I thought as I rolled up the bottoms of the sweat pants to accommodate my shorter legs. *I was just a dalliance.*

Because it was obvious to me now that he'd always preferred someone like Marlis—talented, charming, self-assured, and confident in her own body. Someone who would challenge him, not bow to his every whim. Someone who knew she was every bit as valuable and important as he was.

*Someone more like the woman I am now.*

I tugged at the tight sweat shirt, but it still clung to my curves like a second skin. *It will have to do*, I thought, dumping my discarded clothes onto the bath towel that I'd dropped on the floor.

As I knelt down to pick up the bundle of soggy clothes, a thump drew my gaze to one of the closets. A shoebox had fallen and popped open one of the doors. I straightened and walked over to the closet, planning to simply open the door and shove the box back inside. But when I swung open the doors, I was surprised that the closet was barren except for one gold-and-white sequined evening gown. Empty hangers forlornly filled the rest of the wooden hanging rod. I thought it seemed odd. Even though I knew that this hadn't been their primary residence, I would've expected to uncover more of Marlis's clothes. But there was nothing left in the closet—nothing except one dress and the fallen shoebox.

*Of course, Charles may have already gotten ridden of her things.* I picked up the shoebox. *Perhaps the sight of her clothes was too painful to bear.* As I lifted the box over my head to place it back on the shelf above the hanging rod, the top popped open and something slid out and fell across my bare foot. I picked it up, prepared to shove it back into the box, but paused to stare at it instead.

It was a white hat. Hand-knitted, with bright-blue snowflakes emblazoned around the edge.

Lacey Jacobs's hat.

I closed the closet doors and backed away, still clutching the knitted cap. Without thinking, I stuffed it into the pocket of my borrowed sweatpants and crossed back to the pile of damp clothes on the floor. I wrapped them in the towel and scooped them up before making my way out of the room.

"Ah, there you are," Charles said, pointing to a ceramic mug. "Coffee is ready, and brandy is on the counter. Here, let me have those wet things and I'll toss them in the dryer while you doctor your drink."

I mutely handed over the bundle and crossed to the marble-topped island. As he headed for a small room off the kitchen, I grabbed the brandy bottle and poured a good slug into one of the jade-colored mugs before adding coffee.

"All taken care of," Charles said as he walked back into the kitchen. "Although feel free to wear those borrowed things home if you don't want to change again. I can always pick them up later."

I studied him, admiring his cool confidence while I fingered the knitted cap in my pocket. *He thinks he'll be dropping by my house sometime soon? Of course he does.* He was undoubtedly certain that this encounter was merely the prelude to establishing a new relationship with me.

"I don't mind changing back into my clothes," I said after taking a healthy gulp of my alcohol-laced coffee. "Besides, you said you might be selling this place. Once you move, it might not be that easy for you to run by Aunt Lydia's house."

Charles poured a little brandy in his own coffee. "Oh, I don't know. Maybe I shouldn't be so hasty in making a decision to sell." His brilliant-blue gaze ranged over my body. "I might decide to stay around a little while longer."

I set down my cup. "Well, before you make that decision, perhaps you'd like to explain this." I yanked Lacey's hat from my pocket and dangled it in his face.

Charles blanched. "You snooped through my things?"

"No. A box fell in your closet, and when I went to put it back, I found this." I waved the hat. "I know this belongs to Lacey Jacobs. What's it doing in your house?"

Charles took a long swallow of his coffee before carefully placing the cup on the counter. "I found it. At the accident scene."

"Wait, what?" I dropped the knitted cap onto the marble surface of the island. "You mean where Marlis was killed?"

"Yes. Can we sit down?" Charles motioned toward the main room.

I mutely followed him over to the white leather sofa and took a seat at one end while he sat at the other. "Now, please explain. You found Lacey's hat near Marlis's body? But why didn't the authorities confiscate it for evidence?"

"Because I was the first person on the scene and I never told them about it," Charles said, lowering his head. "I discovered the body."

"Oh goodness, I didn't know that."

"It isn't common knowledge." Charles glanced over at me from under his golden lashes. "You're actually the only one who knows. I called 911 immediately, of course, even though I'd checked her pulse and knew Marlis was already dead."

"You left her there?" I hadn't intended to use such a sharp tone, but Charles just shrugged.

"Yes. You have to understand—I was in shock. I grabbed up the hat from the ditch and just jumped in my car and drove off. That is, I guess I did. I don't really remember much about that day."

"Why didn't you tell the police about the hat, though? I mean, I assume you knew it didn't belong to Marlis."

Charles raked his hands through his hair. "I don't know. I

thought about it, but then there was the funeral, and after that I took off traveling. When I returned from Europe, I found the hat in my car and just stuffed it in that shoebox in the closet."

"You didn't think it might be a clue as to who struck Marlis?"

"Not at first. I guess I just didn't want to think too closely about anything to do with the accident. Then I saw that report on TV about the student who had disappeared . . ."

"Lacey Jacobs."

"Right." Charles glanced at me. "I realized she must've been the one who hit Marlis. But she was missing at that point, and I thought . . . well, I wondered if she'd finally been overcome with guilt and run off into the mountains to do herself an injury."

"You suspected she meant to kill herself?"

Charles nodded. "So I didn't want to bring the hat into the equation. Not until after . . . after whatever happened. When they found her and she was injured and the doctors had to induce a coma, I thought I'd just wait and see what she said when she came out of it."

"If she comes out of it, and with the capacity to communicate. She may not. You know that's possible, right?"

"I know." Charles slid a little closer to me. "Look, Amy, I'm sure you think I should share this with the authorities, but if the girl ends up with brain damage, well maybe that's enough of a punishment. I doubt she meant to hit Marlis. It was just an accident."

I studied his drawn face. He was suffering, that was certain. Perhaps, in his own way, his sparing Lacey further pain was one way he felt he could salvage something from this tragedy.

"She should have reported it, though. As I should report this hat to the authorities as soon as possible. However"—I held up my hand, cutting off Charles's protestations—"I promise not to say anything until after the girl regains consciousness. You're right—she should be given the chance to confess. That would probably go a long way toward mitigating any criminal penalty."

"That's what I thought. She's a young woman with her entire life ahead of her. I'd hate to see her spend the rest of her days in jail over an accident, no matter how negligent she was in reporting it." He swallowed. "Punishing Lacey Jacobs to the full extent of the law won't bring Marlis back. Nothing will ever do that."

"You really did love her, didn't you?" I said as Charles dropped his face into his hands and silently wept. "Hey, it's okay. It's perfectly natural to cry, given the circumstances." I patted one of his heaving shoulders.

"Thank you, Amy," he said, lifting his head as he covered my hand with his. "It means a lot to me that you still care."

I slid my fingers free of his grip and sat back. "I sympathize with your loss. But as for anything else . . ."

"You mean you don't really have feelings for me." Charles pulled a tissue from his pocket and dabbed the tears from his cheeks as he studied my face. "After what I did to you, I suppose that's fair."

"It's not that I don't care at all, it's just that my feelings have changed. I don't love you. Not like I once did." I crossed my arms over my chest as he continued to examine me. "Although to be honest, I don't think I ever truly loved you, Charles. I loved my imaginary idea of you—an image I created in my head. Not the real you." I smiled to myself as I recalled my aunt's words on this subject. It was a lesson she'd learned as well, although later in life than me. "I apologize for that. I wasn't really fair to you either, as it turns out."

"If you say so, although as I told you before"—Charles leaned forward—"seeing the woman you've become, perhaps I should've given our relationship a little more time."

I stood up so quickly that the pillows behind me flew off the sofa.

"Sorry, Charles, but it's too late. That ship has sailed over the horizon. And speaking of things being too late, perhaps you could retrieve my clothes and allow me to change so you can drive me to my car? I really should be getting home before my aunt starts to worry. She'll expect me back from work soon."

Charles did as I requested, saying nothing more about any possibilities of a future relationship between us, although I caught him sneaking glances at me as he drove me to the trailhead.

"You know, Amy," he said as I climbed out of his car. "I've learned that life is rather more unpredictable than one expects. Which means I still have hope that, going forward, we can at least be friends."

"You can always hope," I said, before shutting the door.

Sitting in my own car, I considered my next action. It was true that Aunt Lydia would expect me home soon, but I had another destination in mind. I pulled out my phone and sent her a text.

"Stopping by Richard's," it said. "Don't hold dinner for me."

Because after talking to a man I had once thought I loved, I knew I needed to talk to the one I truly did.

# Chapter Twenty-One

Richard enthusiastically welcomed me but apologized for his sweaty condition. "I've been rehearsing. That is, when Loie lets me. She keeps leaping at my legs." He pointed a toe at the kitten, who just looked up at both of us with her green eyes rounded in innocence.

"Don't be silly, you know I don't mind that," I said, throwing my arms around his neck. "And Loie obviously wants to dance with you."

"Which is cute, but I don't want to trip over her." Richard pulled me so close that I could feel his heart beating under his damp T-shirt. "I certainly don't want to fall and hurt her."

"Or yourself." I leaned back against his arms and looked up into his face. "I just had to stop by and tell you something."

"Glad you did, but what's that?" Richard slid one hand up my back as Loie batted the tassel on one of my loafers.

"I love you." I rose up on tiptoe to kiss him.

"Always good to hear," Richard said, after returning my kiss. "But what brought this on?"

I dropped my arms and grabbed one of his hands. "Stuff that happened today. Let's sit and talk."

"Okay." Richard followed me to the sofa, still gripping one of my hands.

Loie, obviously thinking this was a new game, pranced and pounced, weaving in and out of our legs. It took some fancy footwork to make it to the sofa without taking a tumble.

Richard and I dropped down onto the couch at the same time while Loie jumped onto the coffee table, curving her black tail into a question mark. "Silly cat." The kitten obviously interpreted my indulgent tone as an invitation to leap into my lap.

"That's what she wanted," Richard said as Loie curled into a ball so tight that her little black nose touched the tip of her tail.

I stroked the kitten and smiled as her purring rumbled against my fingers. Leaning back against the sofa cushions, I glanced over at Richard. "I needed to see you because I heard something from Hope Hodgson today that made me lose my mind for a bit."

"Oh?" Richard reached out and brushed a lock of my hair behind my ear. "Did you get caught in the rain? Your hair's all tangled."

"Yeah, but that's not important right now." I grabbed his hand as he pulled it away. "I doubted you. Just for a few minutes, but still . . ."

"What do you mean?" When Richard lowered our clasped hands to my lap, Loie rolled over and pressed her warm body against our entwined fingers.

I explained what Hope had told me about Lacey's involvement with some older man. "I really didn't think it could be you, but she planted this evil little seed, and"—I gazed down at our hands, unable to meet his eyes—"for a moment I almost believed it. Anyway, I started questioning myself and went out for a walk to clear my head. On the Twin Falls trail."

"You got caught in that storm this afternoon?" Richard reached out with his free hand and tipped up my chin. "That was foolish, Amy."

"Almost as foolish as doubting you. But not quite." I met his concerned gaze. "I'm so sorry. I should never have given any credence to Hope's theory. I know you better than that. You'd never get involved with a student."

"No, I never would. Besides, wasn't this supposed to be going on after I met you?" He raised his eyebrows. "You really believe I'd cheat on you?"

"No, and I feel terrible for even imagining . . ." I swallowed. "I just wanted to apologize for doubting you at all. It makes me feel like such a rat."

"Maybe a slightly drowned one," Richard said, squeezing my fingers as he offered me a smile. "Don't beat yourself up. I seem to remember that I withheld some important information from you recently. I can understand why the doubt might creep in."

Loie meeped and rolled over on her back. "Still, I realized how stupid such an idea was after I spoke with Charles."

Richard pulled his hand free and sat back. "Bartos? What were you doing talking with him?"

"Don't be jealous. I was at his home, but I promise it was simply a refuge from the storm." I absently rubbed Loie's soft belly. "His house was the closest option. I stopped there just to dry off and beg a ride back to the trailhead. Anyway, spending more time with him made me realize the difference between the way my heart feels when I'm sure of someone and when I'm not."

"So—sure of me, but not him?"

"Exactly. I never really loved him, you know. Just my notion of him."

Richard slid closer and placed his arm around my shoulders. "I've done that in the past. Created a person in my head and tried to force someone to match that image."

"Yeah. Poor Charles. For all his faults, he never had a chance of living up to the fantasy I had created around him." I snuggled against Richard. "Meanwhile, I know and love you just as you are. Anyway, you surpass all my fantasies."

"Do I?" Richard kissed the top of my head. "Glad to hear it, but it also sounds a little daunting." He grinned as I looked up at him. "Continuing to surpass the fantasies, I mean."

I tapped his chest with my finger. "I think you're up to the challenge."

"I aim to please," he said, before leaning in to kiss me.

As he pulled me closer, Loie meowed and leapt off my lap. "Uh-oh, you just pissed off the cat," I said.

"The cat will get over it."

We didn't talk for some time after that, but after a while, Loie's incessant mewing forced us apart.

"Crap, I forgot to feed her." Richard leapt up and strode toward the kitchen. "Come on, fur ball."

Loie raced after him while I giggled and called out, "Bad daddy."

"Trust me, she's not starving," Richard replied.

After he returned and settled back beside me, I considered how to broach the subject of Lacey again, finally just launching into Charles's tale about finding her hat at the accident scene.

"I can't believe he's never informed the authorities about that detail," Richard said. "It sounds like he's protecting Lacey, but why? He doesn't strike me as a person who'd be concerned about some random young woman's future."

"I know. That seems odd to me as well. Charles is all about

self-preservation. Acting altruistic . . ." I shook my head. "It's out of character, for sure."

"Unless he really is looking out for himself in some way," Richard said thoughtfully.

"What do you mean?"

"Maybe Lacey has something on him? Some dirt he doesn't want exposed?" Richard straightened. "She does know him, at least in passing."

"How's that?"

"Lacey was part of a performance I choreographed to Bartos's music. Remember, I told you about it when we were discussing Charles once. Granted, the collaboration was a one-time event. That joint project didn't last long, and I actually made sure I never worked with him again because he was such a pain."

"I know. I certainly wouldn't forget you telling me about that because it also explained exactly how you felt about Charles. But what does that have to do with anything?"

"I told you that Charles Bartos was rude to all of my students, and for the most part he was. In fact, he was downright mean to most of them. They actually begged me not to allow him to play for any of our studio performances again, and I was happy to oblige that request. But now that I think of it, there was one girl he occasionally praised."

"Lacey?"

"Yeah. He even held her up as an example to the other dancers. Said she didn't seem to need the constant repetition of passages like they did, and that he wished they were all such quick studies." Richard rubbed his jaw. "I shut that nonsense down immediately, of course, but now I wonder . . ."

"When was this?" I asked.

"Two summers ago. Before I was hired at Clarion full-time."

"So she knows him, at least a little. Enough to know who he was if she caught him doing something illegal or immoral." I lifted Loie off my lap and gently placed her beside me on the sofa. "I didn't tell you this before, because . . . well, just because of all the crazy stuff that's been happening lately, but Mona warned me that she had some dirt on Charles. Something she thought would compel him to do what she wanted. I wonder if Lacey uncovered that information as well."

"Could be. But it still seems strange that Bartos would allow her to go scot-free when it comes to the accident. You do think he loved Marlis?"

"As much as he can love anyone." I flicked some dried mud from my slacks. "They were crazy about each other, at least from what I hear. As recently as this past November, anyway. Zelda said she and Walt were at one of Charles's performances, and when they went back-stage to see a friend, they almost fell over Charles and Marlis. Well, she actually just called her 'a lovely blonde,' since she had no idea who she was. But apparently Marlis was draped all over Charles to the point where it almost made Zelda blush. And that takes some doing, believe me."

"Yeah, embarrassing Zelda wouldn't be that easy." Richard sat bolt upright. "Wait a minute, when in November?"

"I don't know. Does it matter?"

"It might." Richard reached over and popped open his laptop. "Does Bartos post his concert schedule?"

"On his website. At least he used to."

Richard handed me the computer. "Can you look that up? I'm really curious about the date of that particular concert."

"Okay." I entered the address for Charles's professional website and pulled up the page listing his performances. "This must be it—a one-shot at the Kennedy Center in DC. That's the venue that Zelda mentioned." I looked over at Richard. "November tenth."

He shook his head. "That's impossible. Marlis couldn't have been there."

"Why not?"

"Because that was the weekend of Fall Dance. November tenth would've been the Friday dress rehearsal, since performances were Saturday and Sunday. Remember—you attended the Saturday show, on the eleventh."

"I remember, but . . ." I stared down at the computer screen. "Marlis played a violin solo as an accompaniment to one of the pieces. She even sat on the stage."

"Right. Deidre's piece. And Marlis was at the dress rehearsal on the tenth too. I remember clearly because I was helping troubleshoot the lights and we had such a time trying to illuminate her while not distracting from the actual dancing." Richard drummed his fingers against his knee. "So she couldn't have been the blonde Zelda saw at that concert."

The truth rose up and swept over me like a tidal wave. "Lacey."

"Had to be." Richard slumped back against the sofa cushions. "That explains a lot, including why she might've wanted to talk to me about something personal before she disappeared. Maybe she wanted my help to deal with her affair with a professor. Maybe she even wanted out but didn't know how to extract herself from the situation." He rubbed at his jaw. "And I just blew her off."

"You couldn't have known she was in such a mess."

"No, but I should've asked. I should have listened."

I stroked his tensed arm. "None of this is your fault. Anyway, they apparently hid it well, especially if it started up a few years ago." I made a face. "Ugh, how old was Lacey then, anyway?"

Richard grimaced. "Eighteen or nineteen, I guess. Legal, but just. Anyway, it isn't right, no matter the age. As a professor, Bartos held a position of authority, and he abused it."

"If that girl at the concert really was Lacey."

"You did hear that she was supposedly hooking up with some older man."

"At least according to her parents. Hope said they never met him, but they knew that much."

Richard's expression grew thoughtful. "I'm pretty sure Lacey still lives in a dorm. Which probably means that she had to meet him somewhere off campus."

"At his place, I imagine." I placed Richard's laptop on the coffee table.

"Maybe. But didn't he and Marlis live together?" Richard shot me a raised-eyebrow glance. "I mean, they could've met there occasionally, when they knew Marlis would be away, but maybe they also hooked up when he was on the road?"

"Based on Zelda's memory, it seems so." I scooted forward as Richard tapped something into the laptop's keyboard. "What are you looking up?"

"My gradebook. It's on the campus integrated system. Password-protected, of course." He shot me a glance. "Lacey missed some days in the studio here and there this fall. I want to see if there's a pattern."

"You mean if it was long weekends or something?"

"Right. And when it started. She never missed a day at the beginning of the semester but started skipping later. Come to think of it, that happened last year as well."

I sat back as Richard scrolled through the records. "But that won't really confirm she was involved with Charles."

"No, but it's more evidence."

I sat back. "So what's the verdict?"

"Well, when she did miss studio, at least this fall, it was primarily on Fridays and Mondays. A long weekend sounds about right."

"Wait, I have an idea." I opened the shallow drawer under the coffee table and pulled out a notepad and pen. "Call out those dates for me."

As I jotted down the information, Loie padded back into the room and over to the sofa. "Watch out—kitten incoming."

Loie jumped onto the coffee table just as Richard pulled the computer onto his lap. "Why'd you want those dates?"

"I want to see if they corollate with Charles's out-of-town performances. Can you pull up his website again? Should be under the history tab."

"Okay, got it."

I handed him the piece of paper before patting my knees to draw Loie to my lap.

"Well, look at that," Richard said, after only a moment. "It matches up exactly."

"Coincidence?"

"I doubt it." He slid the laptop back onto the coffee table. "What do you think?"

"I think Charles was cheating on Marlis just like he cheated on me. And here I thought he truly loved her."

Richard sat back and slid his arm over my shoulders. "Maybe he did. But it seems Bartos is not one for monogamy, whether he loves someone or not." He pulled me close to his side. "If our theory is correct, that could very well be the reason he won't implicate Lacey."

"Because she might confess the truth about their affair in

retaliation." I stroked Loie with one hand while I laid my other hand on Richard's knee. "Or even if she didn't want to hurt him, it would certainly come out when she was interrogated."

"Right." Richard covered my fingers with his free hand. "And with Clarion's new 'no tolerance' policy on such things, Bartos would likely be fired."

"So he *was* just looking out for himself," I said.

"Sounds like it." Richard caressed my fingers. "We really do need to tell Brad Tucker or someone at the sheriff's office about Charles finding Lacey's hat at the scene."

"Yeah, but"—I twisted my neck to look up at him—"could we wait until Lacey is out of the coma? Not to spare Charles, but so she has an opportunity to confess. I mean, if she can. It seems like that might help her case in the long run, and I'd like to give her that chance."

"I suppose. It's only hearsay, anyway. But if she doesn't say anything, and Bartos doesn't speak up either . . ."

"I'll talk to Brad, I promise." I snuggled back against Richard and considered our new theory. If it was true, it explained a great deal— why Lacey might have finally experienced a breakdown leading to her disappearance, and even the dirt that Mona had claimed to have on Charles. It also cleared up my niggling question about why Charles wouldn't report Lacey to the authorities after he found her hat at the scene of a crime.

*If his story was true.*

I pulled away from Richard and stood up, dislodging Loie, who slid from my lap. Landing on her feet, she arched her back and hissed.

"Now look who's disturbed the cat." Richard cast me an inquiring glance. "What's up?"

"I just realized that part of our theory could be very wrong."

Walking over to the bookshelf, I picked up the gold brooch that lay beside a framed photo of Paul Dassin. "I should've known better. After everything we've been through, I should've learned that making assumptions about people is a great mistake."

Richard stood and crossed to stand beside me. "What's wrong with our theory?"

"We've assumed that Charles told me the truth about finding Lacey's hat at the accident scene. But what if it came into his possession in a different way?"

Richard's gray eyes widened. "You mean she left it at his mountain house during one of their secret rendezvous?"

"Or at the loft." I tapped the brooch against my palm. "Charles mentioned something about Marlis jogging early in the morning. He said she'd grab scarves and gloves and such from the hall closet in the dark and that he often teased her about wearing mismatched things when she returned from her run."

Richard's expression grew more thoughtful. "If Lacey had tossed her knitted hat into the closet during one of her secret hookups with Charles and left it there by mistake, Marlis might have been wearing it when she was hit."

I placed the brooch back on the shelf and turned to face Richard. "It might also mean another thing."

"What's that?"

"Think about it. The hat is the only connection to Lacey and the hit-and-run at this point. I mean, she did tell Hope and Chris that she had to have repair work done on her car after hitting a deer around that time, but that could be a coincidence."

"True. It's not uncommon to encounter deer around Clarion, especially out on the side roads." Richard took two steps back and looked me up and down. "Wait, are you thinking what I'm thinking?"

"I imagine so. We only have Charles's word that he was first on the scene after someone else hit Marlis and that he found Lacey's hat there in a ditch."

"He could be lying."

"As he does, not infrequently, it seems. Which means that Lacey may not be the only one who could've run down Marlis Dupre and left her to die. It's possible that Marlis's killer was actually her cheating lover."

Richard whistled, causing Loie to look up at both of us with slitted eyes. "Charles Bartos."

# Chapter Twenty-Two

I returned home, but not until after I promised Richard to tell no one about our suspicions until I could speak to Brad or one of his deputies face-to-face.

"Stay away from Bartos," Richard had said as he kissed me goodbye.

"Trust me, I will," I'd replied with fervor.

I put in a call to the sheriff's office as soon as I reached my bedroom, but of course it was late and I couldn't speak to anyone unless it was a dire emergency. Which it wasn't, I realized. Whatever his guilt or innocence, Charles had no idea that either Richard or I suspected his story about Lacey or his relationship with the girl. There was no logical reason for him to take any action against us. Any meeting with the authorities could wait until the next day.

I called again the next morning and obtained a four o'clock appointment with Brad. Which was fine by me, as it would allow me to work most of my regular shift at the library.

Not long before lunch, Chris Garver appeared at the circulation desk asking for access to the archives.

"Trish and Hope are with me," he said. "They're waiting out

back by my car. We'd just like to collect some of Mona's notes we think she left in the archives. Could we take a look?"

"Sure," I said, glancing over at Sunny, who pointed to herself and then the desk, indicating she'd cover things inside. "I'll escort you."

"Could we also have a little time to check over a few additional files?" Chris asked as we walked outside.

"Something about a treasure?"

He stopped short in the middle of the parking lot. "You figured that out?"

His obvious chagrin over this disclosure, as well as his nonthreatening posture, led me to believe that of the three students, he was the least likely to have been responsible for Mona's death. I shook my finger at him. "You didn't file that document properly."

"Sorry." Chris hung his head. "Yeah, I saw a letter that mentioned gold coins and I told Ethan about it. He decided to do some searching while he was out in the woods. It was just fun, like a game, but then when Professor Raymond got killed . . ."

I lowered my voice as Hope and Trish walked toward us. "So the others also know about the coins?"

"Not sure." Chris's dark eyes widened. "You don't think they could be involved?"

I pressed my fingers to my lips for a second before speaking. "Hi guys, I'm going to open up the archives and let you all work alone for a bit. I trust you," I added, casting Chris a significant look.

"Thank you, Ms. Webber," Hope said as they followed me over to the small fieldstone building. "We were talking about the professor's research earlier and decided that we should at least compile everything she'd collected, and even take some notes on things she didn't get a chance to look at yet. Maybe another folklore specialist can edit it into something that could eventually be published, with Professor Raymond getting some of the credit."

"Perhaps Trish could do that," I said, unlocking the doors and standing to the side as the students filed past me.

"I don't know. Not sure that I have the proper expertise yet," Trish said.

I flicked on the overhead light and examined the graduate student, noting her pinched face and the dark circles beneath her eyes. "You could work with another professor. I just think it would be good to have someone who knew Mona fairly well take over her research."

"I doubt I'll be able to do that," Trish said, before turning away to stare at the shelves.

"Okay then, I'll leave you to it. I'll just need one of you to come into the library and let Sunny or me know when you're done so we can lock up."

"Sure thing," Chris said as he pulled a box off one of the shelves.

When I returned to the circulation desk, Sunny gave me a questioning look. "You left them alone in there?"

"I don't think they'll do any damage. Chris, at least, knows he can't pull another fast one on us."

"You really think he was our culprit?" Sunny's bracelets jangled as she piled returned books next to the computer.

"I do, and he just confirmed it. Not sure about the others, but he definitely saw the letter and told Ethan Payne about it. Which explains why I ran into Ethan out in the woods searching for the coins." I met Sunny's inquiring gaze. "Okay, I haven't had time to tell you, but I had a little adventure after I left work yesterday." Looking up, I noticed one of our regular patrons staring at the nonfiction shelves with a puzzled expression. "But I probably should check with Samantha first. It looks like she may need some help."

"Go ahead. I want to hear your story, but it will keep for later." Sunny opened one of the books and swept a wand over its bar code to check it in. "Dawn is supposed to show up around noon today to put in her volunteer hours, so you can fill me in at lunch."

"Sounds good," I said as I circled around the desk and walked over to assist Samantha Green with some research on starting a small business.

After I helped Samantha pull a stack of journals and books and set her up at one of the reading tables, I rejoined Sunny at the circulation desk. Despite the absence of any other patrons, Sunny and I waited until Dawn Larson arrived to take over the desk before we headed to the break room for lunch. We never liked to leave the circulation desk without coverage. That was a poor service model, no matter how few people were using the library at any given time.

No one was using the children's room, which was adjacent to the break room, but I left the door ajar in case someone needed our assistance. While we ate lunch, I brought Sunny up-to-date about my encounter with Ethan as well as my subsequent meeting with Charles.

"That's why you're talking with Brad this afternoon?" Sunny asked as she toyed with her package of peanut butter crackers.

"Exactly. Richard and I thought that he needed to know about the hat as well as Charles's claim about Lacey being involved in the hit-and-run." I crumbled a few potato chips into my napkin. "I've considered confronting Charles again, even though Richard really doesn't think it's wise."

Sunny frowned. "Neither do I."

"I don't know. The more I think about it, the more I wish I could ask him a few questions before I go to the authorities. I'd like to give him a chance to come clean before I inform on him, just for the sake of our former relationship. But I doubt there's time. I think I'd better get ahead of Charles making any statements about Lacey to the sheriff's office."

"Makes sense," Sunny said, looking over my shoulder. "Hello?"

"What?" I turned my head toward the break room door. "Was someone there?"

"I don't know. I thought I saw a shadow."

I leapt to my feet and dashed to the door, just in time to catch a figure running through the children's room and into the hall that led to the back door.

"I'm going after them," I called out. "Keep an eye on things, okay?"

I didn't wait to hear Sunny's reply. The back door slammed as I reached the far side of the children's room. Just as I ran into the hall, Samantha stepped in front of me and asked another question.

"Sorry," I said as I attempted to slide around her. "I can't help you right now. Go ask Sunny. I think she's still in the break room."

"But you know what I'm looking for . . ."

"I really need to go." I slipped past Samantha and made a beeline for the back door.

The shadowy figure had to have been one of Mona's students. I reached the parking lot in time to see Trish grab something from Chris's hands as he stood in the doorway of the archives.

"Hey, wait!" I shouted, but Trish jumped into Chris's car and took off, tires spewing gravel.

I ran over to meet a bewildered Chris. "What's going on?"

"I don't know," he said, rubbing his shaved scalp. "Trish was shrieking like a banshee, demanding to borrow my car for some emergency."

"Oh crap." I grabbed his arm to steady myself. "Did she say where she was going?"

"No. Just said to wait here and she'd return the car when she was done."

"This isn't good, this isn't good," I muttered to myself.

"Do you know what's going on?" Chris asked. "Trish went inside to find a restroom, then flew out here like she'd seen a ghost or something."

"I have no idea," I lied. I didn't want to embroil Chris and Hope any deeper than they already were, and if Hope, or even Ethan, *had* been involved in Mona's death, I didn't want to tip them off either. It was possible that Trish was going to drive straight to the hospital to tell Lacey's parents what she'd overheard, or even confront Charles over his affair with Lacey. Neither of which was a situation I thought would be improved by the presence of any of the other students. Especially if any of them had a guilty conscience. "Why don't you guys come back into the library to wait? I'll even find you a ride if you want."

"No, that's fine. I think maybe we'll walk down the street and grab some lunch at the diner. Please let Trish know where we are if she comes back looking for us."

"Of course," I said as Hope appeared at Chris's shoulder. "Look, you guys go on ahead. I'll just close up the archives behind you."

I considered my options as I fiddled with the lock on the archives door and concluded that I should probably tell Brad about this turn of events as soon as possible. I couldn't wait until our late-afternoon appointment. If Trish had heard what I'd told Sunny about Charles carrying on a relationship with Lacey and Lacey's likely involvement in the hit-and-run, she might feel that she finally had something she could use to strike back at the man who'd falsely accused her of cheating. Which meant she was probably headed for the hospital.

I pulled out my cell phone and dialed Brad's number but reached only a recorded message. That was no good—I didn't think I could explain the situation in a voice message or text. I could talk to another deputy, but while I believed it prudent to head off any confrontation between Trish and Arnold Jacobs, I also felt the situation required an even-tempered response from someone like Brad. In my experience, few other deputies displayed his wisdom and common sense in sticky situations.

I needed to drive straight to the sheriff's office, explain to Brad what had happened, and ask him to look for Trish. Unfortunately, Aunt Lydia had needed the car earlier in the day, so I'd walked to work. But when I'd called earlier to make sure I'd have access to our shared vehicle around three thirty, she'd assured me that she'd be back by one, so I decided to hurry home on foot and hope that the car was available.

Dashing back inside the library, I ran into the workroom and grabbed my purse, waving aside Sunny's demands for an explanation.

"I need to take the rest of the afternoon off," I told her as I bolted past her. "I'll explain later."

I raced home at a jog and had just reached our house when I noticed a vehicle idling in the neighbor's driveway across the street. The car sped out onto the road and pulled up alongside me. After the car came to a stop, Trish jumped out of the front seat and circled around the hood before I could do anything but gape at her in astonishment.

"Please get in," she said.

"What? Why?" I managed to squeak out.

"I need you to drive me to Charles Bartos's house. I was going to just head straight to his house, and even got halfway there, but then I realized he didn't know me and might not even allow me in the door. So I changed my mind and drove over here to wait for you. I figured he might talk to me if I brought you along." As Trish looked me over, I noticed her right hand stuffed into her jacket, and a lump in the pocket that appeared to be more than fingers.

*Not another gun . . .* "Are you threatening me?"

"If I have to. I hope I don't." Trish pulled back her hand, revealing the butt of a revolver. "I do know how to use this."

"I suppose so. I did see a photo of you in your skeet shooting club."

"You researched me? Guess I should be flattered." Trish slid the gun back into her pocket. "I have a concealed carry permit, by the way, as does Chris. This is actually his gun. I knew he kept it locked up in the car when he went into places like the library or archives, and I decided to take advantage of that fact in order to convince you to accompany me."

"You may have a legitimate right to carry a gun, but threatening me still isn't legal," I said as I walked around to the driver's side door.

I wasn't convinced that Trish would actually shoot me, but I didn't see the need to take that chance. If all she wanted was to talk to Charles, there was no real danger. Unless she wanted to do more than talk . . . I slid my fingers into my purse and felt around for my cell phone as I climbed into the car.

"Hand over the phone," Trish pulled out the gun and pointed it at me as she settled in the passenger's seat.

I reluctantly passed her my cell before buckling up and turning the keys that still dangled from the ignition. "What do you want with Charles? I doubt he'll tell you much."

"I bet he will if I threaten you."

"I don't know if I'd place that wager." I turned the car around at the end of the paved road and headed back into town. "Charles is all about Charles. If he has to throw me under the bus to protect himself, he will."

"We'll see." Trish kept the gun leveled on me as she used her other hand to buckle up.

"I don't see why you want to talk with him so desperately, anyway," I said as I drove through town. "I know you overheard me talking with Sunny about Charles and Lacey, but I have to tell you that I don't entirely trust his account of the accident."

"Neither do I," Trish said, in such a grim tone that I gave her a side-eyed glance. She was so tense that she almost appeared to vibrate.

I tightened my grip on the steering wheel as I turned onto the road that led up to Charles's mountain retreat. "Did you know that Charles and Lacey were an item? I only ask because Mona apparently did. At least, she told me she had some dirt on Charles, and now I think that's what it must have been."

"No, I didn't know anything about that," Trish said. "Not until I overheard you mention it."

"Then why this need to talk to Charles?"

I caught Trish's grimace out of the corner of my eye. "Because he has it all wrong."

Thinking about the conversation I'd had with Richard, I shot her a quick glance. "You think Charles was the one who hit Marlis, not Lacey? Because I've considered that possibility as well—that Marlis was wearing a hat Lacey had left at their place and that's how the knitted cap ended up in the ditch."

"I expect you're on the right track there," Trish said. "But I know for a fact that it wasn't Charles, or even Lacey, who hit that woman."

"How can you be so sure?"

"Because I did," Trish said.

# Chapter
# Twenty-Three

I fought my urge to slam on the brakes. "You were the driver?"

"Yes." A quick side glance revealed Trish's quivering lips, although her hand holding the gun didn't waver. "It was an accident, of course. I was thinking about something else, and the light was still dim. I never expected anyone to be out jogging so early, especially in the cold."

"But if it was an accident, why not call for help? It's still tragic, but you wouldn't have gotten into so much trouble. Now . . ."

"I know. Now I'll be up for jail time." Trish exhaled a deep sigh. "I just lost my mind for a while. Of course, I stopped when I felt the impact. But I saw the jogger's knitted cap sail off her head before she fell, and when I actually looked at the hat in the ditch . . ."

"You thought it was Lacey?" Truth dawned as I lifted one hand from the wheel and flexed my cramped fingers.

"Yes. She was lying facedown, and there was all that blonde hair, and the hat, so I thought I'd hit Lacey Jacobs. I didn't approach the body close enough to see otherwise, just jumped back into my car and drove off. I didn't even know for sure that the person I'd hit was dead, but I knew that since I'd come up on them from behind, they couldn't identify me or my car, so I just bolted." Trish's voice shook slightly on the final word, and she cleared her throat before continuing. "I was in shock, but I admit there was also this voice in my head, telling me it was fate. Or karma. Honestly, for a short period of time, I felt that justice had been served. Anyway, I didn't call 911. I just drove back to my apartment, parked in a spot away from view, and ran in and grabbed up enough stuff for a weekend away. Then I immediately drove to my hometown, where I have a friend from high school whose family owns a junkyard. He always wanted to date me, so I figured I could sweet-talk him into getting rid of the car, no questions asked."

"And you did?"

"I did. I said I didn't want my parents to know I'd wrecked the car, that I planned to just tell them I'd sold it. Then I begged him to do me this one favor. He agreed. He even had a crusher at the yard, so the car is now nothing more than a cube of metal." Trish leaned back against her seat. "Of course, I came to my senses eventually, but by then it was too late to do anything but keep up the pretense."

I clutched the wheel with both hands. "But when you heard who it was, that must've been a shock."

"That was the worst. Not that I ultimately felt right about hitting Lacey, despite what her father had done to me, but when I found out it wasn't even her . . ." Trish's voice trailed off.

I flexed my hands, one at a time. If I could keep her talking, maybe I could convince her that a confrontation with Charles was not a smart idea. "Why did Professor Jacobs accuse you of being part of that cheating scandal? Did you rebuff his unwelcome advances or something?"

"No, nothing like that. He didn't like me from the get-go because I challenged him too many times." Trish adjusted her grip on the revolver before continuing. "And then I called him on his bullying. There was this one student in my class that he constantly ridiculed. I could tell that she had learning difficulties. Well, it was more like she suffered from social anxiety, I guess. Anyway, it was clear to me that she was prone to panic attacks. My mom has that problem, so I can recognize the signs. Anyway, Jacobs just kept after the girl, even when she was hyperventilating, and I called him on it. I even reported it to the dean. That really set him off, so I guess when he got a chance to get back at me . . ."

"He took it."

"Yes, and almost ruined my educational career. I was lucky to get into Clarion after all that mess, even though I was exonerated. But Clarion isn't exactly the same caliber as my previous university, which does impact my future prospects. I've never forgiven Jacobs for that."

"Or Lacey, it seems."

"Which wasn't right. I know that now. But I was so angry . . ." Trish sighed. "I admit that for a brief period of time, I lost my head and simply figured that hurting Lacey, no matter how accidentally, would be my best revenge against her father."

"So now what—you want to confess your part in the hit-and-run to Charles or something?"

"Yes. I want to tell him the truth." Trish straightened and shot me a sharp glance. "Before I turn myself in."

"But why drag me along?"

"Like I said before—because he doesn't know who I am, and I wasn't sure he'd even open the door to me. But I knew he'd ask me in if I brought you along."

"I see." I turned onto the mountain road that led to Charles's house. "But why now? You could've talked to him weeks ago."

"Weeks ago he wasn't planning to tell the authorities that story about Lacey. I was afraid he'd soon spill all his suppositions, which are obviously untrue."

"He told me he wouldn't say anything while she was still unconscious."

"Not sure I believe that. I mean, we don't know how long she'll remain in the coma, or whether she'll have any brain damage when she wakes up. I doubt that Mr. Bartos will wait forever to share his theory. Not when he thinks it could close the case."

I looked over at Trish, whose face was pale and crumpled as paper. "You actually want to protect her?"

"I do. I know it sounds strange, but I don't want that false theory to get out and hit the news. I don't want anyone to think, even for a moment, that Lacey struck Marlis Dupre and drove away."

"But that would all be cleared up when you confessed to the hit-and-run, wouldn't it?"

"Yes, but I know from experience that once people hear about someone being accused of wrongdoing, they remember that story long after the person's exonerated."

I took a deep breath. "That's what happened to you when you were accused of cheating."

"And cleared. But while the media was quick to blast out my name when I was accused, they weren't so diligent when I was exonerated. In fact, it went from headline news to some tiny little mentions. A lot of people never knew that I'd been cleared of suspicion. All they heard or read about was the accusation. That's why I had to leave the university, and that's why"—Trish looked me over before sliding the gun back into her pocket—"I don't want Lacey to be accused of something she didn't do. Despite not really being her friend, I didn't want that smear on her name, especially when she has no way to defend herself."

We'd reached Charles's property. I turned into his driveway and parked in front of the house. "You really want to do this?"

"Yes, I do." Trish unbuckled and turned to face me. "Will you come with me?"

"To protect you? I think the revolver's a better option, although I wouldn't suggest threatening Charles on top of everything else."

"No, as a witness. I want the authorities to know that I confessed to Mr. Bartos before I turned myself in. Not that it will make much difference, but it's something I want them to know."

"All right, I'll accompany you. But keep that gun in your pocket."

"I will," Trish said as she exited the vehicle. "Just so you know—I wouldn't have used it on you."

I climbed out, leaving my purse in the car, and followed her to the porch. "You should've just told me the truth in the beginning."

Trish's thin lips twitched. "I wasn't sure you'd agree, and I knew you were talking to Chief Deputy Tucker this afternoon. Yeah, I overheard that as well."

"Well, despite not approving of being abducted at gunpoint, I promise I won't press charges over this. I figure you're in enough trouble as it is."

"Thanks." Trish stared at her feet as I banged the acorn knocker against the wooden door.

"Amy, how nice to see you again," Charles said as he cracked the door. Opening it wider, he spied Trish, and his expression shifted from pleased to confused. "But who's this?"

"Trisha Alexander," the young woman replied. "We haven't officially met, but it's crucial that I speak with you. I asked Ms. Webber to come along since she's a friend of yours."

I almost corrected her but thought better of it. "Trish is a graduate student at Clarion. She was working with Ramona Raymond on the folklore project."

"Oh?" As Charles stepped back to allow us to enter his house, I couldn't help but notice his hands hanging at his sides. With his fingers curling into fists.

He was definitely on guard. I puzzled over his obvious tension as Trish and I crossed the room to stand beside the kitchen island. "But that's not why she's here today. She actually has something she needs to tell you."

After closing the door, Charles strode over and stood behind the island, facing us. "What, that Mona was lying about me stealing her work? That I'd like to hear."

Trish gripped the rounded edge of the counter with both hands. "I don't know anything about that," she said, staring down at the swirling pattern of the marble.

"Then what's this information you feel so compelled to share?" Charles slid his gaze from Trish to me. He raised his eyebrows, as if indicating that he found this situation ridiculous. "I don't believe we've ever met, Ms. Alexander, and certainly can't imagine what we'd have in common."

"Marlis Dupre," Trish blurted out, without looking up.

Charles instantly froze. "What about her?"

"It was me, not Lacey." Trish lifted her head and stared Charles straight in the eye. "I was the driver who struck and killed your girlfriend, Mr. Bartos. Lacey had nothing to do with it."

Charles swayed slightly before pressing his hands against the marble countertop. "What did you say?"

Trish straightened and lifted her chin. "I hit her, with my car. It was an accident, but then I didn't call for help because, because . . ."

"She thought it was Lacey," I said, meeting Charles's furious gaze. "And they had . . . history."

"But why would she think it was Lacey?"

"The blonde hair, a similar build, and"—I met Charles's intense gaze without flinching—"the hat."

He blinked rapidly. "Hat?"

"The knitted cap you said you found at the scene. You told me you thought Lacey left it there, in the ditch, but that wasn't true." I sharpened my tone. "Marlis grabbed that hat out of your closet without really looking. You said she'd do that sort of thing, remember? But the cap was only there because Lacey left it one day by accident, after she met you for a lovers' rendezvous. Could that be right, Charles?"

Heat rose in his face, flushing his pale cheeks. "I don't know what you're talking about."

"Oh, come on. You were carrying on an affair with Lacey Jacobs, right under Marlis's nose. You couldn't stay true to her any more than you could to me."

Trish took two steps back. "Were you really sleeping with Lacey?"

"No. That's just some fantasy concocted in Amy's head," Charles said without meeting her eyes.

"That's what Mona meant," Trish said, as if talking to herself. She glanced over at me. "She said she had something on Mr. Bartos that would make him give her a cut of the song cycle profits, or at least some recognition, but she wouldn't tell me what it was."

"She told me the same thing," I replied.

"That's irrelevant." Charles circled around the island to stand before us. "And a lot of nonsense. Ramona Raymond was an unhinged, bitter woman who liked to pretend that she knew more about everything than she did."

"She's dead," Trish snapped. "Considering that fact, you could be a little nicer, Mr. Bartos."

"And you could be a little more ashamed, considering what

you've done." Charles glared at Trish. "I still don't understand. You hit someone and never called 911? You just left her lying there, all alone?"

I eyed him, thinking, *You did the same, you jerk.*

"I'm sorry. That's what I came here to say. And when I leave here, I'm going straight to the authorities to confess my crime." Trish tipped her head to the side, studying Charles. "You should come with me. You can bring Lacey's hat as part of the evidence to back up my story. Of course, that will probably mean that you'll have to explain how it came to be on Marlis's head that morning. I mean"—Trish sniffed—"how Lacey left it at your apartment."

Charles took another step forward. "I'll do nothing of the kind."

"Don't you want to close the case on your girlfriend's death?" Trish's eyes narrowed. "Or is this why you never turned in the hat to the authorities?"

I remembered Richard's words about Clarion's "no tolerance" policy. "That's it—you didn't care about protecting Lacey. You simply wanted to keep your affair with a student a secret." I slapped my forehead. "Stupid me, thinking you might actually care about someone else, when all you wanted to do was to protect your own career."

"You . . ." Charles swore and lunged forward to grab my arm. "After everything I did for you."

"What exactly was that?" I grimaced as his fingers dug into my wrist.

"I gave you a polish you never had before. Tried to teach you some sophistication and improve your frumpy ways." He looked me up and down. "Although I see it didn't stick."

"Let go of her," Trish said.

Charles and I turned as one. Trish stood with her legs spread slightly apart and the revolver pointed at my former boyfriend.

"You can't be serious." Charles dropped my wrist and stepped to the side.

"Don't make any sudden moves, and don't underestimate me, Mr. Bartos. I'm quite experienced with handling guns. Ask Ms. Webber."

I nodded. "I found out that she was on a sharpshooter team in high school, so, yeah, she knows what she's doing."

"Really?" Charles sucked in a deep breath. "We have that in common then, Ms. Alexander." He shot me a cynical smile. "I'm afraid I didn't reveal all of my skills to Amy, but then, we didn't share that much about our younger years."

I leaned back against the island to steady myself. "You shoot?"

"Yes. Not so much anymore, but I did quite a bit of that sort of thing when I was young. There wasn't much else to do in my little midwestern town. As a matter of fact, I was quite good. I even tried out for the Olympics." A sardonic grin twisted his lips. "You'd never have expected that of me, would you, Amy? Of course, you never asked. You were so sure you knew me well, but you see—you only scratched the surface."

"Should've scratched your eyes out," I muttered, cradling my wrist in my other hand.

"The thing is"—Charles eyed Trish before striding forward and smacking her so hard that she stumbled and fell to the floor—"I don't think I want either of you sharing your little theories about Lacey with the sheriff's department or the police." He kicked a stunned Trish's hand.

Trish howled as his foot connected. She opened her fingers, releasing the gun, which Charles immediately snatched up with a tissue he'd yanked from his pocket.

"Now," he said, straightening and pointing the gun at Trish. "Get up and join Amy."

I stared at him, and my mouth dropped open. Never in my wildest dreams would I have pictured Charles slapping or kicking anyone, much less a woman, or wielding a gun with such nonchalant expertise.

*But he's right, Amy. You didn't know him. Not at all. You never saw him as the man he is—someone who'd cheat on Marlis just as he did you. Someone who'd seduce a student at his own university. A consummate liar who hid the hat, and his suspicions about Lacey, just to protect himself.* I shivered as I stared into the steel-blue eyes of the man I'd once thought I loved. *What else has he done?*

"I can shoot you faster than you can move, so don't try anything," Charles said, backing over to a coat tree next to the door. Without looking, he pulled a pair of driving gloves from a jacket pocket and slipped them on, expertly switching the gun from one hand to the other as he did so. "Now toss your phones over here."

Of course, Trish still had mine. Wisely, she pulled out only hers at first, chucking it over to Charles.

"And the other one. I assume you took Amy's," Charles said, leveling the gun at Trish's chest.

She sighed and threw my cell at him with so much force it skipped like a stone over water, landing at Charles's feet. He stomped on both phones before kicking the shattered bits into the corner.

"What do you think you're going to do with us?" I asked. "Surely you don't plan to silence us forever. I mean, I may have seen some new sides of you today, but I don't think you're a killer."

Charles's eyebrows rose to the level of the silky hair spilling over his forehead. "Don't you? Well, you're wrong again, Amy." He flashed me one of those brilliant smiles that had so charmed me in the past. "Who do you think shot Ramona Raymond?"

# Chapter
# Twenty-Four

I shared a quick, terrified look with Trish before I could make my mouth form any words. "You can't be serious."

"But I am." Charles advanced on us, the revolver gleaming in his gloved hand. "Deadly serious."

"Why would you do such a thing?"

"She tried to blackmail me. Threatened me with that same ridiculous story about Lacey Jacobs." Charles lifted and dropped his slender shoulders in an exaggerated shrug. "She wanted me to confess that I'd stolen her research for the *Moon and Thistle Cycle*."

"And did you?"

"Of course not. Those lyrics are easy enough to find, and they're in the public domain. She had no claim on any of my profits, and I certainly wasn't going to give her a credit." Charles pointed the gun at me and then Trish. "Just another delusion, like this foolish idea of yours that Lacey and I were having an affair."

He still refused to admit that. I wondered why. "So Mona showed up and tried to pressure you, and what? You just shot her right here?" I stared at the pristine wooden floorboards. That had to be wrong. No way he could've cleaned up the blood without leaving any trace.

"No, I'm not that stupid. We argued and I was fine with that, especially since I knew I was in the right. In fact, the whole sordid encounter would've ended without incident until she lost her cool and hit me." Charles touched the side of his face with his free hand. "Hard enough to leave a mark. After that, I defended myself."

"You shot her?" Trish's question ended in a squeak.

"No, I slapped her back. But then she fled the house, swearing she was going straight to the authorities. I couldn't allow that."

"You chased her down," I said, as I realized how Mona must've ended up in the woods. "But the gun . . ."

"I knew Delbert Frye kept a loaded rifle in the shed next door, so I threw on my gloves, ran out and grabbed that gun, and followed her. That wasn't hard. She made enough noise for three people. And since she'd foolishly parked up at the trailhead and walked down the forest path to reach my house, I had time to catch up with her."

Recalling what Delbert had said about hearing noises, I realized the reason for the self-satisfied gleam in Charles's eyes. "You went out that Thursday morning following Mona's visit and made sure to crash about the woods, didn't you? Just to set up a pattern of noise continuing after Mona's death."

"Why yes, as well as to . . ." Charles waved the gun at me. "Well, never mind about that. Now we're all going to take a little walk."

But I wasn't ready to be marched out to my death, which is where I assumed this was headed. "And after you shot Mona, you simply returned the rifle to Delbert's shed, hoping it would implicate him, I suppose."

"That was one option. I also thought that if the rifle was never found on Frye's property, Ramona's death might be written off as a hunting accident by persons unknown." As Charles looked me over, a little smirk twitched his lips. "You see how you've underestimated me, Amy?"

"I see how I never knew you at all. Oh, after we broke up, I did realize that you were an egomaniac, but a murderer? No, that one slipped by me."

Charles stepped forward and shoved the revolver against my forehead. "Don't mouth off at me. You aren't nearly as clever as you think. Now let's go."

*Neither are you*, I thought, considering the difficulty Charles would face in trying to explain two more deaths or disappearances.

*He won't shoot us in the house*, I realized. *He'll want to take us out into the woods.* I planted my feet, determined not to move.

But the cold barrel of the gun against my temple didn't lessen. *Trish*, I thought, realizing that neither of us would make it if we had no opportunity to escape. *It could be easier for at least one of us to get away in the woods. There might be some small chance . . .*

"All right, we'll walk outside," I said. "But remove that gun from my temple first."

Charles stepped back. "Fine. Just remember that I will be right behind you, and I can shoot one or both of you in an instant if either of you make any wrong moves."

I glanced at Trish, who had one hand on her stomach and one over her mouth, like she might vomit any second. "We understand. Right, Trish?"

The young woman nodded.

"Okay then—onto the deck," Charles said.

Trish and I walked slowly toward the window wall at the back of the house. When we reached the French doors, I flipped the latch and then held the door open as Trish walked through.

Charles grabbed the edge of the door with his free hand. "Now you."

I slid past him to join Trish on the deck.

"We're going to head into the woods. There's a short path from the edge of my yard that connects with the main trail," Charles said, poking me in the back with the barrel of the revolver.

"You really think if you shoot us, anyone will write it off as an accident? The sheriff's department impounded Delbert's rifle from the shed, and hunters don't typically use revolvers," I said as we made our way off the deck and across the yard.

"Shut up and walk," Charles replied.

The moment we entered the woods, the light dimmed and the temperature dropped several degrees. I shuffled my feet, kicking up last fall's decomposing leaves.

Charles poked me with the gun again. "Pick up your feet and move."

"Must be insane," Trish mumbled, with a quick glance at me.

I shook my head. Charles wasn't crazy, just so self-centered that he valued only one thing in the universe—himself. And apparently he was so focused on protecting his career that he was willing to murder anyone who might damage his reputation.

As Trish and I walked single file, with Charles's footfalls rustling the leaves on the path behind us, I swept my gaze from side to side, searching for any means of escape. The sharp scent of pine, mingled with the faint odor of mold and animal droppings, filled my nostrils as I took deep breaths to keep from screaming. I had no doubt that Charles would shoot either one of us if we made too much noise, and I wanted at least one chance at escape before I met that fate.

"Take a hard left into the woods here," Charles said.

Trish glanced back at him. "There's no path."

"Just do it." Charles pointed the gun at her forehead.

Trish and I plunged into the undergrowth, kicking aside clusters of mushrooms and tangled vines.

*He's taking us to a spot where he can shoot us. With the gun Trish took from Chris's car.* I sucked in a ragged breath. Of course. Charles was obviously planning to kill me, then Trish, and somehow make it look like she'd murdered me before shooting herself. Maybe with the motive being my discovery of her secret? Charles probably knew that I'd been involved in solving a few recent murders. Perhaps he thought he could spin a story that involved me telling him that I'd discovered Trish's crime using my research skills and that I'd vowed to confront her about it. It wouldn't be out of the realm of possibility that she'd subsequently shot me, then killed herself when she realized what she'd done.

I followed Trish's slender back, my mind racing. We had to get away from Charles, but how?

"Watch out," Trish said as she held back an arching fountain of blackberry vines. She pointed at a deep gulley off to our right with her other hand. "Can't walk around that."

As I took hold of the vines from her, one of the thorns stabbed me—a jolt of pain that gave me an idea. Maybe a really bad idea, but it might at least guarantee Trish, who was in front of me, a fighting chance. Holding in my pain, I yanked the vines forward, then jumped under them as I let them go. They snapped back like a thorn-studded whip.

Charles's scream told me I'd hit my target. I spun around in time to see him shove the gun into his pocket before clawing at the thorns embedded in his face.

"Run!" I yelled at Trish, while thrusting out one leg and bending my knee to hook it around Charles's calf. As he stumbled, I shoved him off the path. He tumbled into the deep gulley with a thud, but the string of curse words rising up from the ditch told me that he was still alive and kicking.

I couldn't get to the gun without moving in too close, so I just turned and ran after Trish. *If we can get far enough way, or hide, before Charles is able to climb out of that hole and get back on his feet . . .*

It was a long shot, but any chance was better than none. I dashed through the woods, ignoring the vines ripping at my bare lower arms and the rocks stubbing my toes inside my thin leather loafers.

"We need to find the trail," I told Trish when I finally caught up with her. She stopped, pressed one hand against a slender tree trunk, and breathed heavily.

"I have no idea where that is," she said, looking up through the thick canopy of leaves. "And I can't even see enough of the sky to know what's north or south or anything else." Trish met my concerned gaze. "Pretty sure we're lost."

"I imagine we are, but we have to find our way out of here."

Trish vigorously shook her head. "I've done enough wilderness hiking to know we can't just take off in some aimless direction. We could easily wander around in circles and never find the trail. Especially since we can't go back the way we came. Not with Bartos still on the loose." She slumped against the tree and stared at me. "Thanks, by the way. That was risky, but it gives us a chance."

"You're quite welcome. It was somewhat selfish anyway. Sure, I wanted to protect you, but I also really don't want to die today." I glanced beyond the tree where she was standing and noticed some stones rising up like monoliths, their dark-gray surfaces covered in moss. "It looks like there might be caves or at least some rock clusters nearby. What if we see if there's any place where we could hide for a bit? If we're lost, Charles probably is too, so he won't necessarily be able to find us easily."

"That's a thought," Trish said, following my gaze. "Better than stumbling around and running right back into him. And I know there'll be people out looking for us eventually. I mean, I'm pretty sure Chris and Hope will sound the alarm if I don't come back with the car."

"And I know Richard and Sunny and my aunt will alert the authorities if I don't show up this evening. Not to mention the fact that I was supposed to meet with Brad Tucker at four o'clock. He's likely to be concerned if I don't arrive for my appointment and no one knows where I am."

"Okay then." Trish straightened and walked purposefully toward the rocks. "Let's see what we can find."

After a quick examination of the wall of stone, we discovered fissures that created narrow passages leading deep into the mountain.

"It's like the entrance to Mona's underground kingdom of the fae," Trish said as she slipped into one of the passages.

"Not comforting," I replied, squeezing in behind her.

"You don't believe in that nonsense, do you?" Trish slid around a corner. "Here, this is better."

She was a lot smaller than me, so my progress was slower, but when I finally turned the corner, I breathed a sigh of relief. We were in a small cavern that was dry and had a natural air shaft perforating its granite ceiling. Glancing around, I was happy to see another passage that seemed, from the glimmer of light I glimpsed around one bend, to lead straight out into the woods. Which meant we wouldn't be trapped in here with only one avenue of escape. I sank down onto a rock ledge that jutted out from one of the cave walls. "This is great, but how will any rescuers find us?"

"I thought maybe we'd stay here until dark, then try to signal someone." Trish patted her jacket pocket. "There's a small flashlight attached to Chris's key ring. We can use that."

"That might work, but it could also draw Charles to our location."

"But if people are out looking for us, what could he do? Sure, he could still shoot us, but that would be risky, especially if your deputy friend is anywhere around." Trish slumped beside me. "I don't know, I just have a feeling that Bartos won't take the risk and implicate himself that way. I bet he'll just skip town if he doesn't find us soon."

"You're probably right," I said, wrapping my arms around my body. "Ugh, it's cold in here."

"Lucky I wore my jacket," Trish said, eyeing me. "Maybe we can share it? I can take it off and drape it over both of us. We'd have to huddle up, though."

"I'm okay for now. Maybe later, when the sun goes down . . ." I shivered. The idea of staying there, basically underground, brought back painful memories of another dark space where I'd been trapped. At least this cavern wasn't damp and filled with muck, and we could walk out of it whenever we wished.

Trish glanced up at me from under her lowered eyelashes. "You dated this guy, huh?"

"Yeah, for about a year. Looking back on it, I guess I can see hints that he was capable of horrible things, but at the time I just refused to accept it. Sure, he was mean to me sometimes, although he was never physically abusive. But he was controlling and hard to please." I frowned, clutching my upper arms harder. "My boyfriend has always maintained that Charles is a narcissist, but I don't know if he really fits the clinical description. I think he's just an egomaniac."

"He only thinks about himself, you mean."

"Right, but more than that. I don't think he even views other people as humans. Not human on the same level as he is, anyway. I believe that he sees other people as things—objects to be used and discarded whenever he's tired of them."

"Which is why he can shoot someone and feel no remorse?"

Trish stared at the opposite wall, her eyes slightly unfocused. "Not like me. I feel regret every minute of every day for accidentally killing someone."

"I suppose." I dropped my arms so I could slide one of them around her trembling shoulders. "You know what's really weird? He pursued me with great determination when we first met. I was so flattered—here was this handsome, famous, talented guy chasing after me. He even employed the whole flowers-and-candy-and-expensive-dates routine. I was dazzled. But then, after I told him I loved him, it all changed. It was like night and day. He became standoffish and rude and condescending, always telling me what to do and how to do it. I should've seen all the red flags and walked away immediately, but I didn't. I thought it was me. I wasn't smart enough, or thin enough, or sophisticated enough. I just had to improve, to do better, and then he'd treat me like he had at the beginning of our relationship. Only, I know now that I was never going to be good enough again. Once he'd won me, he didn't want me anymore. Not really."

"You never see that stuff when you're in the middle of it. Just like I didn't realize that when I told all those lies, I was only piling up enough stones to bury myself." Trish stirred beside me but didn't pull away from my sheltering arm. "After the hit-and-run, there was a time I truly thought I could get away with it. Strangely, with this whole Lacey wrinkle, I guess I really could have. But my conscience balked."

"Because you have one." I squeezed her shoulder before pulling my arm back. "By the way, I'm willing to be a character witness for you, if you'll have me. I could let the court know that your remorse is genuine."

"I'd like that. Thanks," Trish said, then pressed her finger to her lips. "I think I hear something," she whispered as she stood up.

A loud rustle, like shoes disturbing the piles of dried leaves outside the cave, made me shrink back against the cool wall behind me. As Trish crept over to the passage where we'd entered the cavern, my fingers slid down the side of our natural bench, looking for a loose rock or any other type of weapon. Instead, they encountered something that felt like an old shoe.

I pulled the object up into my lap, surprised by its weight. It was a leather pouch that had obviously been exposed to the elements for some time, based on the crackled texture of its hard surface. The loose knot in the rawhide tie gave way easily under my fingers. I opened the pouch slightly, just enough to glimpse the objects inside.

Coins. I retied the knot and clutched the bag with both hands. The Frye family gold, found at last. Ada and Violet must have hidden it in here before they met their sad end. I clutched the bag with both hands, fervently hoping that Trish and I wouldn't suffer the same fate.

As I looked up from my lap, I noticed Trish walking backward to reach the center of the cavern. Facing her, and striding forward with the revolver pointed at her heart, was Charles.

"Thought you could hide?" Charles swept some debris from his golden hair with his free hand. "What idiots you two are. I knew you weren't smart enough to outwit me, but I didn't realize that you'd conveniently provide a place where I can kill you and not worry about your bodies being discovered. At least, not before most of the evidence will have faded away."

As he aimed the revolver at Trish, I leapt to my feet. Fueled by adrenaline, I used every bit of strength I possessed to hurl the leather pouch at his right arm.

The loud crack of the gunshot reverberated throughout the cavern. Trish fell, clutching her shoulder.

Charles, whose aim had fortunately been thrown off by the impact of the pouch, fell too—backward into the hard surface of the stone wall. He staggered and slumped to the floor, still gripping the revolver.

Uncertain that I could take the gun from him without being shot, I ran to Trish and bent over her.

She pulled me close with her uninjured arm. "Go," she whispered in my ear. "He's dazed, but he'll be up soon. Get out of here."

"He'll kill you," I whispered back, after a swift glance at Charles, who was blinking and rubbing the back of his head.

"No, he'll chase you. He can leave me here to deal with later, since I can't really move very well." She released my arm and fumbled in her pocket, pulling out her keys with the attached miniature flashlight. "Go," she said again, pressing the key ring into my hand.

Charles had come back to awareness enough to mutter something like "won't get away from me."

"Oh yeah?" I raised my voice as I straightened and headed for the wider exit. "Watch me."

I ran out of the cavern, hoping against hope that I wouldn't hear another shot. I didn't. Apparently, Trish's gamble had paid off.

Which meant that everything now depended on me. I had to find help, somehow. Even though I could tell by the cooler temperature and darkening sky that night was falling over the woods. Even though I had no idea where I was.

I was tired and terrified and completely lost, but I had to persevere. I had to find a way to signal for help, no matter how dangerous it might be.

More than my life depended on it.

# Chapter Twenty-Five

I stumbled into a tall cluster of rhododendron bushes and hunkered down for a moment to think. Crashing around the woods was obviously not the best way to escape Charles. I couldn't outrun him. I had to outsmart him.

*Use his own failings against him. He thinks he's more intelligent and cunning than everyone else. Prove him wrong.*

I uncurled my fingers, staring at the key ring. As I shifted it to my other hand, I vaguely registered the grooves the keys had dug into my palm.

I needed only the flashlight. I slipped it off the ring and stuck it in my pocket, then rose to my feet and listened for any noises that could indicate Charles was nearby.

Hearing nothing except the chirping of tree frogs and the rustle of the wind through leaves, I crept out of my hiding place. I moved on the balls of my feet, making as little noise as possible. When I reached a small clearing, I dropped the keys, then circled back the way I'd come.

If Charles found the keys, I hoped he'd think I'd pressed forward, headed down the slope that fell away from the clearing. It's what I would've expected from someone unfamiliar with these woods—to venture down the mountain, not farther up.

I moved silently, determined to reach a spot where I could hide again. There had to be another cave or someplace where Charles wouldn't readily spot me. I had one advantage—Charles and I hadn't interacted for a few years. I was certain he still saw me as that rather awkward girl he'd met in the university library. He didn't know what I'd been through since then, how my courage and resolve had been tested by other criminals and killers. I figured Charles was likely to picture me running wildly through the woods, screaming my head off. He wouldn't expect me to remain calm and think my way out of danger. He didn't realize how much I'd changed.

I'd faced death before. I knew how to fight to survive.

Creeping from tree trunk to tree trunk, I paused every few minutes to listen for any footfalls on the leaf-strewn forest floor. The rush of wings from an owl swooping over my head startled me, and I clapped my hand over my mouth to silence a scream.

I glanced up at the patches of sky that peeped between the shifting canopy of leaves. Fortunately, the moon was nearly full, which meant the woods were dark but not impenetrable. With my eyes adjusted to the limited light, I was able to navigate without using the flashlight.

Surprised that Charles wasn't right on my heels, it seemed that perhaps my little gambit with the keys had worked, at least for a time. Gingerly holding back a spray of thorn-encrusted vines with one hand, I slipped into another thicket and made my way to the pile of scattered boulders I'd spied through the arching vines.

At first glance, it appeared that the stones were aligned to form a solid wall, but closer inspection proved out my hope that there might be a hiding spot among the boulders. The front line of stones extended only halfway across, so between them and the back wall of granite was a narrow passage. I shimmed into this cavity, fighting my natural aversion to tight spaces.

*Down into the cold and dark* . . . No, I couldn't dwell on that memory. I had to control my breathing and force my shivering limbs to relax. I might be holed up in this spot until morning.

*If Charles doesn't find me first.*

I closed my eyes for a moment, picturing my parents at Kurt Kendrick's dinner table. I rewound the memory, mentally admiring how gracefully they'd deflected the barbs cast by Jim Muir, and how they'd hugged me when they left that Sunday, sharing their approval of Richard despite his parents' bad behavior.

*Richard.* I breathed deeply, slowing my racing heart. Behind my eyelids I could clearly see Richard's beautiful gray eyes, so often filled with humor as well as love. And Sunny's bright smile. And Aunt Lydia looking imperious and gracious all at the same time. *I have to get back to them*, I thought, *and I will.*

Something rustled the fallen leaves on the ground beyond the thicket. I stilled all my movements.

"Amy?" a familiar, unwanted voice called out. "Are you here? I thought I noticed a footprint back in that clearing, pointed this way."

*Oh no.* I bit my lower lip to prevent any sound from escaping my parched lips. *Perhaps I'm not as clever as I thought either.*

But Charles wasn't walking toward the jumble of boulders. Not yet, anyway. If he stepped into that thicket of vines, I would hear the crackle of bent branches. That was the point where I'd have to slide out of my hiding spot.

*And do what, Amy?* I pressed my palms against the rough granite of the stone shielding me and considered my options. If Charles moved any closer, I'd have to run. It wasn't likely to be a very success-ful escape plan, but it was the only one I had.

*If he finds me.* If not, I knew I was safer staying put. I fought my natural inclination to flee as I heard Charles call my name again.

"You know I won't really hurt you, Amy," he said in a tone I knew so well. The silky, seductive voice that had charmed me when we'd first met. "So if you're around here somewhere, come on out and let's talk this over. What do you say?"

No rustling of the vines. I stayed in place, barely breathing.

"It's really all a misunderstanding," Charles said. "Yes, I shot Mona, but that was in self-defense. I just wanted to frighten her with the rifle. Force her to abandon her ridiculous vendetta against me. She was trying to ruin me. No one should allow their whole career to be destroyed over such foolishness. Surely you agree?"

I wanted to shout that he was a "lying liar who lied" but clamped my lips together instead.

"If you and I could simply talk this out, I'm sure you'd under-stand." Charles's voice took on a wheedling tone. "I simply showed her the rifle and she lunged at me. Then I had to shoot. I was protect-ing myself, that's all."

*He probably believes that*, I thought, swallowing back a hysterical burst of laughter. *In his own twisted way, he undoubtedly believes that his career, his reputation, is worth more than any number of lives.*

Something blazed, illuminating the stones beyond the crevasse where I was hiding. *Flashlight*, I thought, but instantly realized that Charles's yelp of terror made that unlikely.

Besides, he didn't have a flashlight. At least not one I'd seen. Per-haps he had one on his cell phone, if he'd thought to bring that with him, but the light I'd just seen didn't look like a light from any phone.

I inched over to the edge of my protective shelter and peeked out. A flare brighter than several camera flashes popping at once momentarily blinded me. I shielded my eyes with my hands.

Charles screamed and, by the sound of his heavy footfalls, took off running. When I could make out anything, I spied the back of his jacket as he fled the area.

Pursued by a globe of light.

*No*, I thought, *it can't be following him. That must be an illusion.* I blinked and rubbed my eyes as I stepped out from behind the rocks.

Other globes of light rose from the floor of the forest and sailed up through the tangle of branches and fluttering leaves to hang above the tree tops.

I moved through the thicket to reach open ground, keeping an eye on the surrounding woods to make sure Charles was nowhere in sight.

But I could tell by the crashing sounds I heard fading in the distance that he was still running.

Away from me.

I exhaled a long breath. That was all that mattered.

I knew I still had to be cautious. Slipping from tree to tree, I stayed on high alert for any sound that might indicate Charles's return, but all I heard was the rush of wings as shadowy birds flew away from the brilliant white globes still bouncing above the trees.

The mountain lights. They were real.

They had saved me.

I shook my head. No, it was simply some natural phenomenon, serendipitously occurring at just the right moment. *If it can't be proven scientifically, it's nonsense . . .*

Still, the "nonsense" illuminated the sky above me like paper lanterns released by hidden hands. I zigzagged through the woods, using the blazing balls of light to guide me toward a thinning of the trees.

It was the trail. I grabbed a nearby tree trunk and used it to support my trembling limbs as I caught my breath. Once my legs ceased shaking, I stepped away and studied the path, trying to determine which way to walk to reach the trailhead.

The sound of breaking limbs spun me around. My throat closed up. *Charles found me.* But no, before me on the path stood a deer, with a coat the color of ripened wheat and antlers branching upward like a great tree. The buck turned his head to look at me and our gazes locked. His eyes were dark as a sky without stars. His nostrils flared as he breathed in my scent.

Drawn by a force I could not understand, I moved toward him. The deer stood still, his flanks heaving. "Hello there."

The buck's eyes rolled, showing a rim of white around brown irises. I knew this creature could slash me with his hooves or spear me with his antlers. Yet I felt no fear.

He was a part of these mountains—a natural force that belonged in these woods. Unlike Charles and his gun.

Unlike me. I clutched my upper arms with both hands and backed away. *There is still wonder in these mountains*, I thought, staring into those fathomless dark eyes. *They still echo with magic and mysteries and wild power, despite everything humans have done to tame them.*

The buck snorted and tossed his heavy head before leaping off the trail. I spied only the white flash of his tail as he disappeared amid the trees.

I heard it then—the sounds that had undoubtedly frightened the deer. Human voices, calling my name.

"Over here!" I shouted, pulling the tiny flashlight from my pocket. I waved it over my head. "I'm here!"

"So you are," said a voice off to my left. I turned to face Charles, and the gun.

"There are people looking for me. Sheriff's deputies, as well as my friends." I lowered the flashlight and forced the tremor from my voice. "You can't shoot me and get away."

"Can't I?" Charles's eyes reminded me of something. Yes, the stare of the buck—terrified and threatening at the same time.

I backed away. "They will catch you, no matter where you run. You've overplayed your hand, Charles. But there's still one chance, if you allow me to live. Let me go and I'll stall them. I'll take them straight to Trish and say I never saw you once we left that cave."

Charles gripped the revolver with both hands. "I'm afraid I don't trust you, Amy."

I'd fought for my life against my cousin and her gun and triumphed despite a night spent in a dank, silt-filled well. I'd lived after facing off with a man who would've happily shot me over a painting he thought was worth millions. I could survive this too. I met Charles's wild glare without faltering. "You have no other choice."

"Maybe. And maybe I just want to kill you and don't care if I'm caught." Charles aimed the revolver at my heart. "You always were more trouble than you were worth."

"I know what I'm worth," I said. "And it's more than you ever deserved. And I also know," I added, as the hard ground vibrated beneath the thin soles of my loafers, "that you'd do anything to escape justice." I pointed toward the trail. "Feel that? That's hard-soled boots, pounding the earth as my rescuers run toward us."

Charles swore and fired just as I yelled, "Over here!" and dropped to the ground. The bullet whistled over my head. Before Charles could fire again, I rolled into a ball, hoping he'd only be able to hit my arms or legs.

There was no second shot, only the rumble of boots on the path and a loud crackle of underbrush being trampled underfoot. I lifted my head to meet the concerned gaze of Chief Deputy Brad Tucker. I mutely pointed toward the woods, and Brad nodded.

"He won't get far," Brad said as he helped me to my feet. "My deputies are only seconds behind him, and I've sent out others to set up a perimeter. Now"—he looked me over—"the important question is, are you all right?"

"I'm fine," I said, brushing the dust and leaf meal from my clothes. "But Trish Alexander isn't. Charles shot her. Only in the shoulder, so I think she'll be okay, but she needs help."

"Hold on, let me get the EMTs in on this; then you can show me the way."

"Not sure I can remember. But it's a cavern, in the middle of an old rock fall. Can't be too far away." I rubbed at my temples. "It's somewhere off the trail that leads to Delbert Frye's property."

"We'll find it," Brad said, before barking something into a walkie-talkie. "No cell service up here," he said when he finished alerting emergency services. "Have to go old school."

"Whatever works." I heard someone else call my name and looked down the trail to see Richard running toward us.

I took a few stumbling steps in his direction before he reached me and swept me into his arms.

"Thank God. Thank God," he repeated, holding me close. "You're okay?"

I leaned my head against his chest. "Now I am."

Brad looked over at us with a smile. "Couldn't keep him from volunteering for the search party."

"He tried," Richard said.

"Glad you're here," I said. "You too," I added, with a swift glance at Brad.

"When you didn't show up for your appointment at the sheriff's department, I thought maybe you'd forgotten," Brad said. "But then Lydia called looking for you, and when Sunny told us about you leaving the library in the afternoon . . . well, we knew something was up."

"Sunny also mentioned your visit with Bartos, and how you said you might go back," Richard gently pushed me back while still keeping his hands on my shoulders. "A foolish idea, but enough to send a portion of the search in this direction."

Brad nodded. "And Chris Garver was concerned over Trish Alexander taking off for parts unknown in his car. He and Hope Hodgson also suggested checking the trail. Something about those gold coins you mentioned to me once, Amy."

"Yeah, Chris and his boyfriend Ethan Payne were searching for them. Maybe they thought Trish was too." I plucked a few bits of crumpled leaves from my hair. "Did you guys see the lights? Charles almost caught me, but then these balls of what looked like white fire distracted him."

Brad and Richard shared a glance. "Yes, we saw them. Bouncing over the trees. Gone now." Brad pushed his hat back from his forehead. "Never thought I'd see that in my lifetime. Thought it was just a story."

"Well, I don't know what they are," I said. "But I'm sure glad they're real."

"Me too," Richard said, pulling me to him again as Brad turned aside to answer a call on his walkie-talkie. "Maybe it was the fae, protecting one of their own," he whispered in my ear.

I snorted. "I'm no fairy creature."

"Oh, I don't know. I think there's a touch of magic about you." Richard kissed my temple and tightened his arms around me. "You've certainly bewitched me."

I hid my smile in the folds of his sweatshirt. "Always the romantic."

"Always," he said, before kissing the top of my head.

Brad looked over at us. "We'll need Amy to make a full report, of course. She'll have to share all the details about what happened tonight." Brad lifted the walkie-talkie. "Fortunately, some of my men have found Trisha Alexander, and they say she'll live. She's on her way to the hospital now. Which is where you need to take Amy." Brad added, pointing at Richard.

Richard groaned. "Not the hospital again."

"More waiting." I patted his chest. "But you should be used to that by now."

"I'll never get used to it," he replied, loosening his hold on me but keeping one arm around my shoulder. "Okay, first the hospital and then what? The sheriff's office?"

"Yes. After that you can take her home." Brad tapped the walkie-talkie against his other palm. "You were very lucky tonight, Amy. You really need to stop getting involved in such dangerous matters."

"I don't mean to," I said. "It just happens. I start researching and questioning things and trying to dig up the truth . . ."

"Hmmmm . . ." Brad looked me up and down. "Maybe you're in the wrong line of work. If you insist on sticking your nose into such things, perhaps you should join the force. At least then you'd have the proper training."

"I don't know," Richard said. "She seems to do pretty well without it."

"Luck." Brad pulled his hat back down over his forehead. "That's just luck."

"I thought you didn't believe in luck," I said.

"I don't. Which is why I worry about you."

"You too?" Richard asked with a grin, just as Brad answered another call.

"They got him," he said, lowering the walkie-talkie. "Bartos is now on his way to jail."

Richard's grin faded. "That's good, although I was really hoping for one moment alone with him before he was arrested."

"Why do you think I kept you talking here?" Brad raised his eyebrows. "I didn't want to have to arrest you too."

"Would've been worth it," Richard muttered.

I patted his arm. "It's okay. Wait until I testify against him. We'll get our revenge then, for sure."

A slow smile spread over Richard's face.

"Something about that is particularly amusing?" I asked.

"I was just picturing the elegant Maestro Bartos in an orange jumpsuit."

I chuckled. "Yeah, and with all his lovely hair shorn off."

"Now that"—Richard waved goodbye to Brad before escorting me down the trail—"might be the best revenge of all."

# Chapter Twenty-Six

I spent the rest of the evening in the hospital being checked over by various nurses and doctors in between bouts of questioning by one of Brad's detectives. Late morning, when I was released, I had to go directly to the sheriff's office to make a formal statement. Richard, who'd been waiting patiently through all of this, finally took me back to his house after lunch. After I grabbed a shower and changed into some clothes he'd collected from Aunt Lydia, Richard sat me on the sofa and gave me a glass of wine. Loie, meowing loudly, pawed at my legs, demanding my lap.

I had to admit that the warmth of kitten fur under my fingers was almost as soothing as Richard's arm around my shoulder. As Loie snuggled against my chest, her little paws kneading my flannel shirt, I rested against Richard and exhaled a gusty sigh.

"Feeling better?" he asked, before kissing the top of my head.

"Getting there."

"Want to catch some z's?"

"Later. I'm exhausted, but too wired to sleep right now. I'd rather just sit here, if you don't mind."

"Of course I don't mind. How about a little humor to lighten the mood?" He grabbed the remote and turned on the large television monitor hanging on the opposite wall.

We watched some comedy I couldn't appreciate or follow until the doorbell rang and Richard leapt up to welcome a few visitors. He ushered them in and played host by offering them wine, which they accepted, and snacks, which they did not.

"I just wish I'd had one minute alone with that creep." Sunny, who sat beside me, sipping her glass of wine, patted my knee.

"You and me both," Richard said, taking a seat at my other side.

"It's probably wise that Brad was there to prevent that," Aunt Lydia said. "Or both of you might be in jail right now, along with Charles."

I flashed her a smile. "Yeah, I think he's lucky to have been arrested before Richard found him. Or you," I added, looking over at the man seated in the other armchair.

Kurt Kendrick placed one finger against his nose. "Ah, but I know people . . ."

"In jail? Why doesn't that surprise me?"

He grinned. "I may have a word with someone. But not until we know where Bartos is headed. I confess that most of my contacts are in federal lockup, not the local jail."

Aunt Lydia rolled her eyes. "Yes, I'm sure you wouldn't mess around with small-time criminals."

"If you're implying that I don't mingle with petty crooks, you're right." Kurt leaned back in his chair. "We'll have to wait and see where they incarcerate Bartos."

"That might take some time. And I'll have to testify." I made a face. "Again."

"At least you're safe now," Sunny said, bouncing off the sofa.

"Richard, do you mind if I grab that bottle of wine from the kitchen counter and bring it in here? I think we could all use a refill. I know I could."

"Bring two," Richard said.

"But you need to drive home," I said as Sunny headed for Richard's kitchen.

"No, she doesn't," my aunt said. "She can stay at my place tonight if necessary."

Sunny cast a grin over her shoulder. "I might take you up on that. Although Mr. Kendrick will have to behave more responsibly. Unless you're willing to allow him to bunk at your house too."

"I draw the line at that," Aunt Lydia said, primly tugging down the sleeves of her lavender silk blouse.

"Don't trust yourself, eh?" Kurt looked over at me and winked.

When my giggle turned into a snort of laughter, my aunt turned and stared at me with a haughty expression befitting a queen. "I have no inclination in that direction, as you very well know, Kurt. Please don't give Amy any ideas. Especially when she's giddy from lack of sleep."

"I'm fine," I said, laying one hand on Loie's back and slumping against Richard.

"Sure you are," he said, slipping his arm around my shoulders and pulling me close. "I probably should let Lydia take you home and put you to bed, but I'm selfish and don't want to let go of you yet."

Aunt Lydia gazed at us speculatively. "I thought you could just keep her here, Richard. Unless you'd rather not."

"Is that really a question?" Richard asked, tightening his grip on my shoulder. "By the way, has anyone heard anything more about Trish Alexander?"

"I have," Sunny said, entering the room with a bottle of wine in each hand. She set them on the coffee table. "I brought white and red, just to cover all the bases."

"What did you hear?" Aunt Lydia asked, holding out her glass. "White, please."

Sunny refilled my aunt's glass. "Actually, I just got a call from Brad while I was in the kitchen. Trish is doing well but has to stay in the hospital for a little while longer."

"Poor child." Kurt's blue eyes were shadowed under his white lashes. "I know she must answer for that hit-and-run, even though it was obviously an accident. It's a pity she lost her head and drove off without getting help or alerting the authorities." He ran one hand through his thick hair. "Sadly, she'll probably end up in prison alongside real criminals, like Bartos. Although female, of course."

"Well, they've questioned her but won't do anything more until she recovers," Sunny said, pouring red wine into Kurt's empty glass.

"I'm going to testify for her. As a character witness. I want the authorities to know that she planned to confess before we were attacked by Charles, and that she truly felt remorse." I shook my head as Sunny pointed at my empty wine glass on the coffee table.

"What? You're turning down wine?" Richard tilted his head to give me a comical look of shock.

I swatted his arm. "I'm exhausted. Which also means I'm in no mood for your teasing."

Loie opened her green eyes, looked me dead in the face, and slapped my chin with her paw.

"See—my baby is taking up for me," Richard lifted Loie off my chest and cradled her in his arms. "Good cat," he crooned, before placing her gently on the floor.

I stuck my tongue out at him, but he just leaned in and kissed me on the mouth before sitting back, a broad smile on his face.

Sunny chuckled as she settled down beside me with her glass of white wine. "You *are* a bit giddy, aren't you, Amy? Anyway, Brad also shared some more positive news—Delbert Frye has been released with the department's apologies, and Lacey Jacobs has been brought out of her coma. She's perfectly lucid—there's apparently no signs of lingering brain damage."

"Thank goodness. She's been through enough." Aunt Lydia turned her gaze on me. "You really believe that Charles was carrying on an affair with the girl? From what you said before, he's refused to admit it."

"Yeah, it's so weird. After everything else he told you, why wouldn't he confess to that indiscretion?" Sunny asked, before taking a sip of her wine.

Kurt stretched out his legs over the rug that anchored the coffee table. "Oh, I don't know. Perhaps the idea that he'd betrayed his dead lover with a young student was worse than murder in his mind? Not because he was regretful, of course. But because such a thing might show him in a poor light as well as cost him his job. Men like Bartos," he added, looking at me, "are more concerned with how they appear to others, and their own financial well-being, than any actual wrongdoing."

I leaned into Richard. "It seems you're right. And yes, Aunt Lydia, based on everything I've heard and discovered, I do believe Charles was having an affair with Lacey."

"I guess she'll be able to tell the authorities the truth. Not only about how she got lost in the first place, but also about her relationship with Charles." Sunny swirled her wine before taking a long swallow.

Aunt Lydia finished off her own drink and set the glass on the end table next to her chair. "Charles must have wagered that she wouldn't ever recover and thought he'd never be implicated in the affair. That was a gamble, but I suppose it's why he refused to confirm the relationship, even when he planned to kill Trish and Amy."

I shivered. "I guess. Or maybe he hoped that Lacey would keep his secret, despite everything? I suppose, in his arrogance, he could've thought she still loved him and wouldn't betray him."

"He's enough of an egotist to believe that." Richard pulled back his arm and reached down to pick up the kitten, who was climbing up the leg of his jeans. "While he doesn't actually care about anyone else, he probably thinks people will love him forever no matter what he does."

"Probably," I yawned. "Oh, sorry. I don't mean for you to think you're boring me or anything."

Aunt Lydia rose to her feet. "All it means is that it's time to say our goodbyes."

"Yes," said Kurt, following her lead and standing. "I think it's time we let Amy get some sleep."

Sunny hugged me before leaping off the sofa. "Let me carry these glasses into the kitchen before I follow you all out."

"You don't have to run off." I covered my mouth as another yawn swallowed my final words.

"I think we do." Aunt Lydia crossed over to the sofa and bent down to kiss me on the forehead. "You get some rest. Richard can bring you over for a little light supper after your nap."

Richard carried Loie in the crook of his arm as he escorted my aunt and Kurt to the door, then waited for Sunny to dash back into the room and head outside before locking up.

"It's bed for you," he said, plopping Loie onto the sofa and holding out his hand.

"You coming with me?" I asked, smothering another yawn. "You've been up all night as well."

"I did doze while I waited at the hospital. Anyway, I plan to escort you upstairs and come back down. You need uninterrupted rest."

"Oh, would you disturb me?" I gave him a knowing smile as he hauled me to my feet.

"Without question. Which is why I'm tucking you in and that's it." He guided me toward the steps. "Come on, time for some much-needed sleep."

When we reached his bedroom, Richard swept back the coverlet and held it up so I could easily slide between the sheets.

"I didn't know him at all," I muttered as Richard pulled the quilted bedspread over me. "I spent all that time with him, but he was a stranger." I shivered and clutched the coverlet under my chin.

"He didn't allow you to know him." Richard sat on the edge of the bed. "Don't beat yourself up for not seeing beyond the mask, sweetheart. It seems most people didn't."

Something bounced onto my covered feet. I glanced down the length of the bed. "Hi, Loie. Planning on keeping me company?"

Her bright-green eyes blinked slowly.

"She knows you need her love right now." Richard leaned in and kissed me lingeringly on the lips. "And I hope you know you always have mine."

"I know," I said, my voice as thick as the cotton batting that stuffed the quilted coverlet. "But I do like to hear you say it."

Richard kissed me again before standing up. "Then you're in luck, because I intend to keep telling you that for as long as you'll allow it."

Loie padded up across my body before plopping down beside me and curling into a ball of black-and-orange fluff. I slipped one arm out from under the covers to cuddle her close. "Long time . . ." I allowed my drooping eyelids to close. "That's gonna be a really long time."

"Perfect," I heard Richard say before I fell asleep.

# Chapter Twenty-Seven

On Saturday, I decided to visit Lacey, a plan my aunt did not endorse with any enthusiasm.

"Are you sure you want to do this right now? It's bound to bring up uncomfortable emotions," she said, studying me as I slipped a light jacket over my T-shirt and jeans.

"Yeah, I'm sure. I want to hear the truth from her lips." I grabbed the car keys from the ceramic bowl on the hall table. "I need to know that I was right about her and Charles. Just to settle that in my mind."

Aunt Lydia pursed her lips. "Well, don't forget the flowers."

I picked up the newspaper-wrapped bundle filled with early roses and lilacs that I'd cut from our garden and dropped it into a clear glass vase that had once held an arrangement Hugh had sent to my aunt. "Are you sure you want to give this up?"

"It's fine. Just something the florist bought in bulk," Aunt Lydia said. "I know Hugh wouldn't mind. Now if I gave away that Ming bowl he gifted me at Christmas . . ."

"You'd never do that," I said, knowing that it would always hold a place of honor in the center of the dining room table. "All right, I'll see you a little later. Anything you need me to pick up on the way home?"

"As a matter of fact, there is." Aunt Lydia pulled a piece of paper from the pocket of her slacks. "I was planning to go out later to buy items I need for meals over the next few days, but if you don't mind . . ."

"Oh, that's right." I gave her a knowing look. "Hugh's coming tomorrow and staying over through the May Day festival on Tuesday, isn't he? You must be planning some special meals. I know how he adores your cooking."

A faint brush of pink tinted my aunt's cheeks. "I like to treat all my guests well."

"Some more than others, but I understand." As I took the list from her hand, I leaned in and kissed her cheek. "It's okay. Everyone's thrilled with your relationship. We all think it was about time you found love again."

"Oh, go on with you," Aunt Lydia said, waving me away. "And speaking of love," she called after me as I headed for the front door, "I hope you and Richard have resolved the issues that have cropped up between you over the past few weeks."

"We have." I turned to her and winked before opening the door. "And then some."

"Out," said my aunt sharply. But she was smiling.

* * *

I arrived at the hospital just as Chris and Hope were leaving Lacey's room.

"How's she doing?" I asked.

"Pretty good, all things considered," said Hope.

Chris looked me over. "Sorry about your ordeal, Ms. Webber. I'm really glad you're okay. Trish too." He scuffed his sneaker against the tile floor. "I heard you found the Frye treasure in some cave."

"Yeah. It came in handy, actually." I met his inquisitive stare. "I suppose you know the authorities plan to give it back to Delbert Frye. He doesn't have any children, but I imagine he might share it with his extended family." *Lucky for Alison*, I thought with a little frown.

"Guess that's only fair," Chris said, looking down at his feet. "It really was more like a game for me and Ethan, you know. We weren't serious about keeping the coins. It was just something Ethan found exciting. A treasure hunt—how many people get to go on one of those?"

"I understand," I said. "I wasn't really thinking that you or Ethan would hurt anyone over such a thing, although Ethan with his rifle did give me pause."

"But he's a responsible gun owner," Chris said. "He'd never shoot a person. Heck, most of the time he doesn't even shoot game. He really just likes to go out into the woods by himself to enjoy the peace and quiet and appreciate nature."

"I'm sure," I said, turning to Hope. "Did you get everything you need from the archives?"

"We did. Thanks." Hope glanced over at Chris. "And we have a little surprise. Something to honor Professor Raymond that we're going to announce during the May Day festival. I hope you'll be there."

"I will. Richard's studio is going to be participating in the festivities, you know. The girls, anyway." I shifted the vase of flowers from one arm to the other. "Too bad Lacey can't be there to see them perform, but I guess she won't be up to it."

"Probably not," Hope said. "Although she's trying to convince the doctors to allow her to go. But if she can't make it, I plan to film it on my phone so she can watch it later. Okay, Ms. Webber, I guess we should be going. See you Tuesday."

I nodded and offered my goodbyes before turning and heading into Lacey's room.

She was sitting up, her back supported by two pillows as well as the raised head of the bed.

"Hi, Ms. Webber," she said in a voice as raspy as a frog's croak.

Of course, she'd been intubated for some time, so it was no wonder her throat was raw. I examined her, noting her chopped-off hair, extreme pallor, and hollows under her cheekbones. But despite the ravages of her recent travails, I was surprised to realize something I hadn't noticed before—how much she resembled a younger Marlis Dupre.

*I guess Charles has a type*, I thought with a wry smile. Which made it even more odd that he'd ever taken an interest in me. I looked nothing like the lithe, blue-eyed blondes he seemed to favor.

I shook my head. Maybe I had been just a diversion, or perhaps Charles had been intrigued by the challenge of molding me into an acceptable girlfriend. At least in terms of sophistication, if not body type and coloring.

"Hello, Lacey. I'm so glad to hear you'll make a full recovery."

"Thank goodness." Lacey adjusted one of her pillows so she could sit up straighter. Her blue eyes followed me as I unwrapped the flowers from the newspaper and arranged them in the vase. "I heard what Charles did to you and Trish." Her golden eyelashes fluttered. "I'm so sorry."

"It wasn't your fault." I held up the vase. "I'm just going to fill this with some water. The flowers are from my aunt's garden," I added as I walked into the small bathroom connected to her room.

Returning to the room, I placed the vase on the plastic-topped table next to the bed.

"They're beautiful," Lacey said, her eyes brimming with tears. "Thank you."

"You're quite welcome." I pulled up a metal chair and sat next to her bed. "Charles had a lot of victims. You as much one as anyone."

A tear slid down Lacey's cheek. "I loved him. I really did."

"So did I, once." I took hold of one of Lacey's hands. "He completely fooled me. I guess he did the same to you."

Lacey nodded. "And it's worse than you think." She used her free hand to wipe away more tears. "I've already told the deputies all this, so you might as well hear it too."

"What's that?" I released her hand and sat back in my chair.

"Charles was the reason I was wandering around the woods, injured and disoriented." Lacey met my surprised look with a lift of her chin. "I don't know what he told you, but I went to see him that Friday of the bonfire. That's why I begged Ms. Virts for a ride up into the woods. I knew the secondary trail would lead me to Charles's house and I wanted to see him." Lacey sniffed back a sob. "I was desperate to talk to him."

"Had you seen him since the accident that killed Marlis?"

"No. Not once. Of course, I didn't realize it at the time, but he blamed me for hitting her. Just because he found my silly knitted hat at the scene."

"I know. He told me."

"But the truth was, I'd left the hat at his loft one time when we . . . when I visited him. I guess his girlfriend just pulled it out of the closet and wore it that morning."

"That was something she'd do, according to Charles."

"I guess so, although Charles swore he didn't know what happened to my hat when I texted him about it, even though all the while . . ." Lacey yanked a wad of tissues from the box on the side table. "He never contacted me after the accident," she said, dabbing at her eyes with the tissues. "I thought it was just for the sake of keeping up pretenses. So that when we finally went public with our relationship after I graduated, it wouldn't look like we'd been involved before."

"Had he told you he was going to leave Marlis?"

"Yeah. He said that a lot, even though he never made any effort to do anything about it. Then she was killed, and I realized we had to give it time. But after a while, I got pretty frantic. I hadn't heard from him at all, even after the funeral and his European trip. When I found out he was back here, staying at his mountain property, I decided to visit him. To demand answers."

"So you confronted him that Friday afternoon. But then you disappeared. How'd that happen?"

"At first, I thought everything was fine. Charles seemed glad to see me. He told me that he was actually working out a plan where we could be together permanently, even before my graduation, without causing a scandal. But he said he had to go out of town for some concerts first and begged me to stay at his place until he got back."

"Which you apparently did." I thought back to Brad's comments about Lacey's condition when she'd been found. Her words explained the anomalies. She hadn't been exposed to the elements for days and days. She'd been hiding out at Charles's house until Tuesday or Wednesday of the following week.

"Yeah. Charles told me that I had to stay out of sight for his plan to work. He ordered me not to contact anyone." Lacey blew her nose before tossing the tissues into the trash can under the side table. "He even took my phone. So I 'wouldn't be tempted,' he said."

"Then he smashed your phone and tossed it."

"That's what the authorities assume." Lacey's lips twitched into a grimace. "But like a good little girl, I hid out, waiting for him. I didn't contact anyone. Not even when I saw on TV that people were looking for me." She shook her head. "That's all I had for information, you know. Charles doesn't have a landline up there, and his computer was password-protected."

"You stayed out of sight because you trusted him?"

"Yeah, stupid me." Lacey closed her eyes for a moment. "I still thought everything was fine between us. That we had a chance for a future together. I know he's a lot older than me, but that never mattered. He said we were destined to be together. That we were soulmates."

I flinched. I'd heard those words from Charles too. Early in our relationship, before everything changed. "When did he return to the house?"

"Tuesday afternoon. I was so happy to see him . . ." Lacey buried her face in her hands, and for a moment all I could hear was her breathing. She lifted her head. "But as soon as he came through the door, he verbally attacked me. Said he knew I'd hit Marlis with my car and run away. Shoved the hat in my face and demanded that I confess."

Her eyes were as tortured as an animal caught in a trap. I laid my fingers on her tensed right arm. "It's okay. I get the gist. You don't have to tell me anything more."

"I do. I have to. I want you of all people to know the truth." Lacey shook off my hand and leaned forward, pressing her palms against her knees, which were buried under several thin hospital blankets. "Of course, I had no idea what he was talking about. I said something about losing the hat at his apartment, but he was in such a rage I don't think he even heard me. He said that he'd only asked me to stay at his place so he could 'deal with me properly' after his concerts." Lacey glanced over at me. "That's when I got scared."

"I can understand why," I said, thinking about Charles's face when he'd threatened me and Trish.

"We were standing in the kitchen, near that marble-topped island. He lunged at me and I instinctively fought back. But I guess I lost my balance because I slipped and fell backwards, banging my head. I hit the floor. Everything after that is all mixed up, but I do remember someone else bursting into the house. I guess Charles forgot to lock the front door. Anyway, I looked up and saw Professor Raymond hovering over me."

I sat bolt upright in the hard chair. "Mona was there?"

"Yeah. She screamed at Charles. Something about 'knowing his secret and here was the proof.' I was so disoriented, I'm not exactly sure what happened next except that Professor Raymond pulled me to my feet and somehow dragged me out the back door." Lacey rubbed her forehead. "I don't know how she got away from Charles, but he didn't have a gun or anything at that point, so maybe he just let us go. We staggered across the lawn and into the woods. Everything was flashing before my eyes and it felt like I was in a dream . . ."

"More like a nightmare," I muttered, then offered Lacey an apologetic smile. "Sorry, I didn't mean to interrupt. But one thing I don't understand—wasn't there a lot of blood on you and the floor? You sustained a serious head injury, from what I've heard."

"No, it never bled. Well, not externally. I only had an internal brain bleed. Which is probably why Professor Raymond felt she could move me."

"Just so you know"—I tapped my fingers against my knee—"Charles did confess to killing Mona. He told me he threw on his gloves and took a gun from Delbert Frye's shed."

Lacey nodded. "That makes sense, because he came after us with a rifle. Not immediately, so I figured that he had to take time to grab the gun from somewhere." Lacey took a deep breath. "Professor Raymond really did try to get me away, but I was feeling worse and worse, to the point where I couldn't stand. I slumped to the ground somewhere in the woods and she couldn't pull me up. Then I heard footsteps and Charles's voice and knew he'd found us. I thought I was a goner for sure." As Lacey turned to face me, another stream of tears cascaded down her hollowed-out cheeks. "Professor Raymond screamed at him that I was dead. It was a clever bluff. She knew I wasn't"—Lacey roughly dashed the tears away with the back of her hand—"but I guess she hoped to fool Charles so he wouldn't shoot me."

"But he shot her." I pulled more tissues from the box and handed them to Lacey.

"Yes. I couldn't force my eyes open at that point, but I heard the shot and felt the thud as her body hit the ground." Lacey held the tissues to her face for a moment before looking at me. "I knew, somewhere in my mixed-up mind, that she'd sacrificed herself to save me. So I told myself I had to stay still, to pretend to be dead, until Charles left. Which he did soon enough. I still don't know how he thought my death would be explained, because obviously I couldn't have been written off as a hunting accident. Maybe he was too wound up at that point to care."

"It's pretty clear he isn't as smart as he likes to think," I said, meeting her agonized gaze.

"No, he isn't. Fortunately for me." Lacey tossed the second wad of tissues into the trash. "I came to a little while later. I was still dazed but could see again, even if everything was blurry. I checked over Professor Raymond, but she had no pulse and she was so cold . . . I was sure she was dead, so I just staggered to my feet and walked away, leaving her there." Lacey sucked in a deep breath. "I do feel bad that I didn't stay with her body."

"Don't. If Charles had returned . . ."

"That was the only clear thought in my mind—to get away. So I just wandered. I really don't remember much. I think I hid in some bushes and then under a rock ledge during the two nights I was lost, but I'm not sure. I just know that Charles never found me."

"He did go out looking," I said, recalling Delbert Frye's report about someone crashing through the woods on Thursday morning. "But I think he was also trying to establish a pattern of sounds similar to what happened Tuesday afternoon."

"Always thinks he's so clever." Lacey's tone dripped with bitterness.

"In error, obviously." I took hold of the hand she'd left dangling off the side of the bed. "At some point you fell over Mona's body again?"

"And screamed. That's how those deputies found me, I suppose."

"Thank goodness they did." I examined her drawn face. "It isn't your fault, you know. Charles would've shot Mona regardless."

"I know. It just seems so . . . impossible." Lacey lowered her eyelids, veiling her eyes. "I truly loved him. And we shared so much. I thought I knew him."

Her words hit me like a thorny branch to the face. "I understand. Trust me, I do."

"I thought you might." Lacey twitched her lips into a tremulous smile. "I knew you'd dated him, before Marlis was in the picture."

"And apparently, after," I replied.

"I figured. But I foolishly thought I was different. He told me . . ."

"That you were special? The one he'd been looking for? The love he really needed?"

Lacey ducked her head. "Yeah. That." She tightened her grip on my hand. "I guess we were both fooled, huh?"

"And Marlis as well, poor thing." I squeezed Lacey's fingers before releasing her hand. "It had nothing to do with any of us, you know. It was all Charles. We were just game pieces he moved around."

"I see that now." Lacey leaned back against her pillows and stared up at the ceiling. "I bet he thought I wouldn't recover."

"I'm not sure he thought that through," I said. "I don't know what he expected to happen if you did. He had to know you could blow a hole in all his alibis. Of course, I suppose it's possible he planned to leave the country before that happened."

"Maybe." Lacey's expression grew thoughtful. "He also probably thought it didn't matter. I bet he believed I loved him so much that I would protect him. Despite everything."

"Which just goes to show how wrong he was about you."

"Yeah, 'cause I would have exposed him, even if he hadn't been caught. Even if he'd tried to sweet-talk me into continuing our relationship." Lacey looked over at me, her eyes blazing. "I heard Professor Raymond hit the ground. I touched her cold, lifeless body. After that, it wouldn't have mattered if Charles had crawled to me on his hands and knees and sworn that he'd love me and only me forever. No matter what I felt, or how it broke my heart, I would've still betrayed him. It hurts so badly, even now, but I've vowed to make him pay for what he did."

"And that's why you will get past this and live and thrive," I said. "While he rots in prison."

Lacey nodded. "That's right, let him rot," she said, with the first genuine smile I'd seen on her face during my visit. "Let him be the one to disappear this time. With no one left to care if they ever see him again."

# Chapter Twenty-Eight

On Sunday I got a call from Brad, asking me to accompany him on a visit to Delbert Frye's cabin. He explained that the main purpose of the visit was to return the gold coins. Since they weren't actually evidence in any ongoing case, they could finally be returned to a representative of the Frye family.

"He asked for you," Brad said, when I questioned this invitation.

"Really? That's odd. I could see him wanting you to bring along Walt Adams or some other friend, but me? I've only met the man once."

"Perhaps so, but he said he had a reason. Don't worry, I'll be there. And Richard can come along if you want. I don't think Delbert would mind." Brad cleared his throat. "Alison will be there too."

"Oh? I guess that makes sense. She has an interest in the coins as one of Delbert's only living family members."

"Maybe. I don't know. The old man asked me to bring her along, that's all I know."

"Why don't Richard and I meet you at Delbert's cabin? That way you and Alison won't have to drive out of your way." *And can go home together*, I thought, but of course I didn't say anything like that aloud.

Richard, on the other hand, was quite vocal about his feelings as we drove up the dirt road that led back to Delbert's cabin. "And there goes my suspension," he said as we bounced out of a particularly deep pothole.

"Oh, I'm sure this car can handle a few jolts." I stared out the side window to hide my grin.

"Yeah, but not a moonscape." We hit several additional rough patches before pulling up in front of a log cabin nestled in a small clearing surrounded by towering trees. "Now that's what I call rustic," Richard said as he yanked the keys from the ignition and pocketed them.

The cabin, built from hand-hewn logs, had chinking that was tinted green by moss. A spiral of smoke coiled up from the ivy-draped fieldstone chimney.

"I see Brad and Alison beat us." I pointed at the sheriff's department vehicle as Richard and I crossed the leaf-strewn yard to reach the cabin's weathered front door.

"Well, Brad probably doesn't mind driving that tank fast over these back roads. I, on the other hand . . ."

"I know," I said, sliding my hand through his crooked arm as he knocked on the cabin door. "Admit it—you're still a city boy at heart."

"About some things." Richard looked down at me with a smile.

The door cracked open. "Hello, Amy," Delbert Frye said, eyeing Richard with suspicion. "Who's this?"

"My boyfriend, Richard Muir. He's also my neighbor—he's Paul Dassin's great-nephew and inherited Paul's house."

"The old Cooper place, you mean." Delbert swung the door back and turned away. "Come on in then. Just shut that door behind you."

Walking into Delbert's home was like stepping back in time. The main room was wreathed in shadows. The small windows set into the exposed log walls didn't allow in much light, and there were no overhead light fixtures, only standing lamps that cast yellow ovals of light over isolated areas. Most of the furniture that filled the room looked handmade, as did the faded rag rugs that covered the wooden plank floors. Looking up, I examined the shelf that ran in a continuous track around all four walls. It was set just far enough below the timbered ceiling to accommodate stringed instruments of all shapes and sizes. There were fiddles and banjoes and, of course, a wide variety of dulcimers.

As Richard and I followed Delbert over to a seating area near the stone fireplace, I slid my fingers over the smooth surface of a side table set next to a bentwood rocker. *One of Walt's pieces*, I realized, recognizing the distinctive style.

"Have a seat." Delbert indicated a pine settle draped in a woven wool blanket. "Brad here's been telling me how you discovered my family's old gold coins up there in that cavern. Glad they came in handy against that Bartos fellow."

Brad was seated in an armchair so worn that the springs visibly pressed against the thin floral-patterned upholstery. He fiddled with the rawhide tie on the old leather pouch he clasped between his hands. "Yes, that was fortunate. Otherwise, from what I hear, Ms. Alexander might not be alive today."

"A good twist of fate," Alison Frye said, her ankles primly crossed as she perched on the edge of a ladder-back wooden chair. She waited until we sat on the settle before meeting Richard's eyes. "I do want to apologize, Mr. Muir. It seems I was a bit hasty in suspecting you of any involvement in the Lacey Jacobs case."

"No problem." Richard draped his arm across the top of the settle behind my back. "You were just doing your job."

"We do have to follow every lead in such cases," Brad said. "But I know Deputy Frye feels bad about hounding you, Richard."

"It's okay to call her Alison," I said. "Since you're dating."

Delbert cast a sharp look at his grandniece. "Is that right, Allie? You're seeing the chief deputy now?"

The young woman's cheeks flamed red. "Yeah. I would've told you, Uncle Del, but there hasn't really been time."

Delbert sat on a stool by the hearth. "Makes no difference to me, though now it makes more sense why you changed jobs. Should've figured something was up with that. More than just being ashamed of me, I mean."

Alison clasped her hands in her lap and leaned forward, her gaze fixed on her great-uncle. "You put that out of your head. I wasn't ashamed of you. I knew you'd never actually shoot anybody, for all your bluster."

"Good to know." Delbert grabbed an iron poker and jabbed at the smoldering logs in the fireplace. "I don't want you to think too badly of me, Allie, 'specially as you're about the only family I have left."

"Yes, and that's why she's here today." Brad held up the leather bag I'd discovered in the mountain cave. "You know I came here today to return this to you, Mr. Frye. As well as to apologize again for your arrest."

"Don't worry about that." Delbert leaned the poker back against the rough stones surrounding the fireplace. "It was my rifle that killed that lady, after all."

"But not you wielding it," I said. "That was all Charles Bartos, and it seems he wasn't above trying to frame you."

"Got sorted in the end," Delbert said gruffly. He turned his attention to Brad and the pouch the chief deputy was balancing in one palm. "So the Frye family gold has finally turned up. After all these years of the family searching and searching, there it is."

I leaned back against Richard's arm. "Did you ever look for it, Mr. Frye?"

"No, never cared nothing about it." Delbert waved his arm, indicating the various musical instruments that filled the high shelves. "I have everything I want right here. I never could imagine what I'd spend that money on, so I didn't ever bother looking. Besides"—he met my questioning gaze—"I knew that was blood money."

"What do you mean, Uncle Del?" Alison asked.

Delbert stood and gripped the edge of the timber mantle with one hand. He stared into the flames for a moment before speaking. "That gold was intended to give my great-great-aunt, Ada Frye, and her friend Violet a new life, but all it brought them was death."

I sat up straighter, allowing Richard's arm to slip off my shoulder. "The family did know for sure that they had died?"

"Yes, they knew." Delbert turned and leaned against the stones behind him as he surveyed us. "You may have heard that Ada wanted to escape a bad marriage. That was true enough, but only the family knew how bad it truly would've been. The man her father wanted her to marry was rumored to have beaten his first wife. Maybe even killed her, for all anyone knew. But he owned an adjoining farm that bordered the river, so his property would have provided a constant source of water for our family's livestock and crops. Ada's father wanted that land, or access to it, anyway. Only way he could get it was to offer up Ada's hand in marriage."

I studied the old man's drawn face. He didn't seem to know the truth about Ada and Violet's relationship or, if he did, had no inclination to disclose it. Which was his prerogative, of course. I certainly didn't intend to bring up the subject.

"That's awful." Alison sank back in her chair. "No wonder I've never heard that story. Doesn't shine a very good light on our family."

Delbert looked at her with compassion. "Don't worry about that, Allie. It's in the past. Nothing to do with us." His eyes narrowed. "Although I have kept it quiet, just like the rest of the family, out of shame. But no more. Time the truth came out."

"Playing devil's advocate"—Brad placed the pouch in his lap and reached out to clasp Alison's clenched fingers and pull one of her hands onto his knee—"I know the girls took the coins as a way to start a new life after they ran away, and I understand that finding the money might indicate that they didn't make it over the mountain. But Amy also told me about finding some letter that referenced Violet's cousin, who was willing to help them after their escape. She said she hadn't heard from Violet at the point when she wrote the letter, but maybe she did hear something later. We don't really have any evidence either way, so how can you be sure they didn't make it? They could've just lost the coins somehow."

Delbert cast Brad a sad smile. "I know they died. I know because I heard the story whispered by the old folks at family gatherings and such." His gaze shifted to Alison. "I know because the truth is that Ada's daddy hunted those poor girls down and killed them."

Alison gasped. "You have proof?"

"Not absolutely, but the tales I heard sounded real enough, and my granddaddy swore it was true. Also . . ." Delbert took a deep breath. "I was told that Ada and Violet took refuge here after hiding the coins somewhere. A bad storm blew up and I guess they decided to risk using the family hunting cabin to wait out the weather before continuing on. Anyway, Ada's daddy tracked them here."

"But why kill them?" I asked. "Why not simply drag them back home?"

Delbert rubbed at the back of his neck. "What I heard was that they wouldn't give up the location of the coins and my great-great-grandfather lost his temper and killed them in a rage. Or murdered the one, and then felt that he had to silence the other girl too." Delbert glanced at me, his stare as piercing as if he could read my thoughts. "There were other rumors too. Whispered confidences about the girls being in love with each other. That's something you hear about a lot these days, and now it's not such a big deal, but back then . . . Well, I always wondered if maybe it was another reason my ancestor killed Ada and Violet. Didn't want that stain, as he would've called it, on the family. I could see that happening, although I don't see any real harm in such relationships myself. Love is good wherever you find it, is what I think. You learn that when you lose it." Delbert shrugged. "Anyway, all this stuff is just what I heard, third- and fourth-hand, so who knows? I do know that there's a spot out back, in the woods, that's mounded up a bit, and usually covered in mushrooms. Always thought it kind of looked like a grave." He rubbed at the back of his neck. "But all I'm absolutely sure about is that my daddy and others were constantly searching for that gold. That's how I know they truly believed it was still hidden somewhere in these mountains."

"Now it's yours." Brad patted Alison's hand before releasing his grip and rising to his feet. He crossed to Delbert and offered him the old leather pouch.

Delbert stared at Brad's extended hand. "You can march that straight over to Ms. Webber, Chief Deputy. I'm donating it to the town library and archives. Let them sell the coins and collect the money and use it for good. I don't want nothing to do with it." He glanced past Brad to catch Alison's eye. "That's if my grandniece agrees."

"I do," Alison said with a sniffle. She rummaged through her jacket pocket and pulled out some tissues. "Thank you, Uncle Del.

I think that's the only right thing to do," she added before blowing her nose.

Brad looked from Delbert to Alison and back again. "You sure? It'll probably turn out to be quite a bit of money."

"Like I said, I don't need none. Now, if Allie wanted it, I might think differently, but it seems she don't, so let the library have it." He cast me a faint smile. "They do good work, I hear."

"Wow," I said, sharing a look with Richard. "That could certainly be put to great use. Thank you so much, Mr. Frye."

Delbert smoothed down the front of his white cotton shirt. "I just wonder if maybe you could put up a plaque or something, recognizing Ada and her friend."

"We certainly can. Heck, we can name the archives for them, if you want." I met Brad's approving gaze. "I'm sure the town council would applaud that gesture."

"That would be nice," Alison said.

I allowed my gaze to wander over the room, taking in the beautiful instruments that lined its upper walls. "But I do have one request before I accept this gift, Mr. Frye."

Delbert wrinkled his brow. "I offer up a fortune and you're making conditions?"

"Yes, but this is one I think you won't mind. At least I hope not." I pointed at one of the dulcimers. "Would you play for us, Mr. Frye? I'd love to hear you again."

Delbert's eyebrows shot up, but he chuckled. "Is that all? Why sure, if you want. Deputy Tucker, give that gal those coins and grab me that dulcimer up there at the end of the row, would you?"

As Brad handed me the pouch containing the coins, I asked him the question that had been puzzling me off and on ever since Lacey had been found. "By the way, did you ever figure out who left that footprint outside of Mary Gardener's house?"

Brad lifted his eyebrows. "The bare-toes one? No. It doesn't appear connected to the Lacey Jacobs case, so I just wrote it up as an unsolved anomaly."

Alison shifted in her chair. "I think it was some local kids playing a prank on an old lady."

"Probably," Brad said as he turned away from me to head for the shelf holding the requested dulcimer. "That's as good an explanation as any, I suppose."

"I'm sure that's what it was—some teenagers with nothing better to do. You know the kind," Alison said, meeting my questioning gaze. "They think it's funny to tease a woman like Mary. It's happened before, although not recently. But up until a few years ago, she used to be asked to share town folklore with Mr. Arnold's high school history class."

"Right," Brad said as he crossed back over to Delbert's chair. "There were often incidents of vandalism and other pranks occurring at her house after her school visits."

Alison nodded. "I remember from my own school days that there was a lot of giggling and sneering over her obvious belief in fairies."

"Better to call them the Folk, Allie," Delbert said, shooting his great-niece a sharp glance as he took the dulcimer from Brad's hands.

"Now, Uncle Del, don't tell me you believe in such things," Alison said, catching Brad's eye and giving him a smile as he sat in the chair next to hers.

"I just see no sense in taking any chances," Delbert said. "I've lived in these mountains long enough to know that I don't understand all their secrets," he added before focusing on tuning the dulcimer.

I set the leather pouch on my upper thigh and placed my hand over it. Richard laid his left hand over my fingers and leaned in to whisper in my ear, "After all this time, isn't it ironic that this treasure will finally do some good."

I met his intent look with a smile. "First to protect Trish, then to help the library. I think Ada and Violet would be pleased."

He gave me a smile in return as Delbert launched into a traditional folk song I'd heard many times before. But somehow his rendition was more pure and true than any version I'd ever heard. Perhaps it was the words he spoke before launching into the lyrics.

"This one is for Ada and Violet," he said.

I leaned into Richard, who pulled me close while we listened to Delbert sing the haunting words.

I'm just a poor wayfaring stranger
Traveling through this world of woe
But there's no sickness, toil, nor danger
In that fair land to which I go . . .

# Chapter Twenty-Nine

A light breeze lifted my hair off my shoulders, and bright sunlight warmed my face as I stood beside Sunny at the May Day festival. I flicked strands of dark hair away from my face and slid my sunglasses back up my nose and surveyed the festival, now in full swing.

The vacant lot beside the town hall had been transformed into a vibrant space filled with decorated booths and food trucks. At one end of the lot, an electronic piano, drum set, and other instruments sat on a small stage fronted by a temporary dance floor. A few musicians took their places on the stage, but everyone's attention was drawn to the tall pole draped in a rainbow of wide, fluttering ribbons that had been planted in the middle of the lot.

Richard's dancers, attired in dirndl skirts and bright embroidered vests over puffy-sleeved white blouses, formed a circle around the maypole. Wearing a plain black T-shirt and black yoga pants, Richard stood off to one side, undoubtedly giving them final instructions and a pep talk.

Sunny nudged me with her elbow. "Look at those faces. They obviously adore him."

"And why shouldn't they?" I met her amused glance with a smile.

"I bet half of them have a crush on him, but that's okay, because he's very careful around them."

"I know he'd never take advantage." Sunny tipped her head, indicating the cluster of people standing off to our right. "Unlike some others."

I looked over at Chris, Ethan, and Hope, who flanked Lacey's wheelchair. Lacey, who'd been discharged from the hospital to a rehab facility, had been granted permission to attend the festival for a few hours.

"Hope said that the doctors were reluctant to allow Lacey to come, but apparently they relented. I'm glad, because Chris told me that they have something special planned right before the maypole dance," I said. "Not exactly sure what."

"Something to honor Mona, I bet." Sunny shaded her eyes with her hand. "I see Hugh made it."

"He's been visiting since Sunday. Which means Aunt Lydia has been pulling out all the stops on meals." I patted my stomach. "Which also means I've probably gained five pounds. No festival food for me."

Sunny tossed her hair behind her shoulders. "Nonsense. We have to try those fried candy bars."

I made a face. "You can. I think I'll take a pass."

"Here comes the special announcement, I guess," Sunny said as Chris jogged to the stage and grabbed a portable microphone from one of the musicians.

"Hi." He grimaced as feedback roared out of the speakers on stage and tapped the microphone before speaking again. "I'm sorry to interrupt the festivities, but my friends and I"—he motioned toward Hope and Ethan, who'd pushed Lacey's wheelchair closer to the stage—"have an announcement. It's about a memorial for Professor Ramona Raymond."

"Good idea," shouted someone from the crowd.

"Yeah, we thought so," Chris said. "Anyway, we've collected a little money and plan to raise more. We thought we'd try to get together enough to commission a plaque or even a statue or something that will commemorate the tale of the mountain lights and credit Professor Raymond's research on the story." He waved the microphone toward the crowd. "If any of you want to contribute, we'll be over by the entrance to the town hall until the end of the festival. And after that, you can give any donations to Ethan Payne at the firehouse. Okay, that's all." Chris offered a slightly embarrassed smile as a portion of the crowd clapped. Handing the microphone to the musicians, he made his way over to his friends before they headed off toward the town hall.

"That was sweet," Sunny said. "I'll have to try to give them a little something."

"Me too." I glanced across the field. "There's Walt and Zelda, holding hands. I'm so glad they've finally decided to take their romantic relationship public." I smiled as Walt leaned in to kiss Zelda's cheek. "I also love that fuchsia-pink hat Zelda's wearing. And, oh—there's Brad."

"And Alison. They seem to be joined at the hip these days," Sunny said, without rancor. She drummed her fingers, which were decorated with a different spring flower painted on each nail, against her other wrist. "I think I'll go over and say hello."

"To show you're okay with it?"

"To show that I am a free and independent woman who doesn't need a man to be happy." Sunny gave me a wry smile. "Which I am, you know."

"You are. Always." I hugged her slender waist before stepping back. "Go on. I think I'll watch the dance from here."

As Sunny walked off to talk with Brad and Alison, I focused on the maypole. Richard had moved to the side while the dancers took up the ribbons. Strains of a lively folk tune wafted from the stage.

"Hello," said a voice behind me. "Are you Amy?"

I turned to face the speaker. A tall woman built like a statue of Diana the huntress looked down at me. Brushing a few locks of her chin-length sienna-brown bob behind her ears, she studied me with tea-brown eyes.

"Yes, I'm Amy Webber." I gazed up at her with a puzzled smile. "I don't think I know you."

"No, but I think you may have heard of me," she said, glancing over my head.

"Have I? I'm sorry, but I'm afraid I can't place you at the moment." Turning to follow her gaze, I watched the dancers weave in and out, wrapping their ribbons about the maypole in an intricately designed pattern.

"Amazing that they don't just tangle up their arms and feet, isn't it?" the woman said. "But then, Richard choreographed it, so of course he would make certain that didn't happen."

I shoved my sunglasses up on top of my head as I slowly turned to face her again. "You're Karla."

The stranger's smile lit up her broad face. "That's me. Karla Dunmore. Well, Karla Tansen is the name I use now. It's my married name, which is the only thing I kept after my divorce."

I looked her over, wondering how any company could have turned away this goddess just because of her larger-than-life build. Especially if she could dance as well as everyone claimed. "Does Richard know you're here?"

"Not yet."

I wiped beads of perspiration off my upper lip, aware how

ordinary I must appear in my worn jeans and blue-and-white Lindsey Stirling T-shirt. "He'll be thrilled, I'm sure."

"I don't know. I wasn't very nice to him the last time we met. Maybe you heard about that?"

"I did." I drew a circle in the dirt patch under my foot with the tip of my sneaker. "But he understood. Really, he did. And I'm sure he does want to see you again."

"I hope so." Karla focused back on the dancers. "Looks like they're about done."

"Then you should wait here with me. Richard's bound to come over to join me eventually, and then you guys can talk."

Karla glanced down at me. "Thanks. And"—she touched my arm—"I want you to know, Amy, that you don't have anything to worry about. Richard and I always were, and always will be, just dear friends. I know some people find that hard to believe, but it's the truth."

"He told me that as well," I said, meeting her steady gaze. "And I believe him. But I'm curious—how did you know that Richard and I are dating?"

Karla elegantly swept one hand through the air. "Oh, when Kurt Kendrick called and asked me to attend this festival, he told me all about you and Richard."

I took a stumbling step backward. Kurt's busy fingers, pulling the strings again. "You know Mr. Kendrick?"

"I do. We met a few years ago, when I was trying to set up a dance studio for children with physical or mental challenges."

I gazed up into her honest, open face. "And he helped you fund it?"

"Yes. I didn't realize his connection to Richard at first, but apparently he'd been following both our careers for a while." Karla shrugged. "Not that I had a career for quite some time, but somehow he still knew where I was and what I was doing."

*All his little birds* . . . I shook off the chill that had raised the hair on my arms. "He's the one who told you that Richard would be here today?"

"And asked me to come and talk to him." Karla examined me, her light-brown eyes narrowing. "He seemed to think that Richard needed to resolve his issues with me so he could move on. 'Take the next step' is how he actually put it."

"I'm not quite sure what he meant by that, but I'm happy that you're here."

"Good." Karla beamed at me. "Kurt told me that you were a special person. I can see that he's right."

"Really?" I fanned my heated cheeks. "I don't know how special I am, but I do love Richard."

"Which is what matters," Karla said as applause erupted around us.

I joined in as the maypole dancers took their bows. One of the girls rushed over to drag Richard off the sidelines.

He joined them with obvious reluctance, making one short bow before stepping aside and motioning toward the dancers.

"Now it's time for the rest of you to dance," Richard called out, pointing toward the stage. The musicians switched gears and jumped into a lively rendition of some popular song from the 1940s.

Richard called for his dancers to follow as he jogged over the stage and leapt onto the temporary dance floor. One of the girls jumped up to join him in executing an energetic swing dance.

"He just can't stop himself, can he?" Karla fixed her gaze on Richard and his partner as others joined them on the dance floor. "Sometimes I think he loves dancing more than breathing."

"Sometimes I think that, for him, it's the same thing," I said.

Karla looked down at me, her face wreathed in a smile. "You're absolutely right."

As we watched the dancers, Karla tapped her foot, then swung her leg in a tight circle, bouncing one hip.

"I think you might feel the same," I said, touching her arm. "You should join them." I lifted my chin as Karla met my fierce gaze. "Dance with him."

She didn't say anything, just laid her fingers against my breastbone right above my heart for a second before heading for the stage.

Richard's back was to the audience when Karla reached him. She placed her fingers on his shoulder, and he dropped the hand of the student he'd been partnering and spun around to face her.

*He knows that touch*, I thought, without experiencing even the slightest tinge of jealousy.

As the music faded away, Richard and Karla faced one another, still as the ancient Greek statues their bodies resembled. Obviously sensing the electricity crackling between them, the other dancers stepped off the stage and mingled with the audience.

I spied a tall, white-haired man beside the stage. He whispered something to the pianist, and after a moment the music resumed. But now it was a slow, haunting tune. Something I'd heard just a few days before.

Walking forward, I found a place in the crowd not far from Aunt Lydia and Hugh.

The strains of "Wayfaring Stranger" filled the air as Richard held out his hand.

Karla took hold of his fingers and they began to dance.

"Perfection, isn't it?" said a familiar voice behind me.

I replied without taking my eyes off the stage. "Yes, it is. It's like . . ."

"Two souls dancing as one?" Kurt Kendrick laid his large hand on my shoulder. "I saw them once before, when they were young. A performance at their conservatory."

"And you've followed both their careers since?"

"Yes. Because perfection should be cherished, don't you think?" Kurt lifted his hand and stepped around to stand at my side. "Anyway, I believe such art should be nurtured. It's the only thing worth anything in this world."

"Not the only thing," I said, as Richard and Karla finished their impromptu performance and the audience burst into cheers as well as applause. They shared a beatific smile before turning to take their bows. "Love is worth something too. At least I think so."

"Ah yes, but you know when you are a tin man . . ." Kurt motioned toward his chest. "No heart for such things."

"Don't try that scam on me," I said, turning to face him. "I know you're lying."

Kurt raised his eyebrows. "Am I? You think I have a heart after all?"

"I know you do." I met his amused gaze with a lift of my chin. "You invited Karla here. You've even supported her dance studio."

"I simply thought it would be a worthwhile investment, and that has proven to be true. As for inviting her"—Kurt looked up at the stage—"perhaps I just wanted to see them dance again. Maybe it was just something I desired, merely to please myself."

I leaned in and tapped him on the chest. "Stop it. I'm on to you now. You're as big a romantic as Richard."

"Oh dear, is it that obvious?" Kurt grinned and clasped my hand as I pulled it away. Pressing it back against his chest, he gave me a stern look. "I hope you will keep my secret, Amy Webber. Otherwise, I'm afraid my business affairs might suffer."

"It seems like I am always keeping your secrets, but okay. I won't squeal, as long as you tell me one thing."

"What's that?" Kurt asked as he released his grip on my hand.

"What did you mean by telling Karla that Richard needed to move on and take the next step, or whatever it was that you said?"

Kurt's blue eyes crinkled as a grin spread over his craggy face. "I'm afraid I'm not at liberty to share that information, my dear. Not yet, anyway. But if you will keep my secret, I promise to share what I know someday soon."

"Very well, I suppose that will have to do," I said, lowering my hand.

Sunny appeared at my other side. "Wasn't that amazing? I could watch those two dance all day." She peered around me. "Oh hi, Mr. Kendrick. Good to see you."

"Nice to see you as well, Ms. Fields. But I'm afraid I must leave you both. I brought Mary Gardener with me today, and I'm afraid she's been sitting over there under the trees all alone for quite some time. I'd better head back to her."

"Sure," Sunny said, waving goodbye as Kurt moved away. She pointed toward the stage. "Is that the old partner you told me about? She's absolutely fabulous."

"That's her." As the regular dance music resumed, other peopled flooded the stage.

I squinted to try to pick out Richard and Karla in the crowd, then realized that they were walking toward us. Richard had one arm around Karla's broad shoulders. His face was so bright it appeared illuminated from within.

"Look who I found," he said.

"I found you." Karla gave him a nudge with her hip.

"Well, however it happened, I'm glad," I said, as Richard dropped his arm and strode toward me, leaving Karla standing a few feet away.

He swept me up and off my feet before I could do anything

except throw my arms around his neck. "Best day of my life," he said, spinning me around once before kissing me and setting me back on my feet. "And it isn't even over yet."

"No, and you and Karla should spend some quality time together before it is." I pulled away and tugged down my rumpled T-shirt. "In fact, I think you guys should go out to dinner or something where you can really talk. Sunny will keep me company this afternoon, won't you, Sunny?"

"Sure," said my friend, making a comical face. "Good ol' Sunny doesn't have anything else to do."

"Nonsense," Karla said. "We can all go out together."

I shook my head. "No, you have a lot of catching up to do." Meeting Richard's questioning gaze, I gave him a warm smile. "Go on. I've got Sunny and Aunt Lydia and Hugh to keep me company. Besides, you can introduce Karla to your students. I'm sure they'd love to meet her. Now, shoo." I waved my hands at them. "Oh, and by the way, the two of you dancing . . ."

"Simply amazing," Sunny said with a dreamy smile.

"Yeah, it's that. Go on now and have a good long chat. Just make sure you discuss dancing together again." I pointed my finger at Richard and Karla. "That's an order."

Richard pulled me close and kissed me again. "All right, boss," he whispered in my ear. "But I want to see you later tonight. Will you promise to meet me in Lydia's garden around nine?"

"Okay," I said, kissing him back before I pressed my hands against his chest and pushed him away. "Now go. Talk. Discuss dancer-y things. Or whatever."

Richard and Karla both smiled and offered Sunny and I heartfelt goodbyes before heading off toward the young dancers still clustered by the stage.

Sunny's gaze followed their progress across the festival lawn. "You really do trust him, don't you?"

"Yes, I do." I smiled as Richard's dancers crowded around him and Karla. "Which is the most amazing, wonderful thing."

"Sounds like true love to me." Sunny threw her arm around my shoulders. "Now come on. Let's chow down on some disgusting fried food."

"Lead on, my friend," I replied. "Acid reflux waits for no man. Or woman."

Sunny just grinned and herded me toward the food trucks.

# Chapter Thirty

By the time Sunny dropped me off at the house after the festival, Aunt Lydia and Hugh had already eaten dinner and were lounging in the sitting room, discussing Hugh's latest success in reuniting a stolen painting with its owner.

"There's some leftovers in the refrigerator," Aunt Lydia said as I paused in the doorway.

"No thanks. Sunny and I gorged ourselves on the most unhealthy stuff imaginable, and now"—I rubbed my stomach—"I think I need an antacid, not more food."

"Very well." Aunt Lydia looked up from her seat on the sofa and motioned toward one of the vacant armchairs. "Come join us if you wish. Hugh was just telling me about solving an art theft case from over ten years ago."

"They finally nabbed the culprit after all this time, with your help?"

"Yes, it was quite unexpected." Hugh was seated close enough to my aunt to drape one arm around her shoulders. "Some new technology came into play that helped identify a piece that had been slightly altered to hide its true origin."

My aunt's carefully applied rose-pink lipstick was smudged. I leaned against the door frame. *Talking about art, indeed,* I thought with a little smile. *Not until you heard the front door, I bet.*

"That sounds interesting, and I'd like to hear more about it some other time, but for now I think I'm going to head upstairs and grab a shower. I have a garden rendezvous with Richard around nine, and to be honest I feel like my skin absorbed every bit of grease wafting from those food trucks."

"Very well," Aunt Lydia said. "We can always talk later. I do want to hear about this former partner of Richard's who showed up so unexpectedly today."

"Karla? Okay, but I don't have much to tell that you don't already know." I considered Kurt's admission of his hand in the matter, but no—I'd promised to keep that a secret. "Anyway, see you guys later. Carry on," I added as I headed for the stairs.

I was gratified to hear Aunt Lydia say, "What does she mean by that?" and Hugh's chuckle in response.

After my shower, I decided to throw on the cotton dress I'd worn to Kurt's dinner party. The idea of meeting in the garden under the stars seemed to call for something more elegant than just jeans and a T-shirt. I even blow-dried my hair and added a touch of mascara before I slipped on some backless sandals. But recalling my aunt's smudged mouth, I'd only used gloss, not lipstick. Because kissing would be involved. I was sure of that.

Dashing down the stairs right before nine o'clock, I called out to let Aunt Lydia and Hugh know I was headed to the garden but received no reply.

*Kissing is probably involved,* I thought with a grin.

The garden was bathed in shadows and steeped in the scent of roses. I stood next to the concrete birdbath on the gravel path and allowed the sounds of the night to wash over me. Crickets chirped like a section of untuned violins while the tree frogs contributed their high-pitched glissandos and an occasional owl hoot resonated like a bassoon.

*Perfect background music,* I thought, as footfalls stirred the pea gravel behind me.

"Hello you," Richard said.

I turned around to meet his approving gaze. "Hi. Did you and Karla have a good talk?"

"We did," Richard said, talking hold of both my hands. "But right now I want to focus on you. I really like that dress, by the way."

"I know. You told me that before. Which is why I'm wearing it tonight."

"Well, thank you." Keeping his grip on my fingers, Richard swung our joined hands gently forward and back.

"You look pretty spiffy yourself," I said, admiring his pewter-gray cotton sweater and charcoal slacks. "Is that sweater new? It looks great with your eyes."

Richard smiled. "It is, thanks, and . . . I confess I chose it for that very reason."

"Good choice." I stepped closer, forcing him to pull our clasped hands to his chest. "I didn't really get a chance to tell you earlier, but you and Karla dancing today . . . well, that was just magical. Improvised, I take it?"

"But based on things we'd done before. We know each other's dance vocabulary pretty well."

"I bet." I looked up into his face, noting the set line of his jaw. "Is anything wrong? You seem a little tense."

Richard released his hold on my hands. "No, just a busy and surprising day. Not exactly what I planned."

I stroked the side of his face. "But you did plan this little rendez-vous. Why?"

"To see you, of course. We haven't gotten to spend as much time together lately as I'd like. And . . ." He slipped an arm around my waist. "There was something I wanted to share with you."

"Oh? What's that?"

"Come with me and I'll show you." He turned sideways with his arm still at my waist. "We must walk into the woods," he added, leading me down the path.

"Now wait a minute." I planted my feet. "I think I've spent enough time wandering around the woods lately."

Richard laughed. "We won't wander. I have a destination in mind."

"Okay, but you'd better stay with me the entire time."

"Right by your side," he said, guiding me onto the narrow path that led into the trees that bordered the back of the garden.

We'd only walked a short distance when we stepped into the clearing that held an old arbor draped in native wisteria vines.

Battery-operated lanterns lined the interior of the arbor, illumi-nating the area.

"Oh, it's blooming!" I pulled away from Richard to clap my hands. "I've never seen it like this, covered in flowers."

"I know. That's why I brought you here." Richard walked into the arbor and held out his hand. "It's even more beautiful under the vines."

I crossed to him, exclaiming in delight as I entered the arbor. The moon spangled the ground under our feet with sequins of golden light, while the wisteria vines were hung with leaves and blossoms that created amethyst and emerald chandeliers.

"It's so beautiful," I said in a hushed voice. "Like an entry to a magical world."

"But, I promise, not to the lands of the fae." Richard took me by the hand. "I read that wisteria only blooms profusely for a week or two, and around this time. I've been keeping an eye out for it this year."

"So you could show me?" I glanced down at the lanterns. "You obviously set this up ahead of time. Was it all just for me?"

"Yes." Richard smiled. "Remember—we walked through here last year. That was when we first met, after the vines had already bloomed."

"I remember. You said something about Daniel and Eleanora Cooper probably coming out here to . . . what was it? Oh right—*spoon*."

He tapped my nose with one finger. "Which means kissing."

"I know what it means." I tipped my head and studied his shadowed face. "You really are such a romantic. All this effort because you wanted to kiss me under the wisteria blossoms. Now, I must know—when did you start planning this?"

"The first time we walked through here," he said, his smile fading.

"Wow." I pulled my hand free and stepped back. "Seriously?"

"Absolutely. I mean, I knew I wanted to kiss you under this arbor. What I didn't know yet was what else I wanted."

I stared at him. "Why so serious? And, in case you hadn't noticed, you haven't kissed me yet."

"I know. The truth is, there's something I want to do first." Richard audibly swallowed as he clenched and unclenched his hands.

I clasped my own hands in front of me to still their trembling. "Are you okay?"

"I'm fine," Richard said, his voice shaking. "I'm perfect. Everything's perfect, only . . ."

My response caught in my throat as he bent down on one knee in front of me.

"Amy Alice Webber," he said, his voice vibrating with emotion, "will you marry me?"

I stared at him as the faint scent of the wisteria drifted over me. "Oh. Well, I . . . I . . ." My mouth felt as dry as the garden after weeks without rain. I licked my lips and cleared my throat and stared down into Richard's eyes.

Beautiful and intelligent and honest eyes—filled with a love I knew in my heart was real.

Absolutely, truly real.

"Yes, of course I will," I said, my voice ringing out clearly, and as strong as mountain granite.

Richard leapt up and wrapped me in his arms. He kissed me for quite some time before whispering, "I don't have a ring. I thought you'd probably prefer that we choose one together."

"Yes, together. I like together," I said, and kissed him again before adding, "Always together."

# Acknowledgments

T hanks and overstuffed library shelves full of gratitude to:

My agent, Frances Black of Literary Counsel.

Everyone at Crooked Lane Books, especially my editor, Faith Black Ross. Also, thanks to Matt Martz, Jenny Chen, Sarah Poppe, and Ashley Di Dio.

Lindsey Duga and Richard Taylor Pearson—critique partners extraordinaire.

My husband and most supportive fan, Kevin Weavil.

My family and friends.

All my readers, with deep appreciation for your support of this series.